BOOKISH

BERNADETTE MARIE

5 PRINCE PUBLISHING
5PRINCEBOOKS.COM

Digital ISBN: 978-1-63112-414-3

Print ISBN: 978-1-63112-415-0

Cover design by Marianne Nowicki

Interior design by 5 Prince Publishing

First Edition F070225

For more information about this title, visit: www.5princebooks.com

For Stan,
For believing in my bookstore, no matter what form it takes.

ACKNOWLEDGMENTS

Thank yous go out to:
My loving husband, my supportive 5 pack of kiddos, and my encouraging mother and sister. Without you all, my characters wouldn't have any fun quirks.

To my 5 Prince Publishing team; Cate, who keeps my words and stories straight, Lauren who makes me shine online, and Marianne who makes the book look good with magnificent covers. And to Whitney who makes my stories come to life with her vocal talent. You all form one amazing team that makes me shine.

To my friends Natasha and Andre Gonzalez—incredible authors, supportive friends, and family. Thank you for including me in your successes and sharing the bountiful knowledge and opportunities. Thanks too for answering my questions of freaky hotels when I choose not to go in them.

To my martial arts sisters, Alpha, Jess, Barb, Tasha—the support you all give me on and off the mat is life altering. Tang Soo!

To all the authors who hide indoors and create life-altering stories, to the independent bookstore owners who support those authors, and to the readers that make it possible—I appreciate you more than words can express, but I'll keep trying.

ALSO BY BERNADETTE MARIE

THE ROM COM MOVIE CLUB

The Rom Com Movie Club - Book One

The Rom Com Movie Club - Book Two

The Rom Com Movie Club - Book Three

FUNERALS AND WEDDINGS SERIES

Something Lost

Something Discovered

Something Found

Something Forbidden

Something New

THE DEVEREAUX FAMILY SERIES

Kennedy Devereaux

Chase Devereaux

Max Devereaux

Paige Devereaux

STANDALONE TITLES

The Happily Ever After Bookstore

Liz's Road Trip

Publicity Stunt

Bookish

THE MATCHMAKER SERIES

Matchmakers

Encore

Finding Hope

THE THREE MRS. MONROES TRILOGY

Amelia

CHAPTER 1

Independent bookstores—they're important.

Big box stores sell books. The chain stores sell them too. Even grocery stores and convenience stores, but no one creates an atmosphere quite like an independent bookstore.

Within the walls of The Reading Nook in Pine Haven, Colorado, you'll find my dream of a perfectly curated collection of books. Though I'm a lover of everything romance, I appreciate every genre and every voice. I want every reader that walks through my door to find something to satisfy their need for words. Those who are bookish need places like this—like my store—like independent bookstores of all kinds.

I run my duster over the colorful covers of the romances that I adore. Spines with bright colors, couples in embraces, illustrated covers that mask the true heat to the story within their pages. However, the best part of a romance is that each one has a happily ever after or satisfyingly happy ending. It causes me pause. My store *is* my happily ever after.

"The box is here," Julia shouts across the store as she walks through the front door.

In her arms she carries an enormous, heavy box from

Fitzgerald & Clark Publishing in New York. I can't help but think she looks like a grown child with her two long braids and her overalls, not to mention that wide grin she has on her face knowing that books are inside that box—books that aren't ready for public consumption. The coveted advance read copies—ARCs. She sets it on the front counter and hurries behind it to find the cutter from the drawer.

Pine Haven has been selected as this year's site for Fitzgerald & Clark's annual Book Affair Literary Event. Our little mountain town is going to be the setting for literary loving visitors from all over the world. My little, eclectic bookstore is going to be host to New York Times bestselling authors. This will put us on the map.

Fitzgerald & Clark showcase their top five authors of the year at these events, sparing no expense on them. The hotels are top rated, but the authors aren't on vacation. The publishing house makes them work.

Nothing like taking introverted authors and putting them on display, not unlike a circus animal—monkeys asked to perform for treats and affection. The weeklong event is being held at the Monarch Mountain Resort and weaved into the local businesses as well. There will be discussions, author panels, and book signings. But for us, the small businesses, especially the bookish businesses, there will be sales.

I've attended this event in the past when it was much smaller and was held in New York, but to have it in my own back yard, and to be a part of it, it makes my insides bubble just thinking about it.

"Oh that looks like it's filled with something fun," Anna James, who teaches kindergarten at the elementary school, says as she sets three copies of *The Art of Being A Good Person* by Carley McVee on the counter.

"You're getting more copies?" Julia asks.

"When a kid loves to read a book, and it has a good message, you make sure they have their own copy," she says. "What better reward for reading is there than a book itself?"

Julia and I agree with a nod.

Julia finishes ringing up the sale and turns to me as Anna walks out with her The Reading Nook canvas bag slung over her shoulder.

"How many copies of that book has she bought in the last six months?" I ask Julia.

Her blue eyes sparkle as she looks up at the door and watches Anna hold it for an older couple walking into the store. "I think she's up to fifteen copies."

The Art of Being A Good Person by Carley McVee, which was one of my favorite books growing up, had a resurgence a year ago, after the author's death. A TikTok influencer began to circulate the content and it caught on. I wish the message of the book would have caught on and people would be good to one another. At least for Anna James, *The Art of Being A Good Person* makes a huge difference for her students.

She's now bought, according to Julia, fifteen copies of the beloved children's book to give to her students as rewards for learning to read. The thought warms me throughout. Books as rewards; as it should be.

Finally, Julia picks up the cutter again and takes it to the custom Fitzgerald & Clark Publishing tape that seals the box she'd carried in.

Usually we get an assortment of books prior to release so that we can make informed decisions when purchasing upcoming books. But this care package is filled with items for the literary event.

Julia picks up the advance read copy of Noah Carter's newest release, which, according to the email they sent me, will be launched here at the store.

Julia turns the book over and gazes down at the picture of the man on the back. "He is dreamy," she says drawing out the words and I shake my head.

"He's old enough to be your father," I tell her and she shrugs.

"And the top actor on your hall pass list has always been Ed Harris, and ditto," she says to me and my cheeks heat. She's right, and I can't help it. There isn't an Ed Harris movie I haven't committed to memory and drooled over. Even if he's the bad guy, and he's played his share, he remains on my list of people I'd give up anything to have just one night with.

As Julia holds up the book and begins to leaf through the pages, I study the man on the back of the thriller. I've never met him in person, though I once did have a rather brash exchange of emails with him.

When I was working a summer at my aunt's bookstore in New York City, Noah Carter was supposed to have a signing there. We'd sold hundreds of copies of his very first New York Times Best Selling novel *The Winds of Death*, and he was going to do a reading and stay to sign. But, two days before the event, which my aunt had gone all out for because she was, self-proclaimed, one of his biggest fans, he cancelled.

I intercepted the email, and Noah Carter and I battled it out in a tangle of words via the internet.

The emails were curt, mean spirited, and filled with the kind of vulgar language that says the corespondent on the other end lacks education.

I know for a fact that's not true, but that's how I remember it. Noah Carter is a talented author, but I wouldn't give him much more credit than that. As a well functioning human, he doesn't make the cut.

Needless to say, the interaction left me a bit jaded.

I've read every one of his books, because he's a hell of a writer and sells like gangbusters. No bookstore owner would be crazy enough to not carry him. But I have to wonder, what really goes on in someone's head that only writes of conspiracy theories, terrorism, and death? I mean, I've had to put the book down, sometimes hiding it in a drawer, before I can come back to it. The details are so disturbing that I can't comprehend what I'm reading. How does someone who is a functioning human write such twisted things? It all leads back to my point that he's not a functioning human and he has no decorum when it comes to others.

The headshot on the back cover, however, does show off his best features. I won't admit that to Julia, but she's right, he's dreamy, and more age appropriate for me to be gushing over.

Dark hair that is salt and peppered gives him a distinguished look, and dark eyes peer at you from the back cover as if they're searching into your soul—perhaps looking for your flaw so he can dismember you. There are subtle creases around his eyes that weren't edited out, and a goatee frames a tight smile.

It's enough to have me let out a little noise and Julie looks up at me.

"Is it any good?" I ask her, hoping she didn't know what the noise was for.

"Do I get to read it first?" she asks.

"If you want to."

She hugs the book to her chest. "So he's really coming to that literary event?"

"He's on the list, but don't hold your breath." I expect that two days before he's supposed to sign, he'll back out. I wonder what his excuse will be. Come to think of it, he didn't give an excuse when he'd canceled on my aunt, and wasn't that the start of the chain of emails that had left me questioning his character?

"Can you schedule me the night of his signing?"

I snort out a laugh. "You're going to be on the schedule the whole week. Everyone will be." I lean my hip against the front counter. "Do you have any idea how busy we're going to be?"

Her young eyes go wide. "How big an event is this?"

"Look it up online. The resort will be sold out and so will most of the smaller hotels and private rentals."

She mouths the word wow and I nod.

Julia takes off with the book still pressed to her chest and I pick up one of the other books from the box.

When the email chimes on the computer on the counter, I set down the books in my hand and click to the reader and stare at the incoming email.

"You have got to be kidding me," I say clicking on the message.

To Whom it May Concern,

I am one of the featured authors for the Fitzgerald & Clark Publishing Book Affair Literary Event. I will be coming in two weeks prior to the event next month to work on my newest manuscript. The event coordinator, Katie Stevens, has informed me that your store is quaint and might be the right place for me to work while I am there. I am inquiring about a work space, for me to rent while there. Please advise on the rental price.

Sincerely,

Noah Carter, Author

"You haven't blinked in like three minutes," Julia says, so I blink. "What's wrong?"

"Noah Carter wants to rent space for a few weeks prior to the literary event—here."

I don't miss the grin that spreads across her face from my periphery. "He'd be here?"

Now I look at her. "He's old enough to be your father," I remind her about our earlier conversation.

"Yeah, but he's just your age, or so," she says laying his book on the counter, back cover up. "I heard that little sound you made while we were ogling his picture."

Shit, I didn't think she'd noticed that.

"Are you going to rent him a space?" she asks.

"No," I say quickly and Julia flinches.

"Why not?"

Oh, there are so many reasons.

"Where would I put him?" I look around the tight confines of the store.

"We have the reading nook," she says pointing to the small alcove where we have oversized chairs for patrons to sit and read.

"I'm not displacing my customers."

"The storage room?"

I snort out a laugh at that. "As if."

"Your office?" she suggests, wrinkling her nose.

I look behind us at the door that is slightly ajar. My office is just that—mine. Not because I don't want anyone else in there working with me, but because it's that small.

"I don't know," I say and Julia crosses her arms in front of her and purses her lips.

"He wants to write his next book here. You can say that Noah Carter wrote his next bestseller in your store. It'll be huge. We can keep his picture on the wall with a plaque that says *bestseller written at The Reading Nook*," she uses her hand to imagine the sign like a marquee. "Maybe you can even get him to do his book launch here." She makes a little noise of joy, I assume. "Oh my god, it could be the next big event to come to town. What if they make a movie in Pine Haven?"

I can't help but snort out a laugh at that. "That's a little far fetched."

"Not so much. *Terrorists Among Us* was set in a small town and they made the movie there."

I hadn't paid too much attention to that. The book was fine, but seriously, I could only imagine the ego trip Noah Carter had to have been on to have his book made into a movie of that scale.

"I'll think about it," I say.

Julia picks up the book again and holds it to her chest, just as she had earlier. "You'll do it. You can't let it go now. You will only be able to think about him writing a book within these walls. It's like your literary dream come true."

I watch Julia walk away with the book and I look back at the email on my computer. It wouldn't be the first book written within these walls, just the first book to ever be published.

CHAPTER 2

Six weeks later ...

The event coordinator from Fitzgerald & Clark Publishing arrives today. She texted nearly two hours ago and said she was en route from the airport in Denver.

My best friend since, well forever, Lily, Julia, and I nearly have our noses pressed to the window waiting for the event coordinator to arrive. And when she does arrive, she doesn't disappoint.

A black SUV pulls up in front of the store, the driver hurries out of the car and opens the back door, and out steps a woman who oozes professionalism and screams New York. Red hair cut into a sleek long bob. Black heels, a stark contrast to the few snow piles that still pepper the streets. She has on a long wool coat cinched at the waist and large black sunglasses cover her eyes.

I'm suddenly very aware of how unprofessional I look. I have on a pair of jeans and a sweatshirt with the logo of the store on it.

My wiry salt and pepper hair lands at my shoulders and is pushed back with a headband.

She's big city.

I'm small town, and I feel that to my core.

From the car she pulls out a black commuter bag, and dangles it on her arm as she holds her phone in her hand. She converses with the driver, and he points in the direction of the resort. She nods and then looks at the front of my store.

"New York City in Pine Haven," Lily says with optimism dripping from her words.

"Handsome, broody authors, who are old enough to be my father," Julia says in a sing-song voice grinning at me.

"If you two embarrass me …" I leave the threat open as I move to the door to let in New York.

I pull open the door, and the woman, who was looking at her phone, looks up at me startled, but then smiles.

"You must be Emma?" She holds out a hand to me.

"And you must be Katie?" I ask, holding out my hand to shake hers.

"I am. I'm so glad to be here and to meet you. We are going to shower your town with attention, especially your store. I'm excited to get started."

Her enthusiasm is contagious.

I step back, inviting her into the store she'll be showering with attention.

Katie pulls off her sunglasses and makes a grand gesture of looking around before letting out a whistle of appreciation.

"Oh, this is even cuter than the pictures on the website. Oh, Emma," she says, pressing her hand to her chest. "You know what a gem this is, don't you?"

I can feel the beaming smiles from Lily and Julia and I nod. "I do," I say and Katie nods in agreement.

"Oh, and look at this display," she says, walking toward the banner next to the counter with a picture of Noah Carter's next book and his headshot.

"We've been taking orders in person and online. We look to have quite a crowd for the signing—well, for all the authors," I add, but she knows it's Noah's book that's already making the sales.

Katie nods, looking pleased.

"Is the cafe next door attached to the bookstore?" she asks.

"Mrs. Packer and I put in a door between the two businesses when I took over the store twelve years ago."

"Mrs. Packer," she says on a sigh and leans in toward me. "How old is she?"

"Going on eighty," I say. "And she looks eighty, but don't let that fool you. I've never known anyone with more energy and dirtier jokes."

That has Katie reeling back with laughter. "God, I'm going to love it here. Show me around. I want to hear about every part of your store and this cute town before I head to the hotel and try to get a few hours of sleep."

"I'm happy to meet with you later," I offer, knowing that the time difference and altitude can get to a person.

"Oh, no. I'm ready to hit the ground running."

Katie is an information seeker—an asker of questions. After an hour and a half, I wonder what it's going to be like when she and Julia get into a conversation.

We've toured my store, a few times actually. She's intrigued by my collection of romance titles, since they represent over half of my inventory.

"I'm a romantic at heart," I tell her.

"So am I. I'm a sucker for a good happily ever after. Alyssa Maxwell?" she says the name of my favorite romance author and I beam.

"She's an auto buy for me and I'll reread each title at least four times."

"Ditto. When she started publishing at Fitzgerald & Clark, I got to show her around. I don't often get starstruck, but I did that day."

"Do you usually work with the authors?"

"One of the best and worst parts of my job," she says, but before I can hint at wanting to know the gossip behind that statement, she says, "Let's check out the rest of the town."

She's not here to just shine a light on the five authors who write chart-topping novels, she's here to spotlight Pine Haven. Fitzgerald & Clark gives back to the community and to readers, which makes them one of my favorite houses to work with, as an independent bookseller.

"I have a pair of sneakers in my office if you'd like to wear them," I say as we head out the door. "I know that the hike toward the hotel gets a little elevated."

Katie laughs, her hand pressed to her chest, though she's not out of breath. "Believe it or not, I've been training for this."

"Training for this? What do you mean?"

"Stair climber at the gym," she says. "I did an event in Vail once, I was sick for a week while I was there. Everywhere I went, I had to sit down. So, for the past three months, I've been hitting the climber and treadmill at top incline. My ass is firmer than it's ever been," she says confidently.

Setting the treadmill at an angle doesn't give one altitude of thousands of feet, but maybe altitude sickness is a mind game, and Katie seems to be managing it just fine.

Once we have met everyone in the entire town, we head back to bookstore.

When we walk in, I notice Julia standing at the door to my office, behind the front counter. She looks over her shoulder at me, a crease of worry deep between her brows.

A moment later, I understand the worry when Noah Carter walks out of my office.

"That's really small," he says in a low gruff voice.

"Noah!" Katie nearly shouts beside me. "I thought you were coming in tomorrow. I arranged for a car for you tomorrow," she says pointedly.

He looks toward us, and I don't know what happens in that moment, but his dark eyes flash. The broody look disappears for only a second. If you blinked you might have missed it, but I caught it before it returned.

"Change of plans," he says. "Don't worry. I called the resort and added a night, and I called off the car. Janice gave me the number."

There is a tiny twist of Katie's lips, a smile maybe—as if maybe she knows how he rolls and this is unexpected but not out of character? "Well, okay. Do you need a ride to the resort?"

"I rented a car," he says, his eyes darting between me and Katie.

Katie jerks as if she's realized we're all just staring at the two of them. "Noah, this is Emma. She's the owner of the store, your host," she says as if she's a parent reminding a toddler to be on their best behavior.

"Nice to meet you," he says without moving to shake my hand.

"You as well," I say. "This is Julia and Lily," I offer nodding to the others.

Julia's gaze is between starstruck and frightened. Lily appears to be finding something humorous.

"Nice to meet you all. Thank you for the room rental. I'll bring in a check with me in the morning," he says, as if I didn't hear his commentary on just how small the space was. "I think I'll head back to the hotel for the night. What time do you open?"

All eyes are on me now.

There is an opening time and a time in which I get in.

"We open at nine," I say and his groan is audible.

"But she's always here by seven," Julia offers and I slice her a look.

"Great. I'll be here then," he says before walking to the door and turning around. "Can I give you a ride to the hotel?" he asks Katie, who looks down at her feet.

"I suppose these shoes have done enough walking." She turns to me. "I can't wait to fill you in on all the plans. I'll see you tomorrow as well. Bye, everyone," she says as she waves and follows Noah out the door.

When they're both gone from the store, we all just stand there staring out the window.

"Wow," Julia says.

"Wow indeed," I parrot.

CHAPTER 3

Lack of sleep has me fumbling my keys, my bag, and the cup of coffee I just purchased from Pack-a-Punch Coffee, Mrs. Packer's coffee shop.

It's just past six-fifty, but thanks to Julia, I was worried about getting to the store by seven in case Noah Carter was to actually arrive that early.

Just from history, or the tabloids, I thought that broody thriller authors would be night owls. The kind that don't wake until well past noon, drink coffee and whisky intermittently, and then write up a storm until the sun comes up, and then shut all the blinds as if perhaps the sunlight burns their skin.

"You're punctual," the voice comes from behind me just as I get the old key to turn in the lock. Luckily, I don't startle so easily, and the coffee doesn't take its opportunity to spill all over me.

"Mr. Carter. Good morning," I say, trying to keep the irritation out of my voice.

"Mornin'," he returns eyeing the cup in my hand. "Is the coffee good?"

I look at the cup, as if it isn't in my hand burning through the paper cup. "Yes. Mrs. Packer has a special blend."

He nods. "Super caffeinated?"

I know I'm staring at him now, those eyes deepened by dark circles as if the man hasn't slept in a decade. I guess that's the difference. He goes all day and all night? "She has that option. It's called Ski Bum."

I'm sure the corner of his mouth lifts at that, but it's gone as quickly as it surfaced. Without another word, he walks next door to get his caffeine fix for the day.

By the time Noah walks back into the store, I've dropped my things on the counter, and begun to clean off my desk for him to work. I thought I'd have time to clear out of my private space, but here he is, now standing in the doorway.

"Sorry, I thought—"

"Don't be sorry," he says. "I know this wasn't the plan for you. I appreciate you making space for me without warning. I'll pay you for the extra day."

I don't know why I'm so surprised by this. I guess I had just decided, because of our email exchange so many years ago, that this guy was an asshole in person. Well, to be honest, his mood yesterday hadn't changed my mind. And, he doesn't seem to be a morning person either.

"Is there anything I can help you with?" he asks, scanning a look around the small room.

"Really, I just need to clear off the desk. I can do everything from the laptop at the counter. And you're welcome to use the desktop computer if you need to do research or anything on the internet."

"I appreciate that," he says.

Hmm, so morning Noah Carter has a soft side when he gets going.

I gather up the stacks of papers and move to the door. Noah

steps back and lets me through, and then moves quickly into the office and sets his bag on the desk.

"We have a coffee maker and a small refrigerator of drinks in the back room. You're free to help yourself."

He eyes me coolly. "I'll be fine. I don't mean to disrupt your day to day."

"Oh, and the door sticks a bit. So you'll have to give it a good shove and yank to open and close it."

"Got it," he says, but he doesn't move to close the door. So, I set down the stack of papers I'm carrying on the counter, and close the door myself—pulling it shut until it slams.

Julia arrives just shy of nine o'clock. She's usually what brings me to life with her morning person attitude. The coffee and the two hours I'm at work in the dark and quiet settle me—Julia brings the spark to the day.

"Have you seen that enormous pothole at First and Main? I swear my car nearly got swallowed up by it. It's an actual health hazard," she says. "Oh, and I talked to the librarian at the elementary school this morning at the donut shop. She says that they're going to have Audrey Palmer reading to the kids next month. I told her I'd talk to you about having her come here too."

Without me saying anything to her, she keeps walking through the store, flipping on lights on her way to the back room, just as she does every morning.

"When is Katie coming in this morning?" her voice carries through the store. "I have some ideas on how to set up for the signings. And I think we need to rearrange the thriller shelf."

A moment later the sound of the door behind me being yanked open has me turning.

Noah emerges from the office and looks around the store.

"Disgruntled patron?" he asks, his voice low and gravelly.

I look at him. The dark circles are a bit lighter beneath his eyes, and his hair looks as though he's tunneled his fingers through it over and over. Maybe he wasn't working in there, but was sleeping.

"Employee with too much energy in the morning," I say softly, because my morning voice isn't revved up like Julia's yet.

Noah nods as we both lift our heads as we hear Julia walking through the shelves.

"We're going to need to reorganize the back room," she says from beyond the children's section. "When Dreamy's books get here, we'll need to get them staged."

I feel the prickle of anxiety creep up my spine as I look toward Noah.

"Dreamy?" he mouths.

I can only smile. I'm not about to confirm that she's talking about him.

"Dreamy Noah?" she shouts across the store. "Dreamy Daddy?" Julia continues as she works out a name for him.

Now I make a strangled noise as I see the man next to me stiffen.

"Is she talking about me?" he asks, and when I look at him, his eyes have gone wide and he appears to be mortified.

"She thinks you're, well, dreamy," I say with a little shrug of my shoulder.

"Disturbing," he groans, just as Julia emerges from the cookbooks, her arms stacked with books that she's going to display in the window for the day.

When she sees Noah standing next to me, she goes pale. I'm not so sure she's not going to pass out, but she recovers quickly.

"Mr. Carter, I didn't realize you were here," she says looking confident, but her voice shakes realizing that she just shouted all those things about him throughout the store.

"I am," he says.

"Well, glad to have you here. Can I get you a coffee? A muffin? Mrs. Packer makes brownies, and I know she has some special ones in the back that you can ask for if you're needing any kind of pick me up or rest for a few days."

Again, I hear the strangled noise escape my throat, and Julia looks at me, maybe realizing she might be talking too much.

"I'm fine, thank you," he says. "I was just going to refill my coffee."

"C'mon, I'll show the machine in the back. Mrs. Packer is a bit expensive. I mean, sure, buy one cup, support the local businesses, but then use the machine in the back. More cost effective."

Noah exchanges a glance with me as Julia disappears behind the shelves again.

"Am I safe with her?" he asks.

"She's young enough to be your daughter," I tell him, just as I'd told her about him being old enough to be her father.

"That wasn't my question."

"Well, just keep your distance and yell out *avalanche* if you need a safe word," I say.

"Avalanche?"

I nod.

"I just wanted to practice," he says, returning to the office and retrieving his paper cup from Pack-a-Punch Coffee, with the logo of a fist, which Mrs. Packer's grandson created to go with the overly caffeinated coffee.

A few minutes later Noah emerges from the bookshelves with a new coffee mug, this one branded The Reading Nook.

"Your employee thought I should use one of the store mugs if I were going to be in here," he says, obviously not remembering Julia's name, and as if he's explaining why I'll have to wash that mug later.

"She's conscious of those kinds of things."

He stops at the end of the counter and looks at the display with his book and headshot that announces that readers can preorder their copy here.

"This is disturbing too," he says looking over his picture.

"Why? It's prompting people to buy. You're going to be very busy at the signing."

Noah blows a long breath through his lips and his shoulders drop. "I'm sorry you have to look at this everyday. I don't know what I was thinking when I had that goatee and now it's my trademark I guess."

It's only then that I realize his face is shadowed with growth, but the goatee wasn't there yesterday when I met him.

"You look distinguished," I say, and I hear him chuckle softly.

"I look like someone trying to be someone else," he says as if there is regret from doing that in his past.

"We could take a new picture and stick it over the sign," I offer and watch as he lifts his eyes to meet mine.

"I'm not sure that would be better."

"I'm just saying, if you're worried, no one will recognize you …"

"Well, the anonymity is nice."

And there is a new side to this man that I don't really know at all. I wonder how he's going to make it through this event if he's not comfortable with people looking at him. He's going to be the biggest draw here.

He passes behind the counter, back to the office, and closes the door with some effort.

Suddenly, without even knowing him, I feel protective of him. I look at the sign prominently displayed on the counter. I can't take it down. I'll lose sales. But my mind is now fixated on how I can make it better for him.

CHAPTER 4

It's business as usual, except that Julia seems to be on mute, and the office door has been closed behind me for hours. I can't help but wonder what Noah's process is, locked in my office.

Are his fingers flying across the keys on his computer keyboard? Does he have notebooks full of ideas that he keeps adding to in longhand? Is he researching new and evil ways to off someone?

Will the FBI be knocking on my door because he took me up on my offer and is using my computer for his research?

My thoughts are interrupted when I hear the familiar *yank yank* on the door before it flies back and nearly hits Noah in the face as he opens it.

"It's like a safety net," I tell him as he inspects the doorjamb. "I definitely know if someone is breaking in, or out, as the case may be."

He nods. "I could fix it for you."

I am so taken aback by his comment, I know that my expression is nearly cartoonish. A Scooby-Doo double take, if you will. "You can do that?"

He shrugs. "I can be handy. Do you have tools?"

Ducking under the counter, I pull out an old, red, metal tool box and hand it to him.

He sets it on the counter, opens it, and frowns down at it. "I might need something more than this. Surely there's a hardware store?"

"Across the street and down three spaces."

The corner of his mouth turns up. "You can always rely on small towns to have exactly what you need in a short distance."

"We try to keep up with the times."

"Bowling alley?"

I wince. "Fresh out. For that you have to travel about twenty miles."

"And I was just thinking about how much I liked it here. That's a strike," he deadpans.

"Pun intended?"

"Indeed."

Now the corner of my mouth turns up.

I love a good, witty conversation. I have to assume that if I had a daughter, it would be like talking to Julia. There is a protective stance I take with her, but she's comfortable enough to talk to me about her life. Lily and I can get into some deep conversations, and always have. I can tell her anything—and I mean anything. But as for someone who can share witty banter with me, I've been at a loss for years with that. Who would have thought I would find that with Noah Carter, the author with whom I've only exchanged curt emails?

"I was just going to order a sandwich for lunch from Mrs. Packer's, if you're interested. I'd order you one too," I offer.

He's studying me, and I feel a heat move through me as he does so. I suppose he's trying to see if my intentions are true—you know, the good neighborly kind. Maybe he's trying to decide how he's going to kill me off in his book. Either way, it's been a very long time since a man's eyes searched my face for any kind of truth.

"Does she make those in the front of the store or in the back?" he asks.

"You don't want an herbal sandwich?" I tease.

"Lettuce is as far as I go on the greens with my lunch."

"Understood. You'd like a brownie from the front counter as well, and not from the back?"

"We can save that for another day," he says looking back down at the tool box. "Order up the sandwiches and I'll pick them up on my way back from the hardware store."

"You really don't have to fix my door," I say, a bit worried about his handyman skills.

"It'll be a good break."

"Getting a lot of writing done?" I'm curious, and if we keep up this kind of banter for the next two weeks, maybe I will get to know his process. Maybe it'll give me a process to write too, and I can finish that damn book that is stuck in my computer.

"Sure," he says, turning back to the office and retrieving his wallet. "I'll buy lunch."

"Oh, you don't have to do that."

"I'd feel better about it. The other girl ..." He looks around the store.

"She's gone. She's takes classes at the community college on Tuesdays and Thursdays."

"You run the store alone?"

That has me now questioning his motives. I don't know this man who hyper-focuses on thriller, horror, death, and terrorism. I've read his very detailed words on dismembering a body. Maybe I should have had the store fully staffed for these two weeks. But, I took a self defense class from the local martial arts school. I feel confident that I could effectively kick him in the groin and yell, "Leave me alone!" if I had to. In that instant, I also remind myself that if I'm being attacked, I need to yell fire. People respond when they think there's a fire—go figure.

"We're not too busy in the middle of the week until the summer tourists start to pile in."

"Or the literary seeking crowd in the next few weeks?" he asks.

"For that, it'll be all hands on deck."

A silence falls between us and it's not uncomfortable. Maybe we're both just old enough that it doesn't matter. Like, I'm not out to impress him and he's not out to impress me, so we don't have to fill this moment with more chatter.

Noah walks around the counter. "I don't know how long it will take me at the hardware store."

"Ask for Sam. Tell him what you're looking to do, and he'll direct you right to what you need. I have an account, and you can charge anything to it."

"I got it," he says.

"I'll order the sandwiches and they'll be ready when you get there."

He nods and walks through the door.

I find that my eyes stay laser focused on him as I watch him cross the street and start toward the hardware store. Then, the curiosity of it all fills me, and I have to turn back to the office and look inside.

His laptop is closed in the center of the desk and there is a legal pad atop it. There are no notes, just a few drawings, doodles actually. The air doesn't buzz with productivity. I remember how the office would look when I'd put in hours of writing. Surely it's just his process, and mine is much different.

Picking up a piece of paper from my discarded stack near the printer, I walk back to the counter and write out our orders which I'll hand to Mrs. Packer through the open door between our stores. I forgot to ask Noah what kind of sandwich he wanted, but at least I know I can add lettuce.

The thought makes me chuckle.

I opt to order a tuna sandwich and a turkey sandwich, and I'll let him take his pick. If he doesn't like my choices, he's free to go and order something different.

My phone chimes on the counter and I pick it up. It's Katie.

I'll be in at three to start planning. I have some great ideas for the store, and a list that Julia sent me as well. I can't wait for this event!

I shake my head as I reply back to her letting her know I'll be ready. I hope Julia isn't stepping on any toes. I don't want to stifle her enthusiasm, but this is bigger than our store. Fitzgerald & Clark is putting a lot of money into this town, so I'm not going to get in their way, and neither are my employees.

CHAPTER 5

Twenty minutes later, Noah walks back into the store through the open door to the cafe.

"No take out containers? We get plates?" he asks, a plate in each hand.

"Not only do we get plates and real silverware, when we take them back, we have to go through the kitchen and wash them."

He lets out a little chuckle as he sets the plates on the counter, a bag from the hardware store dangles from his wrist.

"Is this where you eat?" he asks.

"Usually I eat at my desk, but ..."

"We could eat at the desk."

"I don't want to disturb your work."

"I'm not working," he says as he sets the hardware bag on the counter too. "Besides, standing here, I'm looking at myself. And there's nothing worse than eating lunch and looking at a picture of yourself. Though it doesn't look like me."

"A few days of beard growth you'd be right back there."

"And about six weeks of sleep," he says and I study those deeply darkened eyes. "Anyway, which one is yours?"

"I don't mind. I didn't know what you liked and I forgot to ask."

"I see the turkey sandwich has greens."

"Fresh from the front of the store and not the back," I assure him.

"Just the way I like them."

We never do move to my office to eat at the desk or walk to the back room. We fall into that comfortable silence again right at the counter.

When the door to the shop opens, and three women walk in, Noah gathers his sandwich and heads to the office. Once he's deposited his lunch on the desk, he comes back for the hardware store bag.

"What time do you close?" he asks.

"On a Tuesday night with no events, six."

"If you don't mind sticking around for a few minutes, I'll get the door fixed before you leave. I don't want to disturb your customers," he says before turning back to the office and closing himself in. Only, he doesn't fully close the door. This time he leaves it unlatched and I wonder if that was to keep from slamming the door, or so that he doesn't feel so isolated.

I finish my lunch and walk the plate to the backroom so that no one smells tuna fish the rest of the day. At some point, I'll take the plates back and wash them.

When I return to the front, the three ladies that came into the store walk to the counter, each of them have a book tucked in their arm.

"It looks like you all found what you were looking for," I say, noticing the book each of them carries is Alyssa Maxwell's newest romance, which I think is her best yet.

"Is there still room people to join book club?" One of the women asks.

"We have some space available." I reach under the counter for the clipboard that has the signup sheet for this month's book club, in which we're discussing Alyssa's newest book.

Turning the board toward them, I hand the first lady the pen to sign up as I ring up her order.

"You haven't been to book club before have you?" I ask, scanning the barcode on the back of the book.

"No. We came to scope out the town for the literary festival. We're in an Airbnb just up the mountain a ways. Luckily, we booked it again for that weekend too because every hotel room in town and the next twenty miles is filled," her voice is filled with delight at having secured a place to stay.

"It's going to be a great weekend," I say as the third lady touches the poster for Noah's book.

"He'll be here?" she asks, actually running her hand over his picture.

"He will be."

"Sexy," she moans and all three of them giggle. "He'll be doing a book signing?"

"He will be. We'll have the schedule out soon. He's signing his newest book. It'll be release day and you can preorder here and we'll have copies for you."

The three of them exchange looks. "I'll take a copy of his book too," the woman whom I'm ringing up says.

I add it to her order, and then push over another clipboard to gather her information for the preordered book so that her copy is waiting for her when she arrives for the signing.

"I'll need one too," the second woman says.

"Me three," the third woman says, her fingers still lingering on his picture. "Have you met him?" she asks me.

My jaw tightens because I can only imagine he's watching this whole interaction through the crack of the door.

"I have."

The third woman finally moves her hand from the poster,

resting it flat on the counter, pulling herself forward. "Is he as sexy in real life as he is on his website and TV?"

I swallow hard. "He's a nice-looking man," I say, because, shit, I'm not about to tell her he's every bit as sexy and broody as he comes across, knowing he's right behind me. Though, I'm also going to protect his privacy until he has to be on display. If he'd wanted the attention, he'd have stepped out behind me by now.

The third woman studies me coolly. She'd obviously wanted better gossip than that.

I ring up their sales and suggest they go next door to Mrs. Packer's for a latte.

When they hurry off in the other direction, that's when the door behind me creaks open.

Noah stands behind me with his cafe plate in hand. "That was extremely uncomfortable," he says, his voice a bit raspy.

"I guess you're just too sexy for your poster."

I'm surprised when he chuckles at that. "You didn't tell her you thought I was sexy."

Now my throat tightens and I shift a long look at him. *Is he flirting?*

"Well, that would have made the conversation even more uncomfortable, don't you think?"

The corner of his mouth ticks up, and I realize that I didn't say otherwise. Shit.

He sets his empty plate on the counter and studies the list the ladies just added their names to.

"What book are we discussing at book club?" he reaches for the clipboard and looks at it. "*Whispers of the Heart*. Alyssa Maxwell."

"I think it's her best yet," I say and watch as he shakes his head. "Let me guess, you don't read romance." There is some snark in my tone as I take my automatic defensive stance when I discuss romance, usually with men. There is a standoffishness about them when they even say the word. Immediately my spine straightens and I'm defending something that hasn't even been discussed.

I've seen the looks, having been a romance reader my whole life, and having dabbled in the writing of it. Literary lovers and especially horror authors, they don't believe in the happily ever afters or the tropes. There is a look that clouds their faces when the word is even used in their presence. Admittedly, I don't know if he has that look. I'm on autopilot, ready to defend the genre with my every fiber.

Noah pushes the clipboard back toward me. "A good author would read across genres to get a feel for others' voices and the market."

"Are you a good author?" I ask, and immediately wish I could take it back when his lips tighten and his gaze drops back to the clipboard.

Noah pulls the clipboard back to him, as well as one of the pens on the counter. On the book club sheet, he writes down his name before pushing it back to me.

Though his lips are still tight, there's a softness in those shadowed eyes.

With that, Noah walks back into the office, and this time, fully closes the door.

CHAPTER 6

As promised, and promptly at three o'clock, Katie walks through the door.

I can't help but be envious of her professional look and her youthful glow.

Looking completely out of place in her heels and suit, she commands the space around her. She's in charge, and I don't think there is a soul that wouldn't let her take charge of any situation.

Just as she was yesterday, when she stepped out of the car, her phone is pressed to her ear. She walks to the counter answering the person on the other end of the call with, "Yes. Okay. Done. Thank you."

With a strong breath out and a smile now taking over her lips, she pulls off her sunglasses and smiles in my direction. "Who doesn't love event planning?"

It's not so much a question as it is a statement. She loves her job and all the little pieces and parts.

Katie sets an enormous canvas bag on the counter, as well as her commuter bag. She then proceeds to pull out a large three ring binder. "Are we okay to look at this right here?" She looks around the store. "I assume you get busier in an hour or so?"

"I'll have a few people wander in before dinner rush in town."

"Perfect," she says, opening up the notebook. "The next few weeks are going to be glorious chaos. But everything is planned. This is where we get to tweak it so it fits your store and the town."

The door behind me rattles, creaks, and then opens with enough force to have Katie jumping back.

Noah wrinkles his nose as he steps out. "Sorry," he says looking back at the door.

"Old buildings, huh?" Katie says.

"My handyman is going to fix it tonight," I say, looking in Noah's direction.

His eyes go wide, and that's when I notice Katie's expression matches his. Did that come across as intimate? Did I cross a line?

"He said he'd fix the door," I say and Katie smiles that same quirky smile she had when he'd arrived unannounced.

"Impressive," she says.

Noah shrugs. "Least I can do." He eyes her notebook. "Do you mind if I listen in to your meeting?"

Katie opens her notebook. "I don't mind at all. Same as usual, and you've done enough of these to know the drill," she says.

"Sure have," he says, and I wonder if that's why he wants in at this stage.

Is he usually present two weeks in advance? Does he work on location before these kinds of events or is this a special circumstance?

Katie takes a beat before she dives into the specifics of the planning.

Each section of the notebook is dedicated to either one of the locations where an event will take place, or to the author who will be there. I'd like to think my organization skills are good—well, good enough—but Katie Stevens puts my skills to shame.

"There will be five different signings here," she says and then points toward Noah's poster on the counter. "I assume he's outselling the others?"

I notice Noah's body stiffen next to me, but the truth is, she's right. "At least five to one," I say.

Katie turns her smile in Noah's direction. "You never disappoint," she says and I watch as those circles under his eyes darken and he swallows hard.

"There will be a day," he promises. "I think I'm going to go next door and get some coffee ... maybe from the back of the store."

To that I snort out a laugh, but of course, Katie doesn't understand the joke.

"Can I get either of you something?"

I shake my head, but Katie pulls her wallet from her commuter bag. "Iced latte, large," she says handing him a ten dollar bill.

"I'll get it," Noah offers.

Katie shakes her head. "I'd rather pay. And thank you for offering."

Noah puts the bill in his front pocket, picks up his plate, and heads toward Mrs. Packer's.

Katie watches him disappear. "He's not bothering you, is he?"

I can only imagine my expression shows the surprise I am feeling by her question. "No. No, not at all."

She turns a page in the binder. "He's a moody one. I'm used to that. Authors are introverts by nature in a career that puts them on display. It's not everyone's cup of tea. But him ..."

She lets it hang there. "Why is he so moody?" I have to ask. I mean I'm sharing space with the man for the next few weeks.

Katie looks back toward the doorway to Mrs. Packer's. "He always was, I hear. It's not that he's unkind, just comes across as grumpy, abrasive?"

Oh, I've seen the unkind side. Well, via email. I can't say I've seen that in the man that's been hanging out in my office though.

"After his wife died, I guess his whole world took a turn. So instead of a mood, it's just how he is now."

"He lost his wife?"

"Breast cancer, maybe eight years ago."

My heart squeezes in my chest. "That's devastating."

"Almost ruined him. But, he drew from the pain I guess. His next six books have hit the charts at number one on presale and stayed there for weeks. Four of them have been optioned for movies. He's the real deal. So, you put up with his moods and go on."

Because it's playing over in my head, the comment about me not telling the women in the store that I thought he was sexy, I have to ask. "Does he date a lot?"

Katie actually chortles at that. "Carter?" She snorts out his last name. "Are you kidding me? This is the most outside his space I've ever seen him. Usually he holes up in his apartment and never leaves, unless he's doing one of these events or publicity. I think the last time I personally saw him out and about was when I met him on the set of the Today Show. Otherwise, I assume he's holding himself hostage in his apartment."

Opening my own business—my bookstore—for me was a refuge of sorts, just to get me out of the house after my husband left me. Without it, I suppose I would hold myself hostage inside my house too.

I watch as Noah returns from the coffee shop with a large iced latte in one hand, and a large coffee in the other, with a brownie balanced atop it.

He hands Katie her latte for which she thanks him.

He hands me the brownie. "She said this is on the house and it came from the back. She said that with a wink."

I can feel the flush of my cheeks as they heat. "That woman," I laugh and I notice the smile that slides across his mouth.

Katie is watching the interaction with too much interest, so I have to let her in on it.

"Mrs. Packer makes her own edibles. If you order anything from 'the back of the store,' that's what you'll get."

She turns to Noah. "You ordered that?" Her voice rises in volume and pitch.

"Not my style, really," he says, but unoffended. "She was just making friendly, I suppose."

"Does she do that?" Katie now wears a mask of panic. "Are tourists going to come here and get drugged?"

I shake my head adamantly. "Oh no. No. She would never do that. In fact, only a few people know about the back counter. I'm not sure why she sent this over." Except that I can imagine she knows I'm probably stressing this event more than I should.

Katie blows out a breath. "Okay then. I don't want anyone feeling as if that's something they have to worry about."

Noah shoots me a grin as he lifts his coffee to his lips and disappears back into the office, fully closing the door behind him.

I tuck the brownie under the counter. I'll save it for Lily, who doesn't mind unwinding that way. Katie gets back to explaining the event in more detail and flipping through the pages of her well-constructed and organized notebook. I don't know if I'm hanging on her every word so that things run smoothly, or if I'm trying to pick up on tips to become more organized.

CHAPTER 7

I'm not sure what drove everyone in town to stop by, but for a Tuesday afternoon, the store is hopping. Katie had even said she'd come back tomorrow to finish going over things, because I just couldn't give her all my attention. I don't usually have staff on afternoons where, as a rule, I'm not busy. But today, Julia and Lily would have been handy to have around.

Exactly at six o'clock, the door to my office opens and Noah, looking even more exhausted than he had earlier, walks out.

"You knew I had a rush on your books and you hurried out to say hello to your adoring fans?" I say, dripping in sarcasm at the empty store, but his eyes are dull as if he doesn't understand my comment. "I was just kidding. But I did have a run on preorders. You're going to be one busy man at your signing."

Noah rakes his fingers through his hair and just nods. "I'll get to fixing the door now so you can get home."

I watch him as he moves back to the office to retrieve the bag from the hardware store. As he gets the items he'd bought set up, I move to the front door and lock it, then turn the sign to closed. Mrs. Packer closed the door between our places hours ago, but I check to make sure it's locked. She opens much earlier than I do and I've been known to find people wandering my store when I walk in because we've forgotten to lock the door.

When I come back to the counter, Noah is on the step stool sanding down the top of the door.

It's intriguing to me that a man who is good with words is handy too. I don't know why I think those two things don't go together, but obviously they can.

I begin to close out the register and run the day's reports. So far I have enough books ordered for the event, but if sales keep up as they have been, I may have to pull in a few favors to cover the inventory for Noah's book.

"How long have you owned the shop?" he asks from his perch on the stool.

I turn to look up at him, surprised by him starting small talk.

"Twelve years," I say.

"It's a really nice shop," he says, looking around from his elevated view. "I like the children's corner."

I lean against the counter and watch him work. "It's one of my favorite places. I wanted kids to get excited about reading. I thought if it was welcoming, they'd want to be there."

He nods. "What do your kids think about it?"

I cross my arms in front of me, closing myself in, as I do when I find myself talking about kids. "Never had any. It wasn't in the cards," I say and he nods.

"Yeah, me either," he says, and I can hear as much disappointment in his voice as I feel in my heart.

"Your romance area is extensive," he says matter-of-factly as if to get us off the topic of kids, and I have to remind myself not to put up that defense I had earlier. He's not dissing me—yet. He's only commenting on the store itself.

"I would have liked to have had an all romance bookstore," I admit.

"Why didn't you?" he asks as he steps down the step stool and tries the door, then climbs back up and starts sanding again.

I let my arms fall, leaving defensive me behind. "The only other store in town is a used bookstore. I figured this was my opportunity to help the community and host local authors who otherwise won't get a chance in a big store. Independent authors need independent bookstores to support them."

Noah stops sanding and levels a look on me. "The big stores don't carry local authors?"

I have to study him a moment to see if he's asking that as a legitimate question. He seems to be honest about it. "No. The big publishers, like Fitzgerald & Clark, have contracts with the big stores. They fill them, not leaving much room for independent authors."

"I didn't know that," he says, almost apologetic.

Again, I'm studying him and wondering what rock he's been under for the past fifteen years, but then it hits me. The devastated widower rock is probably big enough to have sheltered him.

I shrug. "It's how it works. So, instead of only selling romance, I support everyone. Even those who have contracts with big publishers," I say, smiling up at him, and hoping it comes across as sincere.

"I appreciate everything you're going to be doing for the literary event. I don't get out much, unless I'm doing a book tour or one of these events." He steps off the stool again and tries the door. This time it closes without much effort. "If I didn't do these things, I'd never leave my apartment," he admits as he pulls a can of WD-40 out of the hardware bag, along with a cloth and goes about spraying the hinges, and wiping up the drips.

Watching him, I wonder why it's taken this long to fix that door. What he did wasn't rocket science, but there was a patience to it and I appreciate that.

"I'm not dogging on the big publishers," I say, realizing now, I might have sounded a bit jaded.

"I didn't think you were. I mean, you're still working with

them. You carry all of my books. Multiple copies." He turns his head and smiles wide at me. He'd done some shelf scoping.

"I have to. Too many women come in here looking at the back jacket of your books."

He lets out a grunt. "I seriously doubt that."

Noah tries the door a few more times, shutting himself into the office and then opening it again.

"I think this is good," he says and for the first time, his eyes seem brighter. Oh, he still looks like he hasn't slept in months, but there is an uptick in his attitude. "Maybe it won't scare your customers away."

"It does tend to give Julia a near heart attack when I open it."

"Which one was she?"

"The one who thinks you're a hottie," I tease.

Recognition lights in his eyes. "She's much too young for me."

"I agree. I told her as much."

"Thanks for coming to my rescue. I don't tend to date people when I'm old enough to be their parent."

The banter is comfortable enough I ask, "What kind of people do you date?"

There is a flash in his eyes, and when his cheeks lift with his smile, I know we're flirting now. And yes, I have to think it through, because I don't do this. I don't flirt. I don't date. I don't know what's making me do it with someone who is well known for being a bit standoffish and grumpy.

Noah folds up the step stool and slides it back in the office. He then takes the rag and covers the WD-40 can. "Where would you like this? You might as well keep it handy."

I take the can and set it under the counter with the miscellaneous tools. "I'll pay you back for all of this," I say as he throws the sand paper into the trash.

"No need. It makes me feel useful, and I'm in your space. It's the least I can do." There is a moment between us that is silent as we both seem to be taking one another in. "Well, I should let you get home. I'm sure you have someone waiting for you."

"I don't," I say this so quickly that Noah actually flinches. "I mean, I'm single. No one at home caring when I get there."

There is silence between us again, only this time it's charged with an electricity that isn't comfort. No, this is different.

"So what's good in this town, foodwise?" he asks.

"Other than the greens from Mrs. Packer's?"

He chuckles at that. "Yeah."

"Everything is good. That's one of the bonuses of a small town too. It has to be good or it doesn't stay open. But the bar has good food. The barbecue place is good, and always has a good crowd. There is an Italian place, if you like some ambiance with your meal."

"Ambiance?"

"Dark setting. Candles on the table. High backed booths."

He nods as he takes that in. "More private than the bar?"

Until that moment I wouldn't have considered him thinking about where he could go and not be bothered. I mean, on a normal day, he can probably walk the streets of New York and not even be recognized, especially without the goatee. But in a small town, where people are arriving just to see him, this adds a different layer of concern for his privacy.

"You certainly wouldn't feel on display," I say.

Without another word, he turns back into the office and picks up his commuter bag, which he must have already packed. He turns off the light and slings his bag over his shoulder.

"How far is this place?" he asks.

"On the other side of town. Maybe four miles."

"Your car or mine?" he says and I blink hard.

"Why would we take my car?"

"So we could get to dinner."

"You want me to go with you to dinner?"

His eyes grow a bit wider. "Didn't I ask you to dinner?"

"No."

Now he blinks hard. "Oh. I meant to."

For a moment we just stare at each other, but a laugh breaks out of me. I've had my share of being so in my own head, I start conversations with Lily when I'm halfway through them. Once I start to laugh, then so does he.

"I guess I had other things on my mind," he says.

"I guess you did."

"Will you have dinner with me?"

I study him and wonder why in the world he'd want me to go to dinner with him, but then I realize, neither one of us has anyone to hurry home to.

"I'll drive," I say. "Let me get my things."

CHAPTER 8

"Living in the city, I forget just how dark it can get," Noah looks out the front window of my car, his neck craned, as we drive through town.

"It does make for a pretty night sky, that's for sure. A million stars meet me most nights when I get home," I say as I take the exit toward the restaurant.

"You don't live in town?"

"Just outside of it. Up the mountain about a mile."

Noah sits back in his seat and lets out a sigh. "I always thought I'd like to be remote, but I don't know anything but the city."

"You were born and raised there?"

He nods. "Mom was in fashion. Dad was in finance. New York was the hub of it all."

"Brothers or sisters?" I ask, because I find I want to know this man who seems to be a mystery to all.

"Both," he says. "Sister is ten years older. Lives in Connecticut with her husband. They have three kids and five grandkids. My brother lives the Jimmy Buffett life."

I snort out a laugh. "What's that?"

"He lives in the Bahamas and has a boat charter business."

"No kidding?" I feel my skin warm just thinking about it.

"He was the kid that never played by the rules of societal norms. He was in ballet in elementary school. Did gymnastics and swim through high school. Went to college in Key West and fell in love with the ocean. From there he got a job on a cruise ship and traveled the world for years. Then, he settled in the Bahamas and started a business."

"I love that."

Noah's mouth splits into a wide smile. "He's a nut. He's three years younger than I am, but looks twenty years older with the lines on his face from the sun. But they're happy lines. You know, when you meet someone who is permanently sun-kissed and has smile lines from actually smiling all the time? That's him. He's been married three times, and now lives a glorious polyamorous life."

I jerk a look to him and then back to the road as I pull into the parking lot. "Polyamorous?"

"Sure. They have a huge family there that they've created and it's enviable. When I met my wife, I couldn't imagine someone could love more than one person," he says and his smile softens. "I was consumed by her and loved her so much. So it took me a while to understand that some people have it in them to love multiple people like that and to make a family of it."

I ease into the parking space and put the car in park. "I've never given it much thought."

"I hadn't either. My pea brain could only focus on loving one person."

"I don't think there's fault in that," I say, envious that he had that.

"There isn't. I just get a bit into myself when I think of my brother's family and my sister's. Look what they've built."

We're alone in the dark inside my car. It's a very intimate place to be.

I don't really know this man, but I'm drawn to him, as if we fit together some how.

I place my hand over his, which rests on his thigh. This causes him to lift his head to look at me, a hint of surprise in his eyes.

"Katie told me about your wife. I'm sorry for your loss," I say, knowing now it was a loss that was so much more than losing a partner. He lost out on family, and that loss comes across loud and clear when he talks about it.

His other hand comes to cover mine. "Thank you."

We can only stay that way for a beat before it becomes awkward. He lets go of my hand and I pull back and open my door as he does the same with his. A moment later we're shutting our car doors and walking in silence into the restaurant.

Noah pulls open the door for me and I step inside, noticing that he falls in behind me. I request a table and the server walks us to a booth at the back of the restaurant. If Noah wanted some privacy, he's about to get it.

He waits for me to pick a side and sit before he sits. I've opted to let him have his back to the door, and I figure if that's a problem, he'll let me know.

"Ya gotta love restaurants that are so dark you have to use the flashlight on your phone to look at the menu," he says, doing just that.

"I have to use my phone to magnify the print on the menu," I laugh and he nods in agreement.

"Getting old is a blessing and a curse, right?"

"My ex used to say that, but mind you we were thirty and had no idea what we were talking about then."

That warrants a tiny chuckle from him as he scans over his menu.

A few minutes later we give our orders to the server and sip on our water. Neither of us orders wine.

"You mentioned an ex," Noah breaks the silence with that and I wince.

I don't often talk about him. It's not worth the air in my lungs to do so. But, Noah shared with me his family when I asked. I suppose it's only fair if I share a bit about my life.

"I have an ex," I say.

He puckers his lips and crosses his arms in front of him. "That's all you have to say about that?"

"He's not worthy of a lot of my attention."

"But I study people for a living. I'm going to need more to go on."

"Are you going to write him in one of your books?" I ask, amused with myself.

"How do you think I decide who to kill off?"

Now it's me that laughs. When Noah lets the walls around him crumble a little, he can be enjoyable. Admittedly I didn't expect to have conversations with the man while he was working at my store or even at the event. I certainly didn't think we'd be flirting. And now we're sitting in a dark restaurant getting to know one another. I guess when your eyes open in the morning, you never know what the day has in store.

"My ex," I sigh out the word. "We were high school sweethearts. Broke up and went our separate ways after. He went to college and I followed Lily to New York. She went to college and I worked in my aunt's bookstore."

"Where?"

"Chelsea."

Noah lifts his water to his lips and smiles from behind it. "No kidding? I worked at Chelsea Market after college."

"I guess we've moved to the point of the conversation where we ask how old one another is."

Noah sips his water and sets down his glass. "Fifty-five. No hiding it," he says.

"Fifty-two, and proud of it."

We both chuckle at that. He's easy to be around, and I'm glad.

It was going to be a long three weeks of having him locked in my office if I couldn't stand him.

"So we were probably there around the same time," he says.

"Sounds like it." Now I pick up my water and sip. "I stayed for a bit and then came back. I went back to New York when Lily got married and again when she had her first kiddo. Then again when she had her third. My aunt wanted me to stay and work for her, but this is home and it kept calling me back."

"What's the name of the store your aunt owns?"

I swallow hard. The true and only beef I have with this man is because of my aunt's store. I've held this grudge against Noah Carter for years, and I'm going to reignite that if I tell him the name of the store and he has no recollection of it.

"The Chelsea Book Nook," I say, and the moment I do, there is recognition in his eyes.

"Shit," he mutters the curse under his breath so that it's nearly inaudible.

I watch him silently. He picks up his water again, sips, and replaces the glass before doing the process all over again.

"Are you okay?" I finally ask. I realize I've carried this annoyance over this man for years, but I wonder why it's affecting him so much.

"I thought your name looked familiar when Katie sent me the email about the event," he says, his voice filled with regret.

Again, we sit in silence until he lifts his eyes to me. "I owe you a long overdue apology."

CHAPTER 9

I don't know what to say to Noah as he watches me.

He owes me an apology—I'm sure I heard him right.

He remembers the exchange? That was like thirteen years ago.

I don't want to condone the actions that had set me off, or the emails we exchanged, but is, "it's okay," the right response?

I find that I don't have a response.

Because it seems to keep him calm, he sips his water again. "Thirteen years ago Abby got her first diagnosis," he says and his words pierce my chest.

"Abby was your wife?"

He nods and sips from his water again, only now the glass is empty and he stares at it as if his vice is now his nemesis.

"Stage four breast cancer. Things didn't look good from the start. The day I cancelled the signing was the day they rushed her into surgery." His voice hitches, and the need to move around the table and pull the man into me is nearly consuming. But I sit across from him and watch as he busies himself with his napkin now that his water is empty.

"Anyway, it was unprofessional and so were my emails that followed."

I reach across the table to capture his hand in mine. I can't help myself. "I didn't know."

"Of course you didn't. I was devastated, and you got the fallout. I didn't even realize I hadn't told you, I just became this angry monster."

"You deserved to be," I defend him and he shakes his head.

"No. I didn't. I deserved to be upset and angry, and I was all of those things. I didn't need to be nasty, but it just didn't occur to me."

"Thank you for the apology. I'm sorry you carried it with you for so long."

He gives my hand a squeeze and pulls back as the server delivers our food.

When the server steps away, Noah lays his napkin in his lap. "I've created quite a reputation for myself that I'm a tad grumpy."

I do everything I can to control my face. Yes, that reputation precedes him, but now I wonder if I can fix that. I don't know why I'd even want to take on that mission, but something inside of me wants to.

Picking up my fork and twirling it into my pasta, I look up at the man across from me, still obviously very broken. "Katie said your wife only died eight years ago?"

He nods as he cuts into one of his raviolis. "I got five more years with her. I'd like to say they were happy and it was a blessing, but it wasn't. That fucking cancer ate at her for five years. Five fucking years."

Every word is filled with anger, and that pull to him is even stronger.

"I'm so sorry," I say, and I realize then that I'm crying when I hear it in my voice.

I set down my fork and lift my napkin to my eyes and dab.

Noah lifts his gaze up to me. "This night took a turn, huh?"

"Thank you for trusting me with all of this. It means a lot."

"Yeah, but I think it all started when I asked you about your ex."

I fill my mouth with pasta to stifle my laugh. I chew, swallow, and wipe my mouth before I reply.

"I certainly didn't feel the same kind of love for my ex as you did for your wife," I say, because that came across when he talked about her.

"I assume when you say ex, you mean husband? I know you were high school sweethearts," he reminds me where we left off when we started talking about New York.

"Yep," I pick up my water and sip, signaling the server when he looks in my direction to let him know we need more water. "We got back together after he got home from college and I got back from New York, the first time. Then we got married," I say as the server returns to fill our water.

We thank him, and Noah rests his arms on the table and leans in on them. His subtle way of telling me to continue, I suppose.

"I thought it felt perfectly normal when I'd go back out to New York to spend weeks, months at a time to help Lily when she had a baby, and I'd help my aunt at the store. But I realized, later, that it wasn't normal, it was necessary."

"Necessary?"

"Didn't you ever need a break from your wife?"

He shakes his head. "No."

"Oh. Well ..." That stops me, so I take a bite of my dinner.

He doesn't move from his interested perch. He waits.

I've seen this with authors before. The reason they're good at what they do is because they enjoy watching people. Every motion, every word feeds into their character building, even if they don't mean to do it in the moment. They write human emotion, and what's more raw than someone telling you about their wife dying or the end of a marriage.

"Sean just wasn't ticking all the boxes I needed emotionally.

He never really did. He was just comfort," I say, and lift my glass and sip my water.

"That's understandable."

"Maybe. It was still selling myself short to marry him," I say honestly as I set my glass back on the table and pick up my fork. "He was a good enough guy, until he wasn't."

"And this is the meat of the story," he says easing back in the booth and crossing his arms in front of himself again.

"Are you just listening to my back story looking to add it to a book?" I accuse him and his eyes go wide.

"I didn't mean that—"

"I'm sorry. That was crappy," I say, taking a bite of my dinner.

He watches me with even more interest now, as if my accusation didn't ruffle any of his feathers.

He eases back toward the table and picks up his fork, scooping up a ravioli. "I enjoy getting to know people. That's the honest truth."

"How do you do that when you yourself said you don't get out much?"

"Well, I badger them when I do get around them. Just like I'm doing with you," he says and I laugh.

"Great people skills," I reply.

"I've never been accused of having those."

That has me laughing more as I load up my fork again and shove a bite into my mouth.

There is a smile that crosses Noah Carter's face when he's pleased with himself, and poking fun of himself is one of the ways he does that, I've noticed.

"Why did you find it necessary to spend time away from your husband?" he asks when we've settled, drawing me back to my story.

"He was a narcissist." I set down my fork and pick up my water. "I thought that since his parents were narcissists, it was just something that could be worked around. I mean, he never had a chance, right?"

I sip my water and set the glass back on the table. "He'd tell me I should go to New York to help Lily. Then he'd spend the whole time I was gone letting me know how unfair it was for me to travel without him." I wave my hand in the air. His flaws were just something I didn't want to get into. "Anyway. He was bad for me. He was bad for himself. I'm just glad it didn't work out for us to have kids. No matter how devastating my few miscarriages were, I came to understand there was a reason a baby wasn't born in that marriage. I guess the solace is there aren't more genetically narcissistic people in the world because of me."

"That's pretty deep," Noah says, studying me.

"It's how I coped."

"I'm sorry for your losses."

I feel that in my chest. It's an ache that I haven't visited in a very long time, but with Noah's condolences, it's back. Though, it's not the same. He genuinely knows loss, and his words give me comfort.

Deciding that the conversation needs to just wrap up, I continue. "Eventually, the story goes along that I wasn't enough for him and he left me for someone else. By the time they'd gotten involved, I was disillusioned, and I don't think I even cared. It was a good reason to get out of a marriage that didn't bring me joy and didn't serve me in any way. I was happier across the country working in my aunt's bookstore and dealing with moody authors," I add the jab, and he chuckles at it.

"It was fulfilling enough work that you thought you'd open your own store, with a similar name, so that you could have one on one time with moody authors on your own turf?"

"That was my driving force," I say. "I knew that one day I could convince one of them to fix my office door, and they'd be charming enough to get a free back-room brownie from Mrs. Packer," I tease and he snorts out a laugh.

"Don't let that get in the wrong hands," he says.

I watch the stiffness in Noah soften. Perhaps we've given one another a tiny piece of ourselves and that's worth something. He's someone who is broken from watching a horrible disease take the love of his life. I'm someone who has yet to find the love of my life. My story is a basic story of greed, really. I wanted a family, but my body wouldn't allow that. I wanted a husband, but I wanted to be free to do what I loved to do. He was free to do *who* he wanted to do. Now I'm free to live out my dreams in a cozy bookstore where brooding authors fix my office door, share stories with me, and remind me that I have a pot brownie under the counter. Though I was going to give it to Lily, now I think I'll make sure it goes into the refrigerator for later. That might be just what I need with Noah Carter around.

CHAPTER 10

I'm not sure who I should be more angry with, Mrs. Packer or Noah Carter.

Standing at the front counter of my store, at seven o'clock in the morning, I can see the light on in my office coming from under the door, and there is a large paper cup with the Ski Bum logo that Mrs. Packer has printed on the over-caffeinated beverage—like a warning label.

I pick up the cup. It's empty. Obviously he's been here a long time. This means Mrs. Packer unlocked the door between the businesses and let Noah—basically a stranger—into my store. I set my bag on the counter and turn to the closed door behind me. I'm fairly sure I'm going to find Noah in there writing. Anger begins to boil up in my gut. Just because we had a nice dinner and shared some details of our lives doesn't mean that he has the right to bust into my place of business and make himself at home without me there.

Gripping the doorknob tightly, I push open the door hard, only it doesn't stick, because Noah fixed it.

The door slams open and I fall into the office where Julia leaps out of the desk chair and is upright, screaming at the top of her lungs. Her scream has *me* screaming, and then a moment later I can hear pounding on the door between the cafe and the bookstore.

I can hear Mrs. Packer calling for me, but I'm stuck on the scene in front of me.

"What in the hell are you doing in here? Where's Noah?" My voice is loud and only getting louder as Mrs. Packer's knocking on the other door increases. "We're fine!" I shout across the store and the knocking stops.

"You scared the shit out of me," Julia says, her hand to her chest and not answering my question.

"Why are you here?" I look around the room for evidence that Noah is here too. And what in the fuck is he doing here this early with Julia? "And where is Noah?" I ask again.

Julia's brows pinch in confusion. "I've been here for hours, studying. And I don't know where Noah is," she says, pulling off her headphones and pointing to her stack of books and her laptop. "Besides, you don't come in this early on Wednesdays. Why are you here?"

"Because," I shoot out the answer without backing it up, because, well, I don't know why I'm here so early except that if I have someone using my office I should be there. "Why are you here studying?" I'm still shaking and my heart is racing. Only now the anger and the jealousy are colliding in my brain.

"Samantha had a guy stay last night, and he creeps me out. I was trying to study on the couch, but he kept checking me out. And, in the middle of the night, I'm fairly sure he was trying to open my bedroom door."

Now that maternal instinct, which I never got to use on my own kids, but always kicks into gear with Julia, rises.

"Did you tell Samantha that?"

She shakes her head. "You know her. He'll be a one night person."

"Still, he doesn't sound safe."

Now there is knocking on the front door of the shop, and I step back out of the office to see Noah standing there, two cups of coffee stacked atop one another in one hand while peering in the window. His brows are drawn inward and when he sees me, his eyes go wide.

I hurry to the front door, unlock it, and pull it open.

"Are you okay? What the fuck was all the screaming about?"

"Julia scared the shit out of me. That's all," I say.

He nods rapidly. "Oh, well, as long as that's all."

And we're here in this moment for longer than we should be. The moment where I'm grateful he wasn't fooling around with Julia in my office, and the moment he's glad no one was killing me.

"Hey, Mr. Carter," Julia calls from the counter as she lays down her stack of books and laptop and picks up the coffee cup that had been sitting there.

Noah looks at her, then back at me, before acknowledging her welcome with only a lift of his head.

"Here," he hands me one of the drinks in his hand. "This is for you."

My smile is automatic as I take the cup. "I appreciate it."

"I'm not sure either of us need it now. When I heard you scream, my heartrate spiked."

His sincerity warms me and I step back to let him into the store. "I do still have the brownie from yesterday. That would settle us," I tease.

He lifts a brow. "Not sure that would increase my productivity."

"I'm not sure it will."

Julia makes a show of picking up her items and walking toward the reading nook. "Don't mean to bother the two of you. I know this is your quiet time. Don't mind me."

I watch her salute us with her empty coffee cup and disappear in the nook.

"Do we already have a routine?" Noah asks, his head tilted toward mine.

"You know those young'ns, they always are assuming."

"And you know what happens when you assume," he teases as he walks toward the office and disappears behind the closed door without even a creak.

The UPS guy delivers nearly a truck load of boxes to the back door around nine o'clock. It's safe to say that Julia's studying time has come to an end. However, having finished that entire Ski Bum, she's buzzing around the store unpacking books and stacking them in the back room.

Katie walks through the door just after ten o'clock, and today she's dressed in the most Colorado outfit I've seen her in so far. She has on a Patagonia puffer coat, a pair of designer jeans, and a pair of UGGs.

"I have verification that all of your preorders just landed," she says, pulling her dark sunglasses off of her face.

"Julia is back there now taking inventory. We have our work cut out for us to get them in order and ready."

"No books go out early," she says and I draw a cross over my heart, even though her comment could be taken in the worst way, considering I've done this for the past twelve years, well even more. I know the rules.

Katie leans in close to me. "How is he?"

"Who? Noah?"

"He's not bothering you, is he? I mean, you say the word and I'll pull him out of here. He can work in his hotel room."

"He's a delight. He fixed my office door last night. We even went to dinner after."

She studies me and the hardness in her face softens. "No kidding?"

"No kidding."

"Maybe the lack of oxygen agrees with him," she says just as Noah steps out of the office—with no notice given because the door is so quiet.

"Less oxygen keeps my mood intact," he says sipping from his coffee cup, then shaking it, perhaps realizing it's empty.

Katie's eyes go wide, but the professional side of her loads up a smile as she sets her bag on the counter. "Did you see the New York Times?" she asks him and he nods nonchalantly.

"I didn't," I say, because I don't know what this secret language between New Yorkers is.

Katie pulls a printed piece of paper from her commuter bag and slides it in my direction.

Caught in the Crossfire by Noah Carter is the number one selling book on the list—and it doesn't come out for another two weeks.

I shift my glance toward him, the grin wide on my face is tugging at my cheeks.

"This is amazing," I say, and all he does is shrug.

Seriously, does something like this just become old hat? At what point does it no longer matter?

Katie shifts a glance between us before taking the paper out of my hand. "I've already initiated another order of books for you. You're going to need them," she says and I open my mouth to protest, but she holds up a hand. "Fully returnable if they don't sell. You have credit, and we'll discuss the options when the event is done. This is all riding on my word," she promises.

Noah leans in behind me. "I wouldn't bank on me that hard," he says, but when I look up at him, he's looking at Katie.

Her lips flatten and there is a sadness in her eyes, as if she's heard him discredit his talents too many times.

"Anyway," she continues after drawing in a breath to regroup, "I see that you have a book club gathering this evening?"

"Every other Wednesday," I say. "It's our romance book club."

Noah shakes his head, and I realize just how close he still is to me. "Do you have other book clubs or romance only?"

"It's the only book club I can get people to regularly sign up for," I say, but my voice is a bit strained.

"*Whispers of the Heart?*" he says and I nod, knowing we had this discussion yesterday.

"Well, I wish I could be here," Katie says, breaking the tension that is building between me and her author. "I have to fly back to New York for a few days, but I'll be back Sunday," she assures me, or maybe Noah.

"I can sign you up for the next one," I say.

"I'd love that. There is nothing better than a good romance," she says, and again, it's directed right at Noah. "Now, do you have some time to go over the schedules for the event week?"

CHAPTER 11

Noah had visited Mrs. Packer for a Ski Bum to keep him motivated and then locked himself in the office. Lily brought lunch, but I made the decision not to bother Noah. He's a grown ass man, and he's probably deep in his work. He'll eat when he's ready.

"How's the author?" Lily asks as we open the containers of salad she brought for lunch in the back room while Julia works the front counter.

"Moody. Nice. Handy. Broken," I say in rapid succession.

Lily stabs her fork into the lettuce and then pauses with her fork right at her lips. "So, you've gotten to know one another pretty well?"

I snort out a laugh. "He fixed my office door and then we went out for dinner. It was fine. He told me a little about his wife and I told him about Sean."

Lily chews her bite slowly, studying me. "You never talk about Sean."

"We were just exchanging pasts."

"And when you do that, you still usually leave Sean out of the conversation."

I think about that as I take a bite of my salad, dissecting the conversation we'd had last night and the sogginess of the lettuce in my mouth.

Swallowing hard, I set down my fork, pick up my water bottle, and take a long sip.

"It just came up," I say, setting down the bottle and wondering what I'm going to eat, because that salad isn't going to be it. "He did apologize for the way he treated me when he canceled at my aunt's store for his signing all those years ago."

Her eyes go wide. "Are you kidding me?"

I shake my head. "He remembered my name from the emails. It appears we were in Chelsea at the same time when he finished college and you and I were there. Then we got to talking about the store, and he remembered me."

"I'm surprised."

"So was I."

"So why was he such an asshat?"

I chew on my bottom lip and then look out to the store to make sure the door to the office is still closed. "It was the day they took his wife in for surgery after she was diagnosed with stage four breast cancer."

"Shit."

"She died five years later."

"That diffuses your grudge, huh?"

I shrug. It was never so much a grudge as it was unpleasant in the moment. But I think for Noah, it was so much more. Why would he remember it if it hadn't rattled him for years?

Julia's voice grabs my attention. She's talking to Noah, who has emerged from the office. I'm suddenly not sure how I feel about the door not making noise. I didn't realize just how much of a signal that was. Then again, it was a signal to everyone else that I was coming. How many conversations did I interrupt when I pulled open the door and they stopped talking?

Looking out into the store, I see him walking toward the back room through the shelves of books.

"Hey," he says as he walks to the door, his stride easy. He only stiffens when he sees Lily, and then greets her too.

"Hey," I say, as if I wasn't just gossiping about him—well, was it really gossip?

"I'm going to head back to the hotel for a bit; get some lunch," he says as he looks over our soggy salads.

Was he coming to look for a lunch companion? Nah.

"No problem. I might use the office while you're gone, if you don't mind," I say.

"It's your office. You can always banish me back here or to the children's section."

I shake my head. "The kids that write in that section on their time off are much too advanced for you," I say and he laughs, and it lights in his eyes.

"I really need to step up my game," he says, the grin still in place. "I'll be back later. You're here later because of book club?"

"We'll be here until nine. There will be wine and cheese," I say in offer.

"Intriguing, as much so as the book."

Noah turns and walks back to the office and I turn back to my salad, stick my fork in it, and raise it to my mouth before I remember I don't want to eat it. That's when I catch Lily staring at me with wide eyes.

"What?" I ask as I drop my fork and pick up my water.

"What's going on between the two of you?"

I look out into the store and then back at her. "What do you mean?"

"You're flirting."

"I am not," I say before sipping my water.

"You most certainly are. And he's all in."

I lick the water from my lips and set the bottle on the table, my hand still wrapped around it. "He was flirting, wasn't he?"

"You both were," she confirms. "Shit, I can't remember the last time I saw you light up when a man walked into a room. And that one of all people. Could you get someone more pleasant?"

"I'm not getting him at all. We just talk."

"You talk and it drips with sex."

"We didn't have sex," I say as if she's accusing and her face absolutely lights up with a humored expression.

"I didn't say you were. Wow, Emma. You're fucking all into this guy."

I realize just how loud she's being, but luckily I can hear him talking to Julia, so maybe he can't hear these stupid accusations from the back of the store.

I lean into Lily and whisper, "He's a nice guy, under that asshat."

"He's into you."

"He's lonely."

"He's here and so are you."

"And so are you," I remind her.

"I'm not single."

"I'm not looking," I fire back.

"You don't have to be looking to have an affair with some broody writer."

I shake my head at that. "I'm not looking to have an affair. I'm fifty-two years old. I can take care of anything that a man can, and yes, don't look at me like that. I mean everything," I say as she perks up and I know what's coming.

"He's sweet on you," she says.

"He doesn't have a sweet bone in his body."

"I think you should fuck him while he's here and finish that romance novel you have stuck on your computer. It just might be the thing that breaks you out of your writing funk."

I ease back in my chair. "I suck at writing. That's the writing funk."

"You do not. You just don't believe in yourself. The book is good. It just needs some meat."

I can't imagine she even remembers the storyline. I've been writing that stupid book for so long, even I can't remember what it's really about.

Okay, it's about love, new love, exploring love, falling in love. Bleh, even I think that is sickening. I quit believing in love when my ex-husband's girlfriend walked into the restaurant where we were eating one night and told him she was pregnant. Right then and there, I didn't believe in it anymore. Well, not for myself. Had I really loved Sean, he wouldn't have chosen someone else, and I would have been more hurt when he stood up, pulled her to him, and that was that. Suddenly I was the other woman and I didn't care enough to fight for him. I moved back to Pine Haven two days later and never looked back. I never looked ahead either.

I watch as Noah walks out the front door of the store.

I wonder if he still believes in love after what happened to him. What happens when you actually love someone so much but they're taken from you?

CHAPTER 12

Book club doesn't start until six-thirty, but set-up starts the moment I throw that nasty salad away.

Our reading nook has two oversized chairs where we'll host authors when they are in town for a reading and a Q&A. For book club nights, I sit in one of the chairs and guide our group through the discussion of the book. Instead of rows of chairs, we set up in a circle so it's more intimate. We serve wine and cheeses, and Mrs. Packer, always the first to sign up for book club, brings a dessert that is safe for the masses to eat.

Lily left to run a few errands, and Julia headed to the bar to get herself an edible lunch.

While the store is quiet, and Noah is not in my office, I need to pull up my notes on the book and print them out. I have a well-annotated copy of *Whispers of the Heart*, which is also in the drawer.

I sit down at my desk and readjust the chair because Noah is at least ten inches taller than me. I adjust the keyboard back into its normal position and turn on my computer. I search for the notes on the book and send them to the printer. I check a few emails. And then I open the folder entitled *Falling for You*.

Fifty thousand words scroll in front of me. Fifty thousand words that I've written, rewritten, edited, and still hate. No, I don't hate them, I reconsider as I read the few paragraphs that land on the screen as I stop scrolling.

I'm more in love with this book than I ever was with Sean. Perhaps I always thought this book would be the manifestation I needed to have real love in my life. I've just never felt it was good enough to query to an agent or even independently publish myself. Lily thinks differently—and that's why she's my dearest friend.

"Emma?" I hear Mrs. Packer call my name from the store and I push back from my computer and walk out of the office. "Hello, sweetheart. I brought the dessert over for tonight. Do you have room in your refrigerator for it?"

She hands me a tray of tarts covered in cling film. "Don't these look delicious," I moan.

"They are. Noah thinks so too. I gave him one earlier as a tester."

"You know if you feed strays, they will stay," I tease and she grins up at me.

"I'd keep him," she says with a lot of enthusiasm. "I'd best go finish so I'm ready for book club."

I carry the tarts to the back room and slide them into the refrigerator as Julia walks back into the store, followed by three women who frequently shop here. I return to my office, grab my annotated copy of *Whispers of the Heart*, and my notes, and walk back to the counter to help customers. It's nearly my most favorite part of my job. That and reading all day long when I can. There is nothing better than having all the books you'd ever want to read right at your fingertips. And, when the publishers send advance read copies, it's like having a secret Christmas.

. . .

As is the norm before book club, many of those who signed up come in early. We'll have the next book on sale, and of course the wine and cheeses are out. We won't put out the tarts until book club is over. It makes for a long night, and a dark drive home up the mountain, but it's part of the charm of owning the store and living where I do.

Ten minutes before we start, I pull out my notes and look over them one more time.

"Do you think Evan is swoon-worthy enough for an Alyssa Maxwell book?" the familiar voice has me looking up from my notes.

Noah is leaned against the counter, his grin turning up one side of his mouth.

He's shaved, but has left what looks like the beginning of a goatee. I continue to study him as he moves in, leaning his arms on the counter.

"There is a feeling of duty, ya know?" he says.

"You read this book?"

"Didn't I tell you a good author reads across genres. I'm familiar with this one."

"You're not here for book club, are you?" I ask, remembering he wrote his name on the sheet, but I didn't take him seriously.

His smile widens. "Actually, I took a hike today and I think I worked through my plot problem in my book."

"You're having problems with your book?" I sound like a parrot.

The smile he's been wielding slips. "All authors hit road blocks once in a while," he says as the door opens and more women walk through, each with a copy of tonight's book. "How long will you be here tonight?"

"Until at least nine-thirty."

"Do you mind if I work?"

"I don't mind at all. We won't distract you?"

He shakes his head and walks around the counter. "The only

distraction is knowing there are tarts in the back room. But Agnes promised me one, so don't let someone take it."

"Agnes?"

The grin is back. "Mrs. Packer."

"You're on a first name basis? She doesn't let anyone call her by her first name."

"No one does as many dishes as I do."

"You're doing dishes there?" I ask, and I realize my voice is rising, though not attracting any attention.

Noah leans in close enough that his lips are next to my ear. "She has a thing for me," he says and his warm breath sends a tingle up my spine.

"You're not …" I leave it hang there, pulling back so that I'm looking him in the eye, but our noses nearly touch we're so close.

"She'd be one lucky woman, wouldn't she?"

I swallow hard. "I don't know, would she be?"

Noah gives me a wink and moves past me to the office. "Tell me when the tarts come out. I don't want to miss them."

He shuts the door, and it doesn't make a noise.

I have to draw in a few breaths. Noah Carter confuses me. He's broody, sexy, talented, broken, and fuck he smells so good when he gets close to me. And why does he get close to me? Because he's messing with me, that's why. Or is he?

"Everyone is ready," Lily says as she walks toward the counter. "Are you okay? Is the cheese bad? I made one more stop after I picked it up today. It didn't—"

"No. No, the cheese is fine."

"You're flushed," she says scanning a look over me.

"Hot flash," I say, because it's a good answer for anything when you're my age.

"Your hair isn't wet."

"It was just a warm flash?"

Lily snickers at that. "I keep clean clothes in my car and those body wipes too. I hate getting old."

"The alternative is worse," I say and she nods.

"At least the sex gets better," she says and I choke out a laugh.

"Does it?"

"Does for me. We know each other so well that nothing is off the table. It's all trust and new positions. Well, because of my knee and his hip."

That has me cackling. Lily does love to share tidbits about her sex life, and always has. I've just never had much to add to the conversation.

When Noah moves something in the office, Lily's attention is diverted from me to the closed door.

"Who's in there?" she asks.

"Noah."

"I thought he left hours ago."

"He did. He took a hike and now he's motivated to write."

She nods slowly as I pick up the book and notes and we head to book club to discuss just how swoon-worthy we all think Evan really is for an Alyssa Maxwell book.

CHAPTER 13

Mrs. Packer agrees with Noah's earlier take on Evan, the love interest in the book. "I didn't fall in love," she says.

"How could you not?" Clara Harris, a book club regular, says with a hand pressed to her chest. "He's looking for answers, and she has them. He treats her so kindly, and when they have that kiss …"

"That kiss?" Mrs. Packer grunts. "Oh, honey, that wasn't a kiss. That was a lame excuse to feel her boobs."

A few of the ladies giggle, Mary Lou, a book club regular, covers her mouth in disgust, and poor Clara bats her eyes at Mrs. Packer in disbelief.

"C'mon, girlies, this wasn't her best book and we know it," Mrs. Packer lifts her wine to her lips and drinks down what's left in her glass.

"It was a stretch for sure," Noah says from his perch against one of the book cases.

I don't know how long he's been standing there, but the audible gasps and whispers mean no one knew he was there and now the entire flow of book club has been disturbed.

"See, I told ya," Mrs. Packer says, acknowledging Noah's presence.

I eye him coolly, "She's guarded," I say to Noah.

"Yeah, I would be too if some buffoon stole my career and turned the entire art world against me with his lies," he says. "But some historian wanting access to the letters I found in the attic of my new house, that doesn't warrant the softening of her heart as quickly as it happened."

"Maybe she was just ready," I retort.

"Maybe. I mean, sure, obviously she just wanted sex," he suggests.

Again, those who giggled at Mrs. Packer's take on Evan, and the one that gasped, do the same thing. Mrs. Packer stands, fills her glass, and another for Noah, and hands it to him.

"See, I told you these girls wouldn't get it," she says to him as if they've already discussed the book in great detail.

"What's not to get?" Clara asks. "Alyssa Maxwell is a genius at putting together characters. So, they have sex quickly," she says, with a wave of her hand as it's no big deal. "Not every romance has to be slow burn," she adds, and the comment is aimed toward Mary Lou whose cheeks are a crimson red now.

"But it has to fit the story," Noah says, and the whispers begin again among the other ladies.

They've figured out who he is, and one even has one of his books in her hand and is comparing the photo on the back of it to the man arguing romance during book club.

"How does it not fit the story?" I ask and Noah's eyes scan a look over me perched on my oversized reading chair. His lips twitch before turning up into a smile.

"Our dear artist, Emily, hides out in her house and hardly talks to anyone."

"Normal," I say, thinking that sounds like Noah—or what I've learned about him.

"Sure. Absolutely normal," he agrees. "What's not normal is

the first man she lets into her house makes a move on her by chapter six? And she lets him?"

"The heart wants what the heart wants," I agree.

"The vagina wants what the vagina wants," Mrs. Packer injects and now I feel my skin grow warm.

Noah chuckles at that, but keeps his eyes on me. "All I'm saying is the sex was rushed. It was really good sex," he admits and again the ladies giggle at that and Mary Lou drinks down her glass of water. "I think she needed to gain more trust between the characters. Emily wasn't set up as the kind of woman who would quickly let a man in her bed. The whole premise just seemed hurried." He now presses his hand to his chest. "I love a good Alyssa Maxwell book. I mean, c'mon, *Wisdom Among Lovers* ..." he lets the title linger there.

"Oh, my, god!" Clara holds up a hand in praise. "Gloria and Ruben?" She fans herself and Noah points in her direction.

"That's what I'm talking about," he defends himself. "That romance was exactly what a romance should be. Well paced and thought out. It was sexier than any of her books, but it was done just right."

"I've read it seven times," Clara admits.

"Ten," Mrs. Packer says.

Now Lily has her hand up as if it's her turn to speak. "I have a dog-eared copy in my night-stand. Page one-hundred-seven," she says and everyone breaks out into laughter and she turns toward me. "Don't tell me you don't have that very annotated copy in your night-stand too."

"Probably next to her vibrator," Mrs. Packer adds, and now the flush on my skin turns into a heat that does have my hair going damp.

When I look up, Noah's eyes are still on me. There is a bit of concern that flash in them, but I think he's proud of himself for stirring up the women of book club, and now I have to figure out how to rein them all back in.

He lifts his glass toward me, drinks down the wine, then turns to Mrs. Packer and gives her a wink before returning to the office and closing the door.

The next hour goes between discussing all of Alyssa Maxwell's books and the different pacing of the romances. A few of the women have wandered off among the shelves, and I have no doubt they're looking for Noah, but I don't offer any information on his whereabouts.

Mrs. Packer serves up the tarts and Julia helps a few of the women, who weren't familiar with the other Alyssa Maxwell titles, purchase books and even shows them the scenes we've discussed.

I don't think I've ever had book club go so far off the rails, and yet, I have to admit, it was the most fun I've had in a long time.

"I promised Noah a tart," Mrs. Packer says, handing it to me on a plate.

"He's just—"

She nearly shoves it in my direction. "You give it to him when you're ready," she says before turning, gathering her bag, and heading out of the store with a wave in Julia's direction.

I shake my head as I watch the older woman disappear.

I carry the tart to the back room, set it in the refrigerator and remember that the brownie I was going to save for Lily is still there, and she's already made her exit.

As Julia closes out the register, I take down the folding chairs and stack them in the back room.

"Okay, I'm done," Julia calls from the front of the store, and I watch as the lights begin to go out, row by row.

I walk to the front. "Thanks for staying," I say.

"Are you kidding me? That was the funnest night of book club ever. You should make sure Noah is here for all of them."

Shifting a glance to the office door, I now wonder if he's still in there. "I think we need to have a bit more control."

"Why? Mrs. Packer is the one that starts it anyway. She is the dirtiest old lady, and I think it's just to get under Mary Lou's skin." Julia says on a laugh as she picks up her bag from under the counter. "I mean, you forget that the old lady next door used to be a free-loving hippie."

I don't seem to forget that at all, but I suppose for someone as young as Julia, that might seem odd.

"I'll see you on Friday," she says and heads to the door and I follow so that I can lock it behind her.

That's when Noah opens the door to the office. The light illuminates him from behind, and aside from his wild hair, which he must have been tousling with his fingers, he looks like a god emerging from a cave.

"Is everyone gone?" he asks.

"Yep. Just getting ready to pack up and head out. Oh, and your tart is in the back."

"I thought you'd forgotten."

"Nope, *Agnes* wouldn't let me forget to feed her favorite guy," I tease.

"She does love me," he says stepping out toward me.

"What was with that?" I ask as Noah starts toward the back room and I follow. "Did you guys have that little thing staged?"

"Have what staged?" he says as he opens the refrigerator and takes out the tart.

"That little act you came out with. It totally threw off book club."

"No it didn't," he says, opening the drawer with the plastic forks, taking one out.

"Yes it did."

"Did you sell more books?"

"Yes."

"Then it was successful," he boasts as he digs his fork into the tart.

"So you did work it up?"

He eats his bite and then runs his tongue over the fork. "No. We didn't. We had just discussed the book and both felt it wasn't her best."

I watch as he takes another bite of the tart. It's nearly erotic.

"Besides," he says with his mouth full, "that one lady was way off with her assessment of Emily's quick trip to the bedroom between these two."

Watching him fork another bite of the tart, I hear my stomach rumble, and when he lifts his eyes to me, I know he hears it too.

"These are good, huh?" he asks, taking the bite off the fork.

"Usually. I didn't get one."

He blinks and looks down at the plate in his hand. "Why?"

"Because Mary Lou is not only a conservative snob who comes to romance book club, reads the books, and then snubs the sexy stuff," I say thinking about her near pearl-clutching when Mrs. Packer mentioned Evan getting squished up against Emily's boobs, but I saw the reaction when everyone gushed about the sex scenes in other books, "but she also takes more than her share of treats."

Noah wields the fork in the air. "Why do you let her in?"

"I don't send anyone away. She bought the book."

"But she gets offended when you talk about sex?"

I chuckle. "Every fucking time."

His eyes are light and his smile softens his face. He looks back down at the dessert and then moves toward me.

"You need to try this," he says, taking another forkful of the tart.

"I've had them before," I say.

"You haven't had this one," he says lifting the fork to my lips.

That moment of watching him eat the dessert now blooms

inside of me. He's toe to toe with me holding out his fork with a bite of tart on it.

My tongue darts out to my lip, then my eyes settle on his lips before I take the bite he's offering. And when I take the bite, his tongue brushes against his bottom lip. Warmth pools inside of me, and I'm careful not to sigh. The tart is delicious, but the moment is so fucking intimate I could make some very bad decisions.

CHAPTER 14

"What do you think?" Noah asks, his voice raspy and deep, the fork held between us.

"She doesn't disappoint," I say still breathing in the nearness of him.

He eases back only slightly. "There's only one more bite. It's all yours if you'd like it."

Since I'm so pent up, and eating off his fork was a bit too sexy, I shake my head. "All yours."

Noah takes the last bite and then shifts a glance toward the refrigerator. "I did notice you still had your brownie."

That sexy smile that tugs at the corners of his mouth forms, and that warmth inside of me stirs.

"I do still have it. Would you like that too?" I ask.

His eyes search my face, and I wonder what he's looking for. "Would it surprise you if I told you I've never had an edible?"

"Why should that surprise me? I don't know you."

"Okay, well, I've never had an edible," he says and we both laugh.

I take the plate and fork from him and walk to the trash can, dumping it in. "You're a city boy, how did you avoid that?

I mean, you have mobile pot shops on the street in New York."

He nods. "We do. Let's just say when I'm in New York, I'm hiding in my apartment."

There is a seriousness to his tone.

"Why?" I ask.

He shrugs. "I'm more comfortable there than dealing with people."

"You seem to deal with them just fine, from what I've seen. Except for Katie," I say, holding up my finger. "You two seem to have some kind of history."

His lips purse. "I'm not easy to deal with when people make demands of where I'm supposed to be, and they throw in that quip about how I'm supposed to act."

"She's much too young to be your mother," I say.

"Doesn't keep her from trying."

The space between us isn't enough for me to not feel the energy that resonates off of him. Seriously, there is something about him that makes me want to reach for him.

"Why would she have to rein you in?" I ask.

Noah pushes his hands up into his hair. "You've dealt with me on different occasions," he says, a brow risen so he doesn't have to even mention our emails from my aunt's store.

"Maybe you do need an edible," I tease, and I hope it comes across in such a way.

"Share it with me?" he says, and now I wonder if I look like Mary Lou clutching at my pearls.

"You've never had one?" I confirm.

"Never."

"Pot? Have you smoked pot?"

"Twice in college," he says. "I was more a competitive drinker."

I snort a laugh. "One doesn't just eat the whole brownie on the first time."

"Why?"

"It'll fuck you up," I say, now fully laughing. "A few bites, but you'd have to get an Uber or walk back to the hotel."

"I don't think I'll want to walk after a few bites."

"You can take it with you," I offer.

"I don't want to partake alone."

I look at my watch. "It's nine-forty-five. Seriously, it'll be at least midnight before I know how it affects you."

"Can you drive after midnight?" he asks.

"It's not so strange for me to spend the night here. I sometimes have to if it snows too much and I can't get home."

"Then I'll spend the night here, too."

My body chooses this moment to have that fucking hot flash I'd only alluded to earlier. This is my opportunity to walk to the refrigerator and pull it open. Though, I'm going to look like an idiot standing here as long as I need to, just to cool down.

I can feel his eyes on me.

Pulling the brownie off the shelf, I turn and hand it to him. Closing the door I press my back up against it.

"She doesn't usually make them too strong, but if you don't know how you'll react, I wouldn't take more than three bites."

Noah pulls back the wrapping and holds it to his lips. "You're okay with doing this? I'm not keeping you from anything or anyone?"

Why does my chest squeeze when he says it like that? "No."

"You can do whatever work you want. I won't get in your way."

"If this is what you want to do, I'm fine. But, when you're buzzing around, that is if you're not one of those people who just falls asleep, you have to dust shelves."

"Promise," he says with a smile.

"And this can't be every day. I'll never get any work done if we're high all the time."

"It's Colorado isn't—"

I hold up a finger in warning. "Don't go there."

His eyes smile now as he takes his first bite of the brownie. I watch as he chews slowly. "The couple times I did this in college, I remember it hitting fast."

"This will take at least an hour for you to feel."

"I guess I could start walking back to my room," he says as if that's a disappointing option.

"I agreed to this," I say, holding out my hand to take the brownie and my bite.

"Have you ever had a slumber party in a book store?" he asks.

"Does inventory night count?" I say and it amuses me so much I nearly spit out my bite, but now he watches me as I thoughtfully chew, then hand the brownie back to him.

"Is it stupid that I have this superhero feeling?" he asks.

"It did not affect you that fast," I laugh.

"No, the anticipation. Like Peter Parker after the spider bites him. Or, fuck," he pauses, "why can't I think of another superhero?"

This is just laughter from being tired, but as he takes his next bite, he covers his mouth and continues to laugh.

Noah hands me the brownie and I take my bite. "The Flash getting struck by lightning?"

"Is that what happened to him?"

"That and getting doused with the right mix of chemicals in his lab."

"Right. The lab. People really need to be more careful when they're in *the lab*," he says.

"True. Look at Bruce Banner."

"I already have that angry gene," he admits.

That has me nearly snorting out a laugh and spitting out my brownie.

"Do you feel as if you've been shot with that serum they gave to Captain America?" I ask.

He narrows a look on me, as if he's studying me. "I've never known a woman who knows so much about superheroes."

"I'm a bookstore owner. I read all the books."

"Thank you to the bookstore owners who read my books, and to their employees who think I'm a hottie, even if I'm old enough to be their father."

Another wave of laughter hits us.

We each take one more bite, leaving only a sliver of the brownie left. I take it and throw it in the trash.

"You prove to me that you're a good boy on three bites, and we can discuss asking Agnes for more later," I tease.

"Only I get to call her Agnes," he says playfully.

"Cuz, you're *her* good boy."

His eyes go dark as he looks at me, and that warmth surges through me again. "Oh, I'm a very good boy," he says.

Yep, we're about to be fucked up.

CHAPTER 15

In anticipation of sitting in the oversized lounge chairs once this brownie hits, I set us each out a bottle of water and bags of chips. I know what's going to happen. Lily and I have been in this situation with one of Mrs. Packer's brownies more than once.

When the high hits, we're not going to want to move from the chairs. Drinks and snacks will be too much of a hassle to acquire. There might be some crying too.

If I have it all set up and waiting for us, we can comfortably fall asleep in the chairs and let the high wear off.

"Why isn't Sylvia St. Clare's photo on the front counter like mine is?" he asks, walking toward me with the poster that the publishing house sent.

"Women don't tend to want to kiss her poster like they do yours," I tease.

"I kissed her once. It wasn't bad."

That has my spine stiffening. "You've kissed her?"

"At one of these literary events," he says looking down at her picture. "Like I said, I was more of a power drinker."

"And the more you drank, the more she let you kiss her?" The tremor in my voice annoys me.

"The more I drank, the more she drank. It was a few years after Abby died and I was just lonely. It didn't go any further than that," he says, and I'm thankful. I don't want to care, but for some reason I do.

"Have you dated a lot?"

"A couple times. Dated a woman for a year, on and off." He walks the poster back to where it had been displayed. "What about you? Do you date much?"

"And let someone do to me what my husband did? Not on your life."

I plop down into one of the oversized chairs.

"I thought we had to clean before the high kicked in," he says.

"I'm thinking I want to sit on my ass instead."

He nods and falls into the chair next to me. "What did your husband do to you?"

I shift my eyes to look at him sidelong. Didn't we talk about this? No, I guess we never did get into the meat of it.

"Ex-husband," I remind him.

"Right. My mistake."

"He had himself a girlfriend he got pregnant. She introduced herself to me at a restaurant when she came to tell him she was expecting. He left with her. I moved back home."

"Fucker," Noah says, but his words slur slightly.

"He was a fucker," I say, but all I hear is truth. "I've been on a few dates that Lily set me up on, because she couldn't take no for an answer. But, to be honest, I've spent more time with you in the past three days than I have with any other man in thirteen years."

"Your forties must have been sad."

I turn to him. "Why?"

"It's a great time to not have any obligations to anyone else and just do what you want to do."

"I did," I say, lifting my hands to encompass the store. "I did this. This is my marriage, my family, my baby."

It's been about an hour and my head is starting to numb a bit from the brownie. Noah's hit hard faster, I can tell, because his head is leaned back against the chair.

"Yeah, but you can't have sex with your store," he says.

"Who says Lily was making up the comment about my copy of the book?"

That has him lifting his head, eyes wide on me.

"Don't be a prude," I tease on a grand laugh.

"I'm not a prude. I just didn't expect you to say something like that, out loud, to me."

A giggle rips through me. "I guess I didn't expect to say something like that to you either."

"I have a dog-eared copy of that book too," he admits, and that has me sitting up and slapping his knee.

"You do not."

"I do. Abby and I were figuring each other out as we went. When she was gone, I decided I needed a different way to figure women out."

"So you did that through romance novels?" My giggle turns to a laugh.

"Why not?"

"I guess if I wanted to kill someone and get rid of their body, I'd read one of your books. You're fairly detailed," I say, trying to sober my voice.

"Yeah, but I've never done any of those things."

"And you think Alyssa Maxwell has done some of those things in her books?"

He shrugs. "I just think that it's more likely that a woman has six orgasms from a skilled man and writes about it."

"Maybe that's why I never finished my book," I say easing my head back against the chair.

"That's because you didn't date in your forties," he says, and I pick up my bag of chips, unopened, and toss them at him. Only when he grabs them from mid-air, they pop and explode all over the floor.

The high has certainly set in now, as that sets us into hysterics.

We both slide from our chairs, the laughter rolling between us, and as we come to our knees on the floor we bump heads.

Noah falls back on his ass and I fall against him. "You're high," he says.

"You're higher," I say.

"More high," he corrects.

"Fuck you," I say and the laugher starts again. "I'll get the trash can."

I manage two hands on his chair and hoist my ass off the floor, bumping into him as I do so. He places a hand on my butt and pushes against me. Seriously, it's the most action I've had in years.

I head to the front and gather the trash can from under the counter. By the time I make it back to the reading nook, the chips are in a tidy pile, but Noah isn't there. I drop the trash can and follow his laughter through the stacks of books.

He's standing at the romance section slowly running his hand over every title.

"What are you doing?" I whisper.

"Looking for something," he whispers back.

"We're not in a library," I say quietly.

"Then why are you whispering?"

He sways into me as I move in closer.

Finally, he pulls a Jennifer Zeppelin book off the shelf, then turns to balance himself against the shelf with his back.

"Don't bend that spine," I warn.

"Ease up, Mom. I'll buy it if I break it."

I turn my back to the shelf, just as he has, and balance against it.

Noah flips the pages in the book until he's about three fourths of the way through it. "Have you read this one?"

I look at the book. It's newer, but Jennifer Zeppelin is consistently smuttier than some of the books we read for book club. And I say smuttier as a hot term, as the readers on TikTok have now praised the word smut so much, it's now an iconic way to say *bring on the sex*.

He hands me the book and I start to read—and heat.

This sex scene is four pages long, and being high, it's taking me much longer to read than normal. Then again, it could be the man whose body has begun to sway into mine as I read.

When I'm done reading, I press the book to my chest. My breath is heavy as if I were the one having the sex on the page.

"That's some writing, huh," Noah says still in a heavy whisper, and when I turn to speak, he is face to face with me.

When his eyes drop to my lips, I can't help but lick them and then watch him lift his eyes and lock them with mine.

"I'm going to need a moment," I say, with everything inside of me warm and pliant.

Noah lifts his hand to my cheek. "You're flushed."

"I just had sex," I say, laughing as I let his touch surge through me. I lick my lips again, and his eyes fall to them, again. "Why did you make me read that?"

He runs his thumb over my bottom lip. "Words are powerful."

"I know that. But why now?"

His thumb is still tracing my mouth. "I just wondered what it would do to you."

"Did it do the right thing?"

The corner of his mouth turns up into that sexy smile, and now I'm weaker than I was.

"You're high," he says.

"So are you."

"Oh, I'm fucking toast," he laughs as his fingers slide down my throat. "And I'm attracted to you and unable to not say it out loud."

I'm watching him, willing him to touch me, kiss me, all the while knowing we're both too high for this now. "You're attracted to me?"

"Does that bother you?"

"We just met," I say, enjoying the nearness of him.

"Haven't you ever been attracted to someone when you first met them?"

I study his face. Those dark, line creased eyes are lighter than they've been. The salt and pepper streaks in his hair, and that fine goatee that still needs to grown in so that he looks like the man on the back of his books, makes my body react in ways it hasn't in years.

Then I think about the soft noise I'd made last month when his book arrived and Julia was pining for him—now he's pining for me.

"I'm attracted to you, too," I say, but my eyelids grow heavier the closer he moves to me.

"Sleepover or not, I'm not suggesting we have sex."

That has my eyes opening to take him in. "You're not? You just had me read sex, and then you touched me."

He drops his head to my shoulder on yet another laugh, and I'm not sure he can hold his head up at this moment. "I mean, I'd love to have sex with you, sometime. But right now, I'd just like to kiss you."

"Then stop making me wait for it."

Noah lifts his head from my shoulder, his eyes locking on mine. He turns into me, his arms slipping around me, his body pressing against mine.

"That was the best fucking brownie I've ever eaten," he says.

"You might not even remember this kiss tomorrow," I warn him.

"I'll remember. I won't let myself forget something this good."

That makes me snort. "You haven't even kissed me yet."

Noah takes the book from my hands and places it back on the shelf. "I hope you don't forget the kiss."

"Just kiss me so I know how much I want that sex someday."

Noah skims a hand up my back until it comes to the nape of my neck. His fingers lift into my hair as his mouth hovers over mine. "Don't forget this," he says before his mouth comes to mine, and every part of me spins in different directions.

CHAPTER 16

"What the fuck?!"

I don't know if it's the words that startle me or if it's the violent shaking of my body. But when I wake up, Lily is hovering over me, both hands on my shoulders.

The person next to me bolts up too, repeating the same words Lily was saying. "What the fuck?"

"God, you scared me to death," Lily says falling back onto her ass, her breathing labored. "What in the hell are you two doing? I thought you were dead lying in the corner like this."

I blink a few times. My head is still fuzzy and heavy. I take in my surroundings, and then I take in the man next to me who is scrubbing his hands over his face.

We're still in the romance section, on the floor.

It all comes back to me like a memory I'm watching of someone else.

We kissed. Then my whole body spun until I slid to the floor, and he came with me. Then we kissed some more, and more. If I remember correctly, we had a whole make-out session as if we were a couple of teenagers. It was the most glorious thing to happen to me—ever. And then we both passed out, right there in the romance section.

"We fell asleep," I say, thinking that it makes perfect sense, but I suppose it doesn't at all.

"You fell asleep, on the floor of the store, in the romance section?" Lily's voice is rising. "What in the actual fuck, Emma?"

"Okay," I start to rise to my knees and then to my feet by pulling myself up using the shelf. "I think I've heard that word enough times for today. What time is it?"

"It's nine-fucking-o'clock," she adds it in there for good measure. "The door was locked. The lights were half on. And I find you both in this pile on the floor. God, I almost had a heart attack."

"We ate the brownie," I said, as if that was going to make it all better.

"You ate *the* brownie? What brownie?"

"Mrs. Packer sent over a brownie, and we ate it."

Lily draws in a breath and lets her shoulders drop, then she turns her attention to Noah. "They're good, right?"

He blinks a few times and then nods. "Sure."

"But they fuck you up."

Now he laughs. "Hence the reason you found us on the floor like that, I guess."

Noah looks up at me and there are many looks that settle on his face. There's a secret we're sharing—those kisses. There's some horror that maybe we crossed a line, or maybe it's regret for getting high in the first place. But what I notice most, the black circles are gone under his eyes.

I hold out a hand to Lily and help her off the ground, and Noah pushes himself to his feet.

"I suppose I should go home and get a shower," I say.

"I'll head to the hotel and do the same," Noah says. "I'll be back in an hour or so."

"Hopefully the brownie gives you great inspiration," Lily says, with a mix of humor and annoyance in her voice.

"I think I'm inspired," he says, his eyes leveling on mine. "Can I bring some breakfast back? I'll order something from the hotel."

Lily shakes her head. "By the time you get back, it'll be lunch time."

"I'll take an omelet," I chime in. I need food, and if I let Lily keep talking, I'll end up with a soggy salad again.

Noah nods and starts for the office to collect his things, and only a moment later, he's gone.

That's when Lily turns on me. "What in the—"

I hold up my hand. "We've used the F-word enough for today," I say.

"I'm not sure we have." She leans in. "Did you guys …"

"No," I say cutting her off. "But we kissed."

"You kissed."

"That's what I said."

I find that her grin confuses me more than it should.

"And you got high?" she says, that grin turning into an enormous smile.

"You get high all the time. Why are you busting my chops about this?"

"Because you don't get high all the time. Who are you and what did you do with my best friend?"

"Shut up," I say, moving past her and toward the front of the store.

"I'm not going to. You're going to have sex with a stranger, and I want to know all about it."

"I'm not having sex with him, and I'm not telling you anything."

"Oh, yes you are," she says as she follows me. "You're entitled to this, Em. You need it."

"It was a nice night," I say, gathering my bag from under the counter. "It was fun."

"Of course it was. He's no slouch in the looks department, and he must not be quite as grumpy as he comes across."

Turning to her, I ease against the counter. "I'm in uncharted territory. You're right, he's a stranger. A stranger from New York. He's going to go back to New York."

"I'm so jealous of you right now."

I snort out a laugh. "Why?"

"Because this is what it's all about, right? I mean we're in our fifties. We should be able to have all the sex with strangers we want."

Lifting my brows, I bore a look into her. "We? You're happily married."

"I am. And I'm having lots of great sex," she does a little dance. "But you deserve to have lots of sex with strangers, and you don't."

"It's not my style. It never has been."

"Then make it your style. Make him your style. He's hot, Em."

I feel that flush coming over me again. Yes, he's hot. And from what I can remember of the kisses before we both passed out, his kisses are hot too.

The door opens and two ladies walk into the store. We greet them and they begin to browse.

"I'll be back shortly," I say, hiking my bag up on my shoulder.

"Em, seriously, I know you don't want to get hurt again. But let go a little. That was a long time ago, and some guy is into you. And, yeah, he's going to leave, but have fun for the moment. Maybe it'll lead to something else with someone else. But, don't die on the hill Sean left you on. You're a successful woman who deserves something more than a heavily annotated book in your nightstand."

That has me shaking my head as I walk to the front door. "Oh," I turn back to Lily. "Check out the newest Jennifer Zeppelin book."

"Steamy?"

"O! M! G!" I say much too loudly before I leave the store.

I walk around the back of the store to my car, and I'm more than a little surprised to find Noah leaned up against it.

"I thought you were going to the hotel," I say.

"I wanted a few more minutes."

"For what?"

He stands and walks toward me, lifting his hands to cup my face. "To kiss you some more."

That spinning sensation is back, and I wonder if that's just what he does to me, or if I'm still high.

"Can I kiss you, Emma?" he asks when his lips hover over mine.

"Yes," I sigh out the word before my eyes close and let Noah Carter take me under with a sobering kiss.

It's not a quick kiss and when his mouth opens, and his tongue sweeps against mine, I moan and ease into him.

I want this.

I do need this.

I want him.

I need him.

Noah eases back, his hands still on my face. "I had a great time last night."

Swallowing hard, I study him as he studies me. "I don't usually get high like that."

"I know."

"I don't just make out with strangers either."

"I'm no stranger. I've known you for years," he says, his lips curling up into a smile.

"You're right. You have." If that makes me more comfortable, then I'll accept it, even if I were just a name on an email over a decade ago.

"Let me become less of a stranger in the next three weeks. I'd like to keep doing this," he says as he eases in and kisses me again.

I'm going to fall into this feet first. I'm going to feel things for this man that I know can't be reciprocated, because in the end, he will go home.

It's okay to let go a little, I say to myself as his lips work against mine and my body goes pliant against his. *It's okay.*

CHAPTER 17

The store is extra busy for a Thursday and the strained grin on Lily's face tells me it's been this way all morning.

"You took longer than I thought you would," she says through gritted teeth as I walk around the counter to stand next to her and help her with the line of people waiting to purchase their books.

I'd meant to only take a shower and change my clothes, but I guess last night wore me out more than I realized.

"Sorry. I fell asleep for a bit."

"Well," she turns slightly so she's more whispering to me than talking aloud. "He's in the office. People know he's here. The fandom is starting to just show up."

"The event isn't for weeks," I whisper back.

"Yeah, these are the diehard fans who found out he's here. Not the ones coming for the event."

I look down at the book in my hand that I had picked up to help Lily scan. It's one of Noah's older titles.

"Is he okay?" I ask.

Lily rings up the next sale. "Lying low. Shave and a haircut knock and he'll get out of sight for you to walk in. But I need you back out here in like five minutes. There are a lot of people in this store, Em. A lot."

I walk to the door and give the knock. I can hear him move about. When I think it's safe, I open the door and step inside.

Noah is up against the wall next to the door so that no one sees him when I push it open.

I close the door behind me, and he moves to me, swiftly gathering me up in his arms. "I'm disrupting your business," he says pressing a kiss to my neck.

He's disrupting my life.

The warmth of his breath on my skin makes it hard to concentrate. Every ounce of me wants to do nothing more than kiss him all night again, this time unaffected by anything.

"Why all of the sudden is all this attention on you being here?" I ask.

"I think I got your book club all riled up. Someone posted on Instagram about me. Another posted a picture."

His lips still skim my throat. I can't have this conversation while he's doing this, but I absolutely don't want him to stop.

"Why," I breathe out. "Why now? Does this happen all the time?"

"Only once in a while. They just announced a movie deal too, and—"

I finally push him back so I can look at him. "A movie?"

"Yeah, *Caught in the Crossfire*'s movie rights were sold and it just was green lit."

"Why are you so nonchalant about it?" My voice shakes and it's not even my book or my movie.

His finger traces my collarbone. "Why get excited?"

I think about his reaction to his New York Times Best Seller listing. How can I be a big deal to him if nothing else is?

"I don't understand," I say.

Noah eases back to look at me. "What's to understand? I wrote a book and now it'll be a movie."

"You don't even care that it's a bestseller."

"Sure I do. I'll earn out my advance earlier."

"You know some of us would like just even a taste of this success you're having, and you don't care," I say, my voice filled with an accusation I didn't know stirred in me.

His eyes scan over me. "I don't take it for granted. I just don't get worked up over it."

I squeeze my eyes shut. "Fuck. I'm sorry. That came out of nowhere."

"Emma, what's up?"

"I'm jealous of you and it doesn't even make sense."

I push my palms against his shoulders and move from beneath him. How refreshing that in my fifties I can just blurt out those things that stir me up and bother me. Even when no one has asked or when I think it's a problem. God, this is ugly.

"Why are you jealous?"

"I can't even finish a book I've been writing for thirty years. And it's so easy for you that it doesn't even matter." The words are vile dripping off my tongue, and yet, there they go. It's like a faucet of emotion just opened up, and I'm overflowing.

"Of course it matters and it isn't easy," he defends. "I don't write for just a job. I put a lot of blood sweat and tears into my books. It's all I have," he emphasizes the words hard and they sting, and they shouldn't.

"Don't make me feel stupid. I'm being vulnerable with you," I spit out the words.

"Sweetheart," he says, reaching for my hand. "I don't want to make you feel anything but happy. What's going on?"

I have to dig pretty deep to even understand my attitude and where it's really coming from. It's coming from the fact that the last person to shower me with attention and affection gave up on me. It has to do with the fact that I'm in my fifties, and I've been alone for so long that all of this confuses me. It has to do with watching a man live my dream, and him not caring about the successes of it.

"What are we doing?" I finally say when I'm done sifting through my thoughts.

"We're having a fairly intense conversation," he says.

"I mean you and me. We just met. You leave in three weeks. Why are we touching and kissing? Why are we even sharing the same space?"

Noah pulls his bottom lip through his teeth. "I thought we were interested in one another."

"I am. We are," I stumble over my words. "Then it's over, right? I mean, I don't think I can do this—get involved and then watch you walk out of my life."

As I've seen him do many times, he runs his fingers through his hair, leaving tunnels where his fingers were. "I'll pack up my things and head to the hotel," he says defeated.

Like a child throwing a fit, which I feel I am, I throw my hands up in the air. "No. I don't want you to do that."

"I'm getting a lot of mixed signals here, Emma," he says, his voice strained because of my crazy bantering.

I drop my hands. "I like you. I want to be in your presence and I want to do this thing we're doing."

"But?"

"I had a man think I wasn't enough once. That I was convenient when he needed me. I don't want another who wants me only because I'm convenient."

"Is that what you think I'm doing?"

"It feels like we're using each other to fill a hole. Only that hole is going to get bigger. I can't replace your wife."

There is a moment of surprise on his face before it eases. "I didn't ask you to."

"And you're going to leave," I say again, only louder this time.

"So you keep saying."

Noah moves past me and to the desk where he closes his laptop and slides it into his commuter bag.

"I didn't mean to upset you by telling you my feelings. I didn't mean to set you off by any of my successes, and I certainly didn't mean to disrupt your business either," he says. "I'll make sure Katie keeps me in the loop on things, and I'll be here for the scheduled events."

There is a knock at the door and I open it slightly to see Lily's wide eyes. "I need you. We're slammed."

I nod and close the door for another moment.

"Don't go," I say turning back to him. "I don't know what got into me, but I want you to stay and work."

"Emma—"

"I mean it." I take a breath to collect myself. "What I really want you to do is stock the shelves," I say letting out a nervous laugh and it causes him to smile. "I'm out of sorts and I need to figure it out."

"Take the time you need to do that," he says.

"I don't have time. That's the problem," I say as I open the door and walk back out into the store.

CHAPTER 18

Noah hasn't left the office. I finally made sense, or he's now hiding from me too. Either way, he's still close by.

I've warded off at least a dozen questions about Noah being in town.

"Is he staying here all week?"

"Is he as sexy as he is on the book cover?"

"I hear he's actually quite scary," one woman said and even Lily laughed at that one.

"No, he's not scary at all," I defend him.

"He writes really dark," she continued. "Do you think he's mentally stable?"

I think about the conversation I had with him, and he was more stable than I was. "I think his mental state is just fine. He's very creative," I say and the woman nods.

"I don't usually read thrillers, but my sister got me hooked on his. I've read them all. I can't wait until the next one comes out in a few weeks."

"It's fantastic. You'll really enjoy it."

Her eyes go wide. "You've read it? You have copies?"

Sometimes those advanced copies get me in trouble. But I

find it easy to talk about Noah and what he does. Why I feel pride in it, I don't know. Even though I've been letting him kiss me, okay and I kiss him too, it doesn't mean I really know him.

"They sent us an early copy."

"Can I get one of those?" The woman actually leans in over the counter.

"I'm sorry. They are only distributed to stores so the publisher can get orders," I say, as she doesn't know how the process works, so what does it matter.

"That's too bad. I wish I could be here for that book event. I'd love to meet him. Someone said they saw him in town, but I haven't seen him."

"Are you from near by?"

"Forrest Hill," she says of the town twenty miles away. "It was worth the drive over."

"He'll be sorry he missed meeting you, I'm sure."

The woman reaches over the counter to retrieve a stack of sticky notes, and then proceeds to write her phone number and email address on one of them. "If he does come back, call me. Seriously, I want to meet him."

"If I see him, I'll let him know," I tell the woman and then watch as she picks up her The Reading Nook canvas bag, and walks toward the door to the cafe.

I press my fingers to my forehead and Lily watches me. "That's how it's been all morning. When he walked in, I thought I was going to have to call the police."

"I love that the literary world is so admiring," I say.

"So either he needs to work somewhere else, or he's going to have to appease the adoring fans."

I look toward the office. "I'll talk to him. Maybe this will die down in a day. I don't think this is normal."

Lily shrugs. "Call Stephen King, see what he says."

Most authors walk into the store and have to introduce

themselves to me. No one looks like they do on their book covers —except for Noah Carter, I guess.

The door to the office opens slightly. "Is it clear?"

I look around and the store has emptied but a few people in the romance section and another in cookbooks. "I think you're fine."

"I came to stock those shelves you were talking about," he says and I eye him coolly and then notice that Lily is doing the same thing.

"Are you sure you want to do that?" Lily asks. "Is there some contractual thing that says you can't be signing books before the event?"

The corner of his mouth turns up. "No. Just not the book that was delivered to your back room."

Lily nods. "C'mon, stock boy. Let me show you the ropes," she says, leading Noah toward the back of the store.

Picking up the stack of mail on the counter, I decide it's a good time to sort through it and pay what bills came in.

I walk to my office, sit behind the desk, and begin to sort the papers. Noah's stuff is still packed in his commuter bag.

Laying the papers on my desk, I sort through the bills, flyers, and junk.

Reaching to my computer screen and turn it on. My manuscript pops up. I'd forgotten I'd opened it the last time I was on my computer.

I swipe to the next screen and open my bookkeeping software.

Ten minutes into paying bills, I get an email from Katie.

Emma,

I'm headed back on Sunday, would you have time for dinner? Also, Sylvia St. Clare is arriving early as well. She will be in town the week prior to the event and would like to come into the store to get a feel for it, and to sign books. She likes to sign them and then personalize the ones that are sold at events. She feels it gives her more time to mingle with the reader. I hope Noah isn't giving you any grief. He says he's fine, but then again, that's what he always says.

I'll talk to you soon,
Katie

I ease back in my chair. This email has my muscles tensing. There's so much to unpack here.

Dinner on Sunday when Katie gets back is one thing. I know I'm going to be working with her quite a bit on the event, but why is Sylvia St. Clare showing up early? Well, I know why, and that gets to me too. Is that a clever scheme? If Sylvia St. Clare signs all of my inventory, I can't send it back. What if the crowd coming to see her doesn't buy as many books as Katie decided would sell? I can't return them. And does Sylvia know Noah is here? Is she coming here to be with him? Kiss him? To finish what they started?

There is an ache in my chest, and I hate that it's there. I shouldn't care who he has or will kiss. He's not from here. He's kissing me and then he's leaving.

Heat crawls up my neck and I flip from the email reader back to the screen with my bookkeeping, but the screen with my book flashes first and I go back to it.

I look at the words on the page.

I started this book when I believed in love. Back when I knew the meaning of the word.

But as my marriage crumbled, so did the plot.

My main characters got bitter.

The sex got vicious and sad.

I had no happily ever after.

It didn't matter how many books I read, how many sex scenes

I dog-eared, or how many pivotal moments I annotated, I couldn't get the desire back in me to make the book good.

Writing isn't for me. Selling books that make others happy, that's my calling, I think. That's my happily ever after.

My head pops up when the door opens and I see Noah's wide smile.

Quickly, I turn off the screen, making that sad happily never after disappear so he won't see it.

"Penelope Winters?" he says the name on a questioning laugh.

"What about her?"

"She's a regular?" he says as he walks into the office.

"She comes in twice a week and buys two books each trip."

His smile widens. "Lily says I need a commission."

I ease back in my chair again and cross my arms in front of me. "Why exactly?"

"Today's sale was six books."

I can't help but laugh when he does some little celebration dance, and it's so unnatural, I wonder if he's ever danced in his life.

"And she bought six books because of you?" I ask.

"She sure did. Had no idea who I was, didn't care. When I mentioned thriller to her, she turned up her nose and almost gagged. But, because I'm knowledgeable about the romance genre, she walked out with six, yes six," he states again, "books, including the new Jennifer Zeppelin book, and one of those cute annotation kits that you have at the front counter. So bonus points for showing her the good stuff."

He is so proud of himself that I stand, pull him closer to the desk, secure the office door, and wrap my arms around him. Much as he had earlier, he turns me so that my back is against the door as our mouths come together in a heated kiss that has the temperature of the room rising a good ten degrees.

"Congratulations, Mr. Carter," I breathe out the words as his fingers press into my hips and his mouth moves over my throat.

"Is this my bonus?"

"Does it work for you?"

He lets out a deep groan and it rattles through both of us. "It'll do for now," he says, lifting his eyes to meet mine.

They're dark and full of need.

I know I'm scared to death that this man is going to use me and leave, but I'm all in. I guess this is the adventure.

"For now?" I say, my own breath ragged.

"For now," he says again and suddenly I can't wait for later.

CHAPTER 19

It's noon when I walk into the store. Julia is standing on the front counter, Noah holding her ankles while she strings up a banner.

From behind her, Noah lifts a brow and eyes me coolly as I walk toward the counter.

"What's this?" I ask.

Julia shifts a strained look down at me, her arms still holding the banner over her head trying to anchor it to the ceiling.

"The publishing house sent it for the event," she says.

"We have a ladder in the back," I remind her.

"The brothers came and borrowed it last week," she tells me and I shrug.

"Last week? And they never brought it back?" I'm nearly shouting.

With his hands still wrapped around Julia's ankles, Noah looks at me. "What brothers?"

"Williams brothers. They own the brewery down the street."

Noah nods slowly. "They serve food there?"

I narrow my gaze on him. "They do."

He motions for me to take his place anchoring Julia.

I move in behind the counter, drop my bags, and take up his

position holding on to Julia. "Anything there you don't like?" he asks.

"Not really," I say.

"What about you, Jules?" he says, and I'm not sure what to think of him calling her something other than her given name. Is it a pet name? Did they agree on this? Is she making moves on him? Is he making moves on her?

"I have a poor college girls' lunch in the back," she says straining up on her toes to connect the banner.

"What if you save that for your poor college girl dinner. I'll get you lunch. My treat."

Julia shifts a look down at him and it's all smile. "Pick me out something yummy, Pops," she says, and now my stomach tightens. I don't like this budding friendship at all.

Noah puts his hand on my back, as if it's a gentle reminder that he and I have something going on. And, the way I feel at the moment, I'm fully aware of the something we have going on because it's making jealousy rise in me, and I hate jealousy.

A moment later he's out the door and Julia is walking across the counter and I'm following like an Olympic gymnastic spotter.

"What's been going on this morning?" I say as she lifts the other side of the banner into place.

"Couple sales. Noah signed a few books. Mrs. Packer fed him breakfast, but she didn't offer me any," she says with a humph. "Then he locked himself in the office for a few hours. He didn't know you came in later."

I hadn't thought about telling him that last night when we left the store. Of course, I hadn't been thinking of much when we sat in his car and made out, again like teenagers hiding in the alley. The very thought of the steamed up windows and his roaming hands over my body makes my body heat all over again.

I clear my throat and my mind, my hands still holding on to Julia. "You two seemed to have talked a lot this morning."

"What makes you say that?"

"The pet names," I say, trying to keep the strain out of my voice.

"What pet names?" she looks down at me, her arms still lifted over her head.

"Jules? Pops?"

She laughs as she refocuses on her task. "I didn't come up with those, Mrs. Packer did when she brought him breakfast."

That has my stomach tightening again. I should have known that. For what ever reason, Mrs. Packer can't remember Julia's name, so she always calls her Jules.

"Why Pops?"

Julia lowers her arms, looks at the banner, and then at me. I realize she's done and I can step back now. She lowers herself off the counter and looks at the banner and then back at me.

"She told him he was too old for me,"

"Why would she say that? I mean why would she think that you two—"

Julia laughs. "Because she and I talked about how sexy *I* thought he was before he showed up. And then she told me how sexy *she* thought he was when he did show up. And then she told me *you* were having an affair with him, and she called him Pops."

I know my eyes are wide and my face has gone pale when Julia reaches for my arm. "Are you okay?"

"She said that?"

"Yeah, is she wrong? I mean Noah just laughed it off, took his breakfast sandwich into the office and closed the door."

I blink hard and stare at her. No one but Lily knows what's been going on. I don't even really know what's going on.

"I ... Well ..." I don't have words for this.

We're both pulled from the conversation when Noah knocks on the front door, obviously in need of assistance because he has a Kraft bag hanging from his wrist, a tray of drinks, and the ladder under his other arm.

Julia runs to the door, opens it, and takes the drinks and the food as Noah carries the ladder into the store.

"They forgot they had it," he says. "Are you missing anything else? They had a storage room filled with things that look like they might belong to all the other businesses on the street."

His eyes settle on me, and his expression turns to worry.

Julia sets the food and drinks on the counter. "I'll put the ladder back. And I'll let you divvy out the food."

She takes the ladder from him and starts for the back of the store as three women walk in the door. They each have a The Reading Nook canvas bag, and though I can't place them, it tells me they're repeat customers.

I give them a warm smile and welcome them, but Noah is still watching me, assessing me.

"We should take this to the back," I say, looking down at the food.

He only nods, grabs the food and drinks, and hurries off to the back of the store while I busy myself cleaning off the front counter and waiting for the women to make their selections.

As is sometimes the norm, the store has a constant flow of people, and lunch gets forgotten. Eventually, Julia returns from the back room and relieves me from the front counter.

"Go eat," she says.

I start for the back of the store, fix a few shelves on my way, pick up a random piece of paper from the floor, and eventually make my way to the break room. Noah sits at the small table, his takeout container unopened, his arms folded in front of him, and his eyes closed.

I quietly take the seat across from him and open the container that waits for me.

As soon as I do, Noah's eyes pop open.

"I'm sorry. I didn't mean to wake you," I say looking down at the BLT he's brought back for me.

"Damn, didn't realize I'd fallen asleep. Where's Julia?" he asks and I'm glad he knows her real name.

"She took over out front. We've been steady since you got back."

"I must have been horrible company," he laughs and then opens his box.

"Why are you so tired?" I ask, picking up one of the halves of my sandwich and taking a bite.

A thin smile forms on his lips. "I was up a lot last night. Making notes. Thinking things through. Then around one, I checked my email and Abby's sister had emailed me. Her daughter is graduating this year and she wanted to send me an invite, but wasn't sure if I'd moved."

I chew thoroughly, not wanting to choke or appear thrown by what he's told me.

When I swallow down my bite, I pick up my drink and take a big sip, only to begin coughing.

"Are you okay?" Noah sits up as if he's going to move toward me and start slapping my back.

I nod frantically as I cough until I get myself under control, and he eases back slightly. "What is that?" I choke out the words.

"Sweet tea," he says.

"Oh," I blow out a breath and push it away from me. "I didn't even know you could get sweet tea in Colorado," I laugh.

"You don't drink sweet tea in Colorado?"

"Um, no. We're very pure here," I say. "No sugar."

"Then it's undrinkable," he says matter-of-fact.

"Acquired taste, I guess."

"I'll keep that in mind for next time." His smile widens and he lifts his sandwich from the box and takes a bite.

I study him. The dark circles under his eyes are deeper today. What would it take to make this man relax?

"Do you keep in touch with Abby's family? I mean, do you talk to them often?"

He shrugs as he chews, then wipes his mouth and takes a sip of his drink. "It's gotten to be less in the past few years. Out of sight out of mind, I guess. Her sister lives in Virginia, so we didn't see her too much. Her mom is still in the city, so I'll have dinner with her for birthdays and such."

"I think that's nice. Even when I was married, my husband always came down with some kind of sickness and didn't attend birthdays or special events. Red flag, huh?"

Noah reaches across the table and covers my hand with his. He doesn't say anything. I guess there's nothing to be said. We both lost when it came to love. Noah brings a comfort to me that I didn't know lived inside of me, and that's exactly how I'll have to think about it. It lives inside of me and it's awake now. Because he'll be gone, and I'll still need to retain my comfort.

CHAPTER 20

The UPS delivery and the pile of Amazon packages behind the counter surprise me. Katie has sent more books for Noah's signing. She's sent another case of Sylvia St. Clare's books too, and I hope she's giving me the same deal as she did on Noah's, especially if Sylvia signs all of these.

Lily wanders in around five and claps her hands together when she sees the Amazon packages piled up.

"Oh, goodie. Now we can decorate."

"Decorate? What is all of this?" I ask.

"Katie gave us a budget to get things to decorate the store. We're going to brighten up the romance section," she says as she tears into the first box. "I think we should move things around a bit."

"Why?"

"Well, right now the romance section is like the milk and eggs at the store."

"Milk and eggs?"

"You have to walk through the whole store to get the most purchased items in the store. So, you pick up cookies and bread and shit you don't need."

"Romance is milk and eggs," I chuckle following along.

"Right. So let's put the less purchased things like poetry at the front, minus your end-caps and special tables."

"And where do I go?" Noah asks from the doorway of the office where he's leaned up against the door jamb, his ankles and arms crossed casually.

The circles under his eyes are even darker now and I wonder what this trip is doing to him physically.

"Oh, hell, you'll always be in the window, a stack on the counter, and a dedicated table. But, your backlist will be at the back. They'll have to go through the store to get the goods. More eggs," she says, continuing her analogy.

"I'm the goods," he says to me with a smile.

"Oh, she knows," Lily says in a suggestive voice as she digs into her box.

When I turn my head to look at Noah, he's grinning back at me. And when he winks, I just want to scoop him up and hold him while he naps.

"Twinkle lights!" Lily says as she pulls out a box. "You can't have too many twinkle lights."

I shake my head and laugh as Noah ducks back into the office and I go about opening the new boxes of books and entering them into inventory.

Lily and Julia have been flitting around the store all evening, sprucing up the place. Because I don't have an eye for it, I let them rearrange the way they want and add twinkle lights to everything they touch.

Lily upped the display in the window to add more of Noah's books as well as Sylvia St. Clare's, and of the other authors who will be at the event. When we turn the sign to closed at eight o'clock, Lily and Julia pack up and head home and I gently knock on the office door and push it open.

Again, I find Noah sitting up in the chair, his arms crossed in front of him and he's asleep.

I can't help but wonder why he's paying me for this space when he's obviously not getting any work done.

He must sense me because his eyes flutter open and he smiles up at me. "Seems like you keep catching me like this," he says.

"You need to sleep at night," I say.

"That's been my mantra since I was ten, but I'm a horrible sleeper," he admits as he sits up and scrubs his hands over his face. "What time is it?"

"Just past eight."

"I guess I've been here all day, huh?"

I move to the desk and lean against it. "Did you get some writing done?"

He shrugs, stretches, and stands from the chair and pulls me to him. "What are your dinner plans?"

Placing my hands on his chest, I study his face and wish I knew him better so I'd know what was going on behind those eyes.

"I was just going home to have some chili that's in my slow cooker."

He lets out a low hum. "What's the view like from your house?"

That makes me laugh. "Right now? It's dark. In a few hours, it'll be pitch black."

"So no view, but stars?"

"So close it appears that you walk out into a wall of them."

Noah tucks a strand of my hair behind my ear and lingers his hand on my cheek. "I know it's forward of me, but will you take me home with you?"

"You're a fan of chili, huh?"

"I might be," he says as he runs his thumb over my bottom lip.

"Don't you think you should get some sleep?"

"I think I'd rather spend some time with you, if you don't have other plans. I know I'm sucking up your alone time this week, but ..."

"I don't mind," I say quickly, perhaps too quickly. Alone time is all I've had for years. Having someone want to spend it with me is a bonus I hadn't seen coming.

The corner of his mouth ticks up. "I'll drive myself and I promise to leave."

Licking my bottom lip, I consider that. "You know, neither of us has to answer to anyone else."

He watches me and processes that. "No. If anyone can claim to be adults, it's us."

A small laugh escapes me. "I'm trying not to be offended that we're calling ourselves old."

"Fifties are not old anymore. My grandmother still danced until she was ninety-eight. She only stopped when her boyfriend in the home died. He was one-hundred and three. She died at ninety-nine. Ten days before she'd have turned one hundred."

"That would be my goal," I admit. "Not to die in a home, but to be dancing well into my nineties."

Slowly, Noah begins to sway us. "Do you dance now?"

"Almost never."

"Then you have to start if you want to keep doing it until you actually are an old lady," he says, taking my hand and twirling me in a circle and then back to him.

Pressed against him, I breathe him in.

I've spent more than a decade alone, without a man. Oh, a few have wandered in and out of my life, but I don't need one. And I certainly don't want to need this one—this one, who will leave me.

But I want him. And, fuck it, I'm plenty old enough to make some bad decisions and go on.

Placing both hands on Noah's face, I draw him in and kiss him. "If you don't know the road up to my house, it's hard to navigate in the dark."

He studies me for a moment. "So you don't want me to follow you home?"

I shake my head. "It's better if I drive," I say and swallow hard. "And then you stay."

The corner of his mouth ticks up again, and the darkness around his eyes seems to lift.

"I snore," he says.

"So do I," I say, and he laughs.

"You're sure?"

"I'm sure."

Noah brushes his lips against mine again. "There may be rumors," he teases.

"We've already been caught sleeping on the floor of the romance section. I assume rumors have already started, and those are the rumors we're about to fulfill."

Now I watch his throat work as he swallows hard. "I don't want to pressure you."

"No pressure. I'm asking you to come home with me."

"Maybe we should get some provisions," he suggests as he clears his throat and I know he's not telling me we need a bottle of wine.

"On our way out of town," I tell him and he draws in a deep breath.

"I love chili," he says.

"So do I. Maybe it'll be as good for breakfast," I say, not wanting to stop long enough to eat it tonight. Right now, I just want to get this man home.

CHAPTER 21

"You're right," Noah steps out of my car and scans the horizon. "Like a wall of stars."

I pull the bag of groceries we'd stopped for, and other items, from the back seat and grab my personal bag too. "Oh just wait. We'll go out on the back patio and turn off all the lights."

"Gets better, huh?"

"So much better," I promise, drawing out the words for emphasis.

Noah slings his commuter bag over his shoulder, meets me at the front of the car and takes the groceries from me. I unlock the front door and push it in.

The house is old, small, and forever will have that rustic smell of wood that has sat up in the mountains for years—mixed with the smell of the chili that's in the slow cooker.

"How long have you lived up here?" he asks as he looks around and I walk toward the small kitchen, turning on lights as I go.

"Twelve years. I bought it when I moved back. The store keeps me social. The mountains, they keep me grounded."

Noah sets the bag of groceries on the counter, and then deposits his commuter bag on one of the kitchen chairs.

"You're not afraid, up here by yourself?" he asks, looking out the window into the vast darkness.

"Once in a while my door camera catches a bear or a mountain lion."

His eyes are wide when he turns back to look at me. "Seriously?"

"Sure. I'm in their territory."

"What about people?"

I shrug. "I get a few hikers who get lost, or the occasional car that wanders off the road."

"And that doesn't scare the shit out of you? That's how I start my murder scenes." His voice has risen and I'm not sure if that's out of excitement for the situation or out of fear for my well-being.

"And that's why I read you when I'm at work only—morning and mid-day," I add.

He chuckles, more relaxed now. "I have six scenarios playing in my head as we speak." He moves back to the window and cranes his neck to look out further. "Shit."

I watch him. He's processing something. There is a glow to his aura that I haven't seen yet. Creativity is brewing.

He takes an old leather notebook and a pen out of his bag and begins to write.

I retrieve two wine glasses from the cabinet and a bottle of wine from the refrigerator that Lily and I had started last week. All the while, Noah is frantically making notes, now sitting at the table.

Pouring the wine, I set a glass in front of him, and for a moment, he lifts his head and acknowledges me. Then he's back to writing.

I move about the kitchen, putting away the few things we

picked up at the store. Leaving the box of condoms on the counter, I push them back out of the way. We're prepared, but it doesn't need to be the centerpiece of our dinner.

Setting out the few items that will go with the chili, I take down two bowls and fill them from the slow cooker. As I turn around to set them on the table, Noah is sliding his book back into his bag.

"Sorry," he says, reaching for the bowls.

"Sorry for what?" I ask, turning back to the counter to collect the other items.

"It's been a while since I've had a burst of excitement over an idea."

Setting the items on the table, I take the seat next to him. "Tell me you've been working this whole week."

Noah shrugs, just as he has the few times I've asked. "More than I was back in New York. But if I don't get something solid soon …" he lets it linger.

"Well, hopefully being up here will be inspirational," I say as I take a few crackers from the sleeve on the table and crunch them up in my chili.

When I shift my attention back to him, he's staring at me—gazing is more like it.

"I really like you, Emma," he says.

I brush the crumbs off of my fingers and reach for a napkin from the holder on the table. "And I like you too, Noah," I say in his formal tone. "Eat."

That sexy slight smile is on his lips as he turns his attention to the chili.

Once dinner is finished, Noah helps me clean up and store the leftovers. Then, as promised, I turn off all of the exterior lights, leaving only a lamp on in the living room, and we take our wine outside to the deck.

"Wow," he says, drawing out the word. "You weren't kidding."

"It's magical, isn't it?"

"That's one way to put it." He leans against the railing looking out into the vastness. "You're lucky if you can see a star in New York."

"You're right in the heart of it all, huh?"

"Certainly am. Don't get me wrong. I have a lot of good feelings in New York. It's where I belong. The noise. The people. The bustle."

"I thought you said you don't get out much," I say, sipping my wine.

"I don't, but I know it's there, ya know?"

I nod. I do get it. Just like at the end of the day I know the stars are here for me.

But as the wine warms my chest, my body chills in the air thinking about how he loves what he has back home. I can't give that to him here. The pace is much different.

Noah sets his wine on the small table next to us, and then does the same with mine.

"Where is your nearest neighbor?" he asks.

"Half a mile down the mountain."

He turns to look but shakes his head. "I can't see anyone."

"Exactly."

"So if I started to seduce you right here in the dark, no one would see us."

My breath hitches in my lungs. "Is that your plan? To seduce me?"

Noah brushes his thumb over my lips. "I think you deserve seducing."

"Do I?"

"More than anything," he says, leaning in to brush his lips to mine. "Remember, we're not old. I'm not hesitant. You're not shy."

That has me chuckling. "I'm not shy? How do you know that?"

Now he runs his finger over my collarbone. "I don't date a lot, but when I have, I've stayed in my age range. And I find that women, when they clear a certain age, think of themselves as undesirable."

I swallow hard. I've thought that for years.

"The truth is," he continues as he brushes his lips up my neck and down again, "women only get better with age."

"Is that so?" My voice quivers as I ask, my eyes close, and my fingers grip the sides of his shirt.

"There is a softness to you," he says as he begins gathering my blouse in his hands. "And I mean that in the very best way."

"I'm glad you find that an attractive feature."

"Oh, I do," he says as his hand skims under my shirt and rests against my side.

I suck in a breath. "You know, my hair used to be auburn before all of this silver peppered it."

"I never would have noticed your auburn hair," he say with his lips hovering over mine.

"Liar."

"Okay, if I'd met you when my hair wasn't grey, maybe. But, sweetheart," he pauses a breath away from me, "you're perfect."

I pull him to me. It might be something he says to all the women my age, it might be how he really feels. I don't know. But in this moment all I want to do is show him every curve and every imperfect part of me.

My fingers nimbly begin to unbutton his shirt, and his hands gather my blouse.

When I can, I push his shirt from his shoulders, and he recovers to lift mine over my head.

There is something primal that escapes him as he looks down at me in my bra—my average, bought off of Amazon bra. "Perfect," he says as he moves to unbutton my slacks.

"Are we really going to get naked outside on the patio?" I ask as he moves into me, his lips on my chest, his erection pressed against me.

"Are you remembering neighbors you forgot about?"

I let out an airy laugh. "No. I just thought we might like a blanket on the ground."

His smile is bright, even in the dark.

"I like how you think."

CHAPTER 22

Half naked, I run into the house and pull two of the oversized pillows off of the couch, as well as a worn quilt that my grandmother made years ago. Deciding that isn't something I want to get dirty, I throw it back on the couch and run to my bedroom for my comforter instead.

When I return to the patio, Noah is refilling our wine glasses.

"You have a tattoo on your back," I say, noticing its outline, but unable to make out what it says.

Noah stiffens. "I do."

I drop the pillows and the comforter on the ground and move to him, before he turns back.

Running my fingers over his skin, moving him so I catch the moonlight, and I stiffen too.

Abby in a heart with her birth and death dates on it.

"It's a beautiful tribute," I say, running my fingers over it.

"It's a buzz kill when you're trying to impress a half-naked woman."

I move so that I'm standing in front of him. "Reasons to date older women, part two," I begin as I reach for my glass of wine and take a long sip, "we understand that other women came before us."

Noah reaches for his glass and smiles from behind it. "Some women understand that."

"You had something not many people get to have. I understand that."

"You do?"

"I do. I'm envious of it," I admit.

"Jealous of my career. Envious of my relationships. What else are you hiding?"

I shove him gently in the shoulder and he captures my hand.

I swallow. "I'm trying very hard to be mature about all of this. I know that it's fast and we're old enough to handle it. I also know you live thousands of miles away, so this is temporary."

Even in the dark I can see disappointment flash in his eyes.

"It doesn't have to be," he says.

"I'm not going to stake more than the next two weeks on it." I wrap my arms around his neck, holding tightly to my wine glass so that it doesn't pour down his back. "I might seem like a jealous person, but I'm not petty."

"I didn't think you were."

"Have you had lots of women see that tattoo?"

His lips flatten. "A few."

"Did it bother them?"

"Maybe."

I tighten my arms around him and his hand comes to the bare skin at my waist. "I'm not bothered by it. She was a lucky woman. And in this moment, I am too."

There is a beat before he kisses me again. A beat of understanding. A beat of hesitation. I don't know why we lingered there, but now it's just us and the wall of stars.

He moves us to the small couch on the patio, setting our drinks on the cafe table next to it. Old cushions give under us as he sits, and pulls me down to him, straddling him.

Noah's hands move up my back, holding me in place. My hands are on his stubbled cheeks, and my lips work against his.

"You're okay with this?" he says, traveling his lips down my throat to my chest where he peppers my covered breasts with kisses.

"I am," I say, refusing the urge to be sassy about it and saying something like *I invited you didn't I?*

There is a groan that escapes him as he moves his hands to my hips and grinds me against him. I watch his face contort the urges rising in him.

Noah lifts his fingers to the clasp on my bra and releases the fabric that separates us.

"Fuck," he growls out the word as my bra drops between us, and he scoops up my breasts in his hands. "I was wrong," he says and I press my hands to his shoulders to study him again. "I can't do this here."

Noah stands from the couch, me still wrapped around him.

"What are you doing?" I feel the rush of anxiety surge through me. I'm enveloped in the arms of some man I don't really know, who writes about horrific murders, and I'm half naked clinging to him. The edge of the deck is a mere foot away, and he could easily deposit me over the edge and no one would hear me cry from the depths of the rocks and trees below.

"I don't want to do this on your deck. I want to take my time with you," he says carrying me back into the house. "I want to make love with you, not just crazed sex in the dark."

I know when I shift my weight back to look at him, the weight transfer adjusts, and a moment later I find my back pressed to a cold wall so he can keep me upright.

"You're not going to murder me in the dark?"

Noah blinks hard. "Why would you say something like that?"

To his credit, he hasn't let go of me and dropped me on my ass yet. "You still want me?"

"Fuck, Emma. What's going on in that head of yours?"

"Drama," I admit. "Don't hold it against me."

He smiles from the corner of his mouth. "I plan to hold myself against you all night long, if you'll still have me."

"Down the hall to the right," I say as Noah readjusts me and I hold on tightly. As we lift from the wall, I stop him again. "Go back," I say, and he takes a few wobbly steps backward.

I reach out to collect the condom box from the counter. "Okay, now."

Noah chuckles. "This was easier in my thirties," he says as we start down the hallway.

"You're not commenting on my weight are you? I mean, you are the one that picked me up."

"Shhh," he says as we get to my room. "I want us to enjoy every moment of this night. And no, it wasn't a comment on you at all," he admits and I wonder if that was more a comment on his abilities.

Noah lays me on the bed and I let the box of condoms fall from my hand. I take in the moment of him looking down at me. I want to remember it, because in the end, this is all I will have of him someday—and that's okay.

"You're beautiful, Emma. So beautiful."

There is a twinge in the back of my throat—tears. Fuck no. I'm not going to cry now.

"Thank you," I say softly.

"I want to please you," he says as he begins to pull my unbuttoned slacks from my legs. "I want to touch you. Taste you."

There is a strangled noise that escapes me and I nod.

Noah moves back to my mouth and kisses me.

"Relax. Let me love you tonight. I promise it'll be a night you'll never forget."

CHAPTER 23

When I push open the front door to the bookstore, I am met with two sets of inquisitive eyes—make that three. Mrs. Packer hurries through the joined door with a tray of coffees and a plate filled with pastries.

"Oh, don't you girls tear into her until I'm here for it," she says hurrying toward the counter where she deposits the plate and the coffees. "Now."

Julia and Lily study her and then turn their eyes back to me.

"Spill it," Lily says.

"Don't spare one detail," Julia says.

"And if it wasn't good, make that shit up," Mrs. Packer says.

I coolly eye each of them. "What has gotten into you three?" I ask, moving past them and toward my office to deposit my things.

They all follow me, cornering me in the office.

"His car was here all night long," Lily says.

"He got out of your car this morning, in the same clothes he wore yesterday, and got into his car and drove toward the hotel," Julia confirms.

Mrs. Packer picks up one of the pastries off the counter, takes a bite, but keeps her wide eyes on me—waiting.

"I am fifty-two-years-old. I don't have to answer to anyone about who I spend time with," I say.

"Bullshit," Lily says. "You've nearly been a hermit for the past decade, so when something good happens, you have to tell us everything."

"Where is that written?" I ask, crossing my arms in front of me.

"Best friend code. You can look it up online. It's there. And if it's on the internet, it's real," Lily confirms.

I shake my head. "Are the three of you going to hold this vigil the whole day until you get answers?"

"Yes," Lily and Julia say at the same time.

"Yeah, so hurry. I have customers, but I need a fix," Mrs. Packer says, taking another bite of the pastry.

I let out a small laugh. "I had a wonderful evening."

Julia lets out a groan. "That's not going to cut it."

"What details do you want?"

"All of them," she says. "You know I've dreamt of him, so please tell me it was at least that good."

I pull in my lips because a wide smile will burst from me if I don't.

These three women are my everything, and have been for the twelve years I've been back in this town. If the tables were turned for either one of them, I'd be standing where they are now begging for the same details they are.

"There was wine. Some dancing. Dinner, which I made. And," I let out a breath and let that smile escape, "I've only had three hours of sleep, and I'll need a new box of condoms because we nearly ran out."

Mrs. Packer is the first to let the whooping begin. "I knew he'd be a stud."

"He was a stud," I confirm with a laugh.

"Tell me it wasn't all missionary, shit," Lily says wrinkling up her nose. "I mean you know every damned detail of my sex life, and even though I'm in a committed marriage, you know for a fact there is some kinky shit in there."

Mrs. Packer turns to Lily. "Please begin to share that with me from now on. I could use some kinky sex stories."

I shake my head. "Ladies," I scold as the front door opens and two women walk into the store.

Lily raises her brows at me.

"Okay, it wasn't all missionary. Very little," I choke out the words, whispering, but smile through it all. "There was certainly a lot of exploration going on between us. How's that?"

Lily shrugs, but there is a smile ready to burst from her. "It's a start. But you're happy?"

"I'm so fucking happy," I say and it resonates in my words.

"Okay, I won't castrate him and throw him off a cliff," she says, letting that smile surface as she turns toward the store and heads off to help the customers.

Mrs. Packer finishes her pastry as she watches me, and Julia, cheeks pinked, turns to the register and signs in.

I turn back into my office and close the door. I did bring a few of the condoms we didn't use with me. I think my office would be a nice place to explore some things too.

Noah strolls through the door from the cafe an hour later. He has a cup of coffee and a wrapped brownie.

I watch him walk toward me, his eyes laser focused on me, and not the three women comparing the back of his book jacket to the man on a mission.

When he walks behind the counter, he finally acknowledges Julia before he steps to me and kisses me solidly on the mouth.

"Mrs. Packer sent us a brownie," he says looking down at the wrapped treat in his hand.

"She did, did she?"

"She was being very strange when I stopped in. I'm afraid of what she laced this brownie with," he admits.

"Why would you worry?"

"I have a feeling she beat you down for details. So, am I being poisoned or Viagra'd?"

I snort out a laugh and pull him in to the office, closing the door on the women who keep watching Noah's every move.

He's quick to set down his coffee and brownie and pull me into his arms.

We fit.

Not just our bodies, but everything about him fits into my life. And, when I think like that, I go right to the fact that he'll be gone in a few weeks and this will be over. But in this very moment, we fit.

"I don't know which one of us is distracting the other from working," he says as he feathers kisses down my neck.

"I have employees. But you should get some work done."

"Katie gets back tomorrow, right?"

"Uh-huh," is about all I can say with his mouth on me and his hands gripping my waist.

"Yeah, she, my agent, and my editor are harping on me. I guess I should get some work done."

I ease back from him. "I'd be happy to read what you've been working on," I offer.

Noah's lips flatten. "Everyone wants a free book," he says, but I can't read his tone. "I'm kidding. If I write something worthwhile, I'll let you read it."

I'm not sure how to take that. He's been here a week. Surely he's been writing up a storm. But, when I think about the times I've asked him how his writing is going, he usually just shrugs and changes the subject.

I hear the bells above the door chime, and then chime again. Saturday is our busiest day of the week. I know that Lily and Julia are giving me some grace, but that will wear thin soon.

"I should get back to work," I say, pressing one more kiss to Noah's lips.

"Give me a name," he says.

"A name?"

"Yeah. Give me a name. Let's say a name of a woman, late thirties, two kids, and a husband who is deployed."

Studying him, I watch as his eyes darken, just as they had when he was aroused. His lips twitch between anxious and happy.

"Susan Black," I say.

"Just a name you made up?"

"Off the top of my head," I promise.

Noah gives me a nod, steps away from me, and opens the office door. "I have work to do."

CHAPTER 24

I don't see Noah the rest of the day. In fact, I hate to admit it, I forgot he was in the office until I was turning off the lights in the store and I opened the office door to grab my bag.

The collective yelp from both of us diffuses any guilt I might have had forgetting he was there. He obviously forgot I was around too.

"Sorry," I say pressing my hand to my chest.

"I think I was too deep into this to realize how late it was," he says.

I can't help but want to see what he's writing, but that's when I notice that my computer screen is on. He's not writing. He's reading.

He's reading my book!

"What are you doing?" I ask frantically as I nearly fly across the desk to turn off the screen.

Noah's hands come to my waist as I push him up against the wall in the chair.

He's laughing, but this isn't funny.

"You're on my computer," I shout.

"You told me I could use it to do research," he rebuts.

I turn to look at him, as I'm pinned against the desk and him in the chair.

"I did tell you that. I didn't say you could search my drive."

Noah holds up his hands in surrender. "That was on the computer when I turned on the screen. I didn't go looking into anything."

"You … Seriously …" My words trail off because what he's saying comes rushing at me. I had opened the file. I had worried over it the other day. "Shit."

Noah is watching me with wide eyes and a smile that is trying to surface. "It's really good," he says.

"It sucks."

"No. I wouldn't say that."

"Oh, but you wouldn't say it's awesome."

He reaches for me, resting his hands on my hips as he eases the chair closer to me. "I would say that if you let me. I could help you work through it and make it perfect."

"Proof that it's shit."

Noah stands, his hands still on my hips and the chair pushed against the wall.

"It's not shit."

"I don't have even an ounce of the talent you do. I don't want you to read any more of it."

He studies me. "Emma—"

"I'm serious," I say, turning from him and turning off the computer without doing it the proper way—and that's when I see his legal pad of notes.

I pick it up from the desk and study it.

This has nothing to do with his own work, he's written explicit notes about my book. My book!

"You had no right to do this," I say shaking his legal pad.

"I was only—"

"You were only snooping."

The lines around his eyes deepen. "You know that's not true."

"I have proof," I say, holding up the pad.

"You have proof that I took and made notes to help you with something that I think has a lot of potential."

"Proof that you saw something you should have ignored and you didn't."

His fingers go to his hair, just as they always do when he's frustrated.

"Emma, I'm sorry."

My jaw hurts from clenching it so tightly.

"Maybe you should go for the night."

His lips part as if he might say something, but then he doesn't.

Taking the notepad from my hand, he tears off the pages he'd written, and drops them on the desk. Then he takes his laptop off the desk, picks up his bag, and walks out of the office without even putting his computer into the bag.

A moment later, I hear the door open and close, and I fall into the chair.

My eyes sting and tears clog my throat. He had no right to do what he did. What the actual fuck?

He was supposed to be in my office working on his own book and instead he's editing my book? A book I've been working on for decades. A book that will never see the light of day. A book that he never should have seen!

I push up from the chair, rush out of my office and out of the store to the back lot hoping to find him still climbing into his car, or maybe sitting there thinking about what he did. But he's not here.

Pinching the bridge of my nose, I stomp back to the front door of the shop and yank on the door. It doesn't open, instead my fingers slip from the handle, and I jolt backward. The only problem is, there's a piece of sidewalk that is uneven, and my heel catches on it, flinging me to the ground on my ass, my elbow skidding on the cement.

"Fuck!" I shout as I reach for my elbow, cradling it to me.

My ass throbs, and it's just late enough that there is no one on the street, well on my side of the street. There's an entire patio filled with patrons enjoying barbecue and beer across the street, but no one seems to notice that I've flung myself to the ground in a rage of—what—irritation at myself.

The tears are back, my elbow is bleeding, and from my seat on the sidewalk, I realize the door locked behind me. My keys are inside. My phone is inside. Dammit, could this day get any worse?

I cover my mouth with my free hand and let the sobs surface.

"Oh, my gosh. Are you okay?" two women rush down the street toward me.

"You're bleeding," one says.

"Did you fall? This sidewalk is horrible," the other says as they both crouch down next to me.

I blink rapidly to ward away the tears. "I'm okay. I guess the sidewalk won this battle," I try to laugh, but it doesn't come through.

"Where's your phone? Should we call someone?" the woman closest to me asks.

"I'm actually the owner of the bookstore. I've locked myself out."

The woman sits flat on the ground next to me and smiles. "What a shitty day."

I suppose that it ended that way, but when I think about how I woke up, I cry even more.

"Oh, honey. Did you hit your head?" the other woman asks.

I shake my head and blow out a breath. "No. Just having a moment, I guess."

The woman sitting next to me pulls her phone from her pocket. "Would you like to use my phone to call someone?" she asks as she hands me her phone.

I nod and dial Lily's number. Luckily, she's the kind of person that answers every call. She enjoys the challenge when it's a spam caller and she can keep them going as long as possible.

"Yep?" she says, because she's not expecting to know the person on the other end.

"Hey, it's me," I say, and then add, "Emma."

"Where are you? Whose phone are you on? This is a local number, not Noah's."

"Would you give me a moment to talk?" I say and I don't know if it was meant to be humorous or filled with the irritation boiling up in me. "I borrowed this nice woman's phone, so listen. I locked myself out of the store and then fell on that broken piece of sidewalk."

"Shit! I'm going to that city council meeting next month and complaining about it again," she says.

"Lily, are you listening to me?"

"Sweetheart, I already have my keys in my hand and I'm unlocking the car. I'm on my way. Tell me you don't need me to call 9-1-1."

"You don't need to call 9-1-1. We would have already done that."

"I would have hoped so," she says and I hear the engine of her car roar to life. "You're okay?"

"Banged up, but okay."

"I'll be there in ten. Sit and play Candy Crush on that phone or something just to keep that woman there with you."

I laugh and I realize no matter how things end up with Noah, I always have Lily, and she will always have my back.

CHAPTER 25

Lily sets a cup of tea on the coffee table in front of me before sitting next to me, her legs tucked up under her.

She brushes one of my peppered curls behind my ear. "Are you ready to tell me how you locked yourself out of the store?"

I've been sobbing since she picked me up off the sidewalk and poured me into her car. Now, seated on her sofa, where I will sleep, she watches me and waits.

"He crossed the line. He read my book," I say, my lip quivering.

"He read your book."

"Yes."

"I've read your book," she reminds me.

"It's not the same. I let you read my book."

She crinkles her nose and shakes her head. "I don't think you did. If I remember correctly, you had a huge ream of paper that you protectively hovered over and I stole it."

I blink at her, pick up my tea, and study her as she smiles at me.

"I didn't *let* you read it?" I ask.

"No. But it was good. And I know you've rewritten it ten times since I read it, so I'm sure it's even better."

I worry my lip as I lift my cup to my mouth. "You think it was good?"

"It was good, Em," she says with that irritated edge of *I've told you this a hundred times already,* kind of tone.

I sip my tea and shake my head. "He had no right. Besides, he had an entire list of things to fix."

Lily puckers her lips and studies me. "So a New York Times Best Selling author has notes on your manuscript that sits on your computer. You know, a man who has published, how many books? Oh, that's right, people clamor for his attention and make his books into movies. I'm sure he doesn't have anything constructive to say about your book. I mean, how would he know how to craft a good book? Nor would he have connections to make one of your lifelong dreams come true. What a fucking bastard," she says, picking up her own tea and sipping as she stoically watches me over the top of her cup.

I'm not wrong.

He crossed a line.

He should have been working on his own book. Doesn't he have a deadline?

He was wrong to do what he did, only now, I wonder what those notes say.

"I'm going to head out," I say, setting my cup on the table, but Lily is shaking her head.

"You're not going anywhere. Your elbow is the size of an orange and needs to be iced. That huge bandage on your arm needs to be changed. Your ass is sore. Your attitude sucks. Your car is still at the store, and you just need to stay right where you are, sleep off your pissy mood, and go back tomorrow."

I adjust the ice under my elbow and think about tomorrow. Katie returns and we have plans for dinner. I'm not sure I'm up for that, but I won't back out.

I can't imagine I'll even see Noah tomorrow. Why would he want to be anywhere near me after I acted like I had?

Lily picks up the remote to the TV and aims it at the screen. She scrolls through the channels and stops on *Sweet Home Alabama*.

I move in closer to her and rest my head on her shoulder.

There are no more words between us. Until I fall asleep on her couch, and wear one of her dresses to work tomorrow, I'll sit in the quiet with my ride or die friend and let her comfort me and my mixed up emotions.

I haven't heard from Lily yet, but I suppose that I'll get that text any minute. It's just past six o'clock in the morning and I basically snuck out of the house, but the thought of looking at those notes that Noah left on my desk kept me up most the night.

Luckily, she only lives a mile from the center of town, and she leaves the keys to the store in her key bowl by the door. The walk was good to clear my head. Not that I'm thinking any straighter.

"You're super early," Mrs. Packer says from the doorway of her store as I walk up to my store.

"I am. What are you doing here? Are you opening on Sundays now?" I ask as I slide my key into the lock on the door.

"Planning," she says. "I'll be open all week during your book event thing."

That makes me smile. "It'll be an epic week."

I unlock the door and push it open, closing and locking it behind me. Without turning on any of the lights, I walk to my office where the door is open and the light is still on from last night when I ran out of the store.

The notes Noah tore from the pad still lay piled on the desk.

I reach for them, but then pull back my hand as if they'll burn when I look at them.

Instead, I sit down, turn on my computer, and bring up my manuscript.

I read a few pages and then look over at the notes.

They're just words. I shouldn't have gotten so mad that he read them.

Gnawing on my bottom lip, I pick up the notes and look over them.

There are a few notes that mention the scene and the names of the characters all starting with the letter C. That actually makes me chuckle, because I had never thought about how confusing that could be.

He has a few questions written down about storyline and I study them. Everything he has written down makes sense. If I took these questions and addressed them, would I feel better about the story?

I take his first question and scroll through the manuscript until I find what it is he's talking about.

Reading through the scene, I realize I have a gaping hole in the story.

There is a flutter in my chest as I work through the scene trying to address the items he'd noted. Then I move to the next item.

Before I know it, I hear the chimes above the door between the cafe and the bookstore, which means Mrs. Packer has opened the door. I look at the time and realize I have spent the past two hours working through Noah's notes after I'd gotten so angry at him.

"Em, are you in there?" I hear Lily say.

"I'm in my office."

A moment later she's standing in the doorway. "You snuck out," she says.

"I did. Thank you for the dress and the care."

"How's the elbow?"

I lift my arm to look at the scrape. "It's okay."

"It's a good thing Mrs. Packer is watching out for you and told me where you were."

I ignore that and look back down at the notes.

"What are you doing?" Lily asks.

I wince and wrinkle my nose. "Working through Noah's notes."

"Interesting. You were mad enough you sent him away and then hurt yourself, and now, here you are, working through them?"

Shrugging, I smile at her. "He's had a few good points."

"I'm sure he has more than a few. Don't be such a bitch when you see him," she says before she turns and walks back out into the store, turning on the lights and getting the store ready to open.

I sit for a moment and think about what she said. I was a bitch to him. I owe him an apology, a very sincere one.

CHAPTER 26

We've been unusually busy for a Sunday, and again, there are a lot of readers in town who aren't planning on being at the event but are here looking for Noah.

However, Noah isn't around. In fact, I haven't seen him or heard from him, and I can't blame him.

Here I was worried about having an affair with a man who was going to leave town, and now I'm just a woman who had a one night stand with a man and then went bat shit crazy on him.

My phone chimes in my pocket and I take it out and check the message. It's from Katie.

I'm back in town and at the hotel. Meet me here at the restaurant for dinner? Six?

I look at the time, it's just past three. We close at four on Sunday, which will give me just enough time to go home and change into my own clothes.

I'll be there, I reply, to which she sends a smiley face emoji.

"Where's your tenant?" Lily asks as she brings a stack of books from the back room to the counter to add to stock.

I shrug. "Really? You're surprised he hasn't shown up?"

Lily grins as she sets down the books. "He just doesn't realize that your sass is part of your charm."

I snort out a laugh. Only Lily could get away with saying things like that to me and I'd find it funny.

The lobby of the resort bustles with people checking in for the week, and those heading into to town.

Katie stands at the entrance to the hotel's restaurant, her phone in her hand, and probably the most casual outfit I've seen her in yet—a pair of jeans, a crisp white button-down shirt, a beaded mala around her neck, and three-inch high heels.

I've always had a more bohemian style. I look down at my mountain-dweller style of jeans, boots, and a sweater—it is still March in the Rocky Mountains.

With my coat draped over my arm, I walk toward her, very aware that somewhere in this building, Noah has taken refuge away from me.

"Hi," I say to draw Katie's attention from her phone.

"Oh, hey, Emma," she says tucking her phone into the purse. "I got us a reservation. I wasn't sure how busy they would be."

"Never a bad idea," I say as I follow her to the host stand and she gives them her name.

We are seated and Katie orders a bottle of wine and a candied pecan chicken salad.

"I assumed you knew the menu," she says looking at me as if she might be terrified that she quickly ordered as we were seated.

"I'll have the same," I tell the server. "It's a good salad."

"I studied the menu online. I hate waiting for servers to come back to the table. You never know if they will."

I think that says volumes to the difference between small town mountain living and New York City.

"When I was driving up to the hotel, I saw your store window.

It looks fantastic. Have you been getting a lot of business with the display?"

The server returns with our wine and fills us each a glass.

"We have had more business. It appears there are quite a few people who came early, but don't plan to be here for the event. Many of them have heard that Noah is in town, and they are trying to run into him."

Katie shakes her head as she picks up her wine glass. "Tell me he's being gracious and not an ass. I hadn't considered readers clamoring for him."

She hadn't?

"He's been delightful," I say, but even I hear the choked sound I make with it, so I quickly pick up my glass and sip my wine.

"Delightful. That's not a word I associate with Noah Carter."

When I'm with Noah, I see a sensitive man who understands people. Maybe not how to deal with them, but he's studied them and he knows how they tick. After reading his comments about my romance novel, he understands deep emotion too.

Then, there's the man I've been intimate with. Nothing that night showed me the side of the man that lines up with how Katie views him. He was gentle, sincere, and gracious in his giving.

But I know he has a reputation for a reason. So what makes him different when he's with me, or in my store, or here in this town?

Katie takes another sip of her wine and eases against the back of her chair. "I just hope he isn't in your way or giving you any trouble. He'd better be working. His editor has been expecting pages from his new book, but he hasn't sent over anything."

I swallow hard. "He's been putting in a lot of hours," I say, but there is some truth to when I ask how productive he's been, he only shrugs. "I'm sure he'll have something soon."

"He'd better. He has a lot riding on this book. I mean, the

world still wants to hear from him. He sells, but he's hard to work with."

I feel as if I'm part of a gossip session I shouldn't be part of. Sure, if this was a week ago before I'd studied those dark eyes or kissed those talented lips—maybe. If it had been before we'd eaten that brownie and slept on the floor of my store, which only led to us sleeping in my bed—and more.

Again, I pick up my wine and sip as Katie pulls her phone from her purse.

"Let's talk about the literary event," she says as she scrolls through her phone. "There is going to be so much going on in the next two weeks. I'm so excited for your store."

I listen as Katie talks about the different events that will be happening during the week. Each author will give a talk and do a Q&A. There will be a panel with all of the authors, and then of course there will be the events at my store. Each author will do a book signing and a reading. I have to admit, I'm giddy to see my store filled with people. I mean, that's the image in the dream I've always had, and now it'll be a reality.

"I'll come by tomorrow and we'll scope out the store for the best layout for the readings. You might have to move some shelves around, or maybe we can work with your neighbor and use her dining area for seating," she draws out the last words and makes a note in her phone. "What's her name? I'll reach out to her."

"Agnes Packer," I say as the server brings our salads.

"Right. Since the stores are connected, maybe we can get enough seating in her place and then the bookstore doesn't have to move anything, and that'll allow for better sales for you," she says with a rise of her brows.

"Well, I'm all in for that," I say, but all I can think about is standing next to Noah as he signs the thousand books I have in my back room.

The thought warms me. But then I think about how I acted yesterday and now I wonder if he'll want me involved at all.

CHAPTER 27

I watch Katie rush through her dinner, answer texts as they come in, and take notes on her phone as she talks about the event and keeps making new plans.

As soon as dinner is over, she pays the bill and stands.

"Thanks for meeting me," she says as we walk from the restaurant. "I'm so excited about all of this. I'll come by the store tomorrow morning and I'll talk to Mrs. Packer as well."

Then she pulls me in for a hug and hurries toward the elevator, leaving me to catch my breath because the entire evening has been a whirlwind watching Katie process plans, and her excitement about the event that will transform the town. She loves her job. She's amazing at planning and organizing timelines. And though I was there, I'm not sure I participated. I just watched and admired this fireball of a woman.

I shrug on my coat and head through the lobby.

"Emma," the voice comes from behind me.

It's Noah's voice.

I turn to find him in one of the oversized chairs, his legs crossed, and a beer bottle poised between his fingers. He stands and moves to me.

"Hi," I say on a breath, not sure how he's going to react at me.

"You got cornered for one of Katie's business dinners, huh?"

I look toward the elevators where she disappeared. "Yeah, she had some plans to go over."

Noah looks down at his beer and then sets it on the table next to the chair he'd been seated in. "Listen, I wanted to apologize. I had no right—"

I lift my finger to his lips to stop him from talking, and then realize just how intimate it is.

I lower my hand. "I'm the one who's sorry. I never should have lashed out like that."

"I invaded your privacy," he says.

"I invited you in."

He narrows his gaze on me as if he doesn't understand my about-face. And, why would he? We've known one another a week.

"I'm just saying, I shouldn't have acted that way," I say, easing closer to him to see what happens.

His hand comes to my waist and settles there, then he leans in and presses his forehead to mine. "We're okay?"

"We're okay," I say. "Your notes were helpful."

His mouth curls up into a smile. "You actually looked at them?"

"I did. The manuscript's worthless. I'll never finish the book or do anything with it but—"

"Why not?" he asks easing back. "It's a good book."

"It's a pipe dream."

"It's a perfectly good dream."

"You don't understand," I say and his brows lift. "Okay, well, you probably do understand, but I'm fifty-two."

"And?"

"And …" I trail off. And what?

"What are you doing now?" he asks running his hand down my arm until he grasps my hand in his.

"Heading home."

"You still like me after having dinner with Katie?"

Again, I look toward the elevators where she'd disappeared after dinner. "Why wouldn't I?" I ask, looking back at him.

He shrugs. "I'm short with her when she demands my time. I just figure she—"

I touch his arm. "She only knows one part of you."

"And you know more than that?"

I ease in even closer. "I know more than that."

"Come up to my room," he says, his voice low.

"I really should be—"

"No you shouldn't," he cuts me off. "Stay with me tonight."

I swallow hard. "You still want to spend time with me? I showed you all of my crazy, and you still want me to come up to your room?"

"I welcome your crazy," he says running his other hand down my arm, but when he gets to my elbow, I jump back as if he'd hit me. "What happened?"

I grip my arm, but a laugh escapes me. "I had an accident. No big deal."

"An accident? Let me look," he says, his voice filled with concern.

I shake my head. "You'll see it," I say, reaching for his hand, starting toward the elevator with him in tow.

I push the button and the door to one of the elevators opens.

Two others file into the elevator with us, so we stand next to one another, our hands clasped.

When the elevator stops, we step out and I let Noah lead me to his room.

"I've never been upstairs in this hotel," I say. "Never had a reason," I confirm without him questioning it.

"It's a lovely view of the town. I can see your store. I know when you're parked out back."

We stop in front of his room and he shoots me a smile as he unlocks the door with his card.

"So you spy on me?" I tease.

"I think about you," he says as he pushes open the door and I step inside. "But, if you don't mind me asking, why didn't you go home last night?"

I turn to him as the door closes. "You know my car was there all night?"

"Yeah."

I move to him, wrapping my arms around his waist. "I slept at Lily's."

"Why?" he asks, lifting his hand into my hair.

I shrug. "I followed you out to your car," I say.

"I never saw you."

"No. You were faster to get away."

"I'm sor—" This time I silence him with my lips pressed to his, then I step back.

"I followed you. Then found out I locked myself out of the store and then I fell on my ass," I say, shrugging off my coat, letting it fall to the floor, and then reaching for the hem of my sweater to pull it up and over my head.

Noah's eyes widen at first, but when I turn so that he can see the back of my arm, he lets out a groan.

"What the hell happened to you?" he asks, moving to me and touching the sensitive skin.

"I told you," I say wincing at his touch. "I fell on my ass."

"I've seen your ass. This isn't it," he teases. "Seriously, is this because of me?" he asks, studying the scrapes and bruises surrounding my elbow.

I turn so that I'm facing him again. "No, this is because of me. This is all because of the fit I threw."

"Emma—"

"I'm serious. I acted like a child."

"And again, I crossed a line."

I worry my lip as I study him. I know every line around his eyes, and his beard is fuller than it was even yesterday. Lifting my hand up into his hair, I comb my fingers through the salt and pepper strands.

If you'd asked me when my husband left me if I thought I'd find a man I'd like to couple with again, I'd have said no. And, once I passed fifty, I was damn sure it would never happen.

But here stands Noah Carter, only a week ago he was just a name on a book jacket and a signature on curt emails. Now, well, now he feels like my whole world.

"When I came back to the store, I yanked on the door, but since the door was locked, I stumbled back and fell over a piece of the sidewalk," I say.

Noah presses a kiss to my bare shoulder. "I'm sorry."

"Lily fixed me all up and made me sleep on her couch."

He nods slowly, moving his kiss from my shoulder to my throat. "So I'm going to owe Lily an apology too?"

"Why—why would you do that?" I ask as my eyes grow heavy and close.

"Because I'm sure you were still mad and had a lot of not great things to say about me."

"No, no …" It's becoming harder to make sense of my words. "She was fully on your side," I assure him.

Noah eases back and I open my eyes to look at him.

"Seriously?" he asks.

"Seriously. She thinks you could offer me a lot when it comes to my book, and that I shouldn't have acted like I did."

"Your attitude was fair," he says. "But I would like to help you with it. It has potential, and it would give me something to do."

I lick my lips which have gone dry. "You have something to do. Katie says you owe your editor pages."

Now he fully takes a step back and tunnels his fingers through his hair leaving deeper grooves than I had. I'm sure he could never play a fair game of poker. His tells are too strong.

"I'm stuck, Em. The words aren't coming. I thought being here would help, but the first words I even got written were last night after I left you."

"So me yelling at you helps?"

He snorts out a laugh. "No, me helping you seems to have helped. I don't want to help you for my own selfish reasons, but I want to see you succeed. It just so happens that reading your story, which is so different than mine, opened a closed door."

"So you were missing romance in your book?"

He blinks hard and smiles. "I was missing romance in every aspect of my life."

I pull my lips in to keep them from quivering. He found romance in me? Is that what he's saying?

"I've been missing romance in every aspect of my life too. Maybe that's why I can't finish the damn book the way I want it."

Noah reaches out his hand and I take it. He pulls me toward him until we are flush. Lifting his hand up into my hair, he rests his other hand on my hip.

"Let's work on it together. It'll be our project while I'm here."

"We have a project for while you're here," I remind him.

"Let me work on this with you. I have lots of connections. I mean, I can't just walk you in and get you a contract, but maybe I can help you bypass the slush pile."

"Why do you want to do this?"

His hand moves to my cheek. "Because you mean something to me, Emma."

CHAPTER 28

The need for caffeine already hits me by nine o'clock. Mondays are always hard, even if it's a routine day. But after a night with Noah, in his hotel room, and an early morning to drive home to shower and change, now I'm dragging.

The door to the store opens and Katie walks through. She looks like New York again, only, she's smartly dressed in sensible boots since it snowed last night enough to make the sidewalks sloppy.

When she pulls off her dark glasses, her eyes laser-focus on me.

"Is he in there?" she asks, nodding toward my office door.

"No. He had some things to do," I say.

"Good. Let's talk," she says, walking behind the counter and straight into my office without allowing me to invite her in.

Julia is watching Katie with wide eyes as she arranges the table by the door. I give her a shrug and follow Katie into the office, where she shuts the door once I'm inside.

"Why did I see you leaving the hotel this morning?" she asks, or accuses. I'm not sure with her tone.

This is again when I remind myself that I'm fifty-two years old and don't owe some maybe-forty-year-old an explanation.

"Is there a problem?" I ask.

She lets her shoulders fall as she pinches the bridge of her nose. "Just tell me you weren't with Noah."

"Why?"

When that's my response, her brows lift and she drops her hand. "Why? Because that would be bad."

"Why would it be anyone's business?"

"So you were with Noah?"

"I said it wouldn't be anyone's business."

Leaning herself against my desk, she looks up at me. "He needs to work. He's been so blocked, and sleeping with the man isn't—"

"It's no one's business who the man sleeps with," I reiterate. "He's going to get his work done."

Katie studies me. She has no idea what to make of my side of this conversation.

"Emma, I'm not judging."

I don't say anything to that, because, yes, I do think she is judging.

"I guess a better question would have been, is Noah okay?"

And with that question, what I had assumed was judgment, becomes clearly simply her caring for the broken man she works with.

"I think he is. Yes, he said he's been blocked, but he's been writing," I assure her.

A smile finally forms on her lips. "He's had a rough go. I sometimes forget it's not a personality flaw."

I force my shoulders to ease. "He's extremely talented, and sometimes that gets mistaken for irritating."

That causes her to laugh. "You're right. I should know that. I work with enough authors and creatives that I need to remember that." She stands, moving away from the desk. "I'm going to go talk to Mrs. Packer about using her store. And let's meet in a few days to walk through questions to ask during the author talks."

"I'm running the author talks?" I hear my voice rise in pitch.

"Didn't we discuss that?" She laughs again. "We think it would be best since it's your store and there will be many of your customers. Are you comfortable with that?"

I quickly give it some thought. "I guess I am."

"Good. I find when the authors interview one another, sometimes they try to hijack the conversations to promote their own work."

Her phone rings at that moment and she fishes it from her bag as she opens the office door and steps out into the store.

Julia looks in at me from the counter. "Noah is in the back room. I think he's hiding," she says in a near whisper.

That makes me chuckle. "I have no doubt," I say as I watch Katie walk among the shelves while she takes her call.

As soon as she disconnects her call, she gives me a wave and disappears into Mrs. Packer's store.

I take that as the all safe to find Noah.

Just as promised, he's in the back room—hiding.

"Is she gone?" he asks as I slip through the door and shut it behind me—locking it too.

"For the moment. You're not afraid of her, are you?"

"Not in the least. I just don't need to engage in conversation. I brought you a coffee, by the way," he says pointing to the cup on the table.

"Thank you." I pick up the coffee and take a sip. This might get me through the next hour before I need another. "She knows I stayed at the hotel last night."

Noah studies me, his eyes coolly searching my face. "She said that?"

"She asked me about it. I told her it was no one's business why I was at the hotel."

"She knew though?"

"She knew, but I didn't say anything about it. I'm too old to have to answer to anyone."

That has the corner of his mouth ticking up. "They're afraid I'm not working, aren't they?"

I shrug and sip from my cup again. "I told her you're working. They don't need to know the ins and outs of your life. You don't owe that to anyone. And, if they fire your ass, there's always the option to publish yourself."

He actually snorts out a laugh at that.

"What?" I say. "It's completely viable."

"It is. And wouldn't they all shit the bed?"

That has me puckering my lips. "The office is open for you if you want to work."

"What I want to do is go back to the hotel," he says, moving toward me and wrapping me up in one arm, both of us holding coffee cups out to not spill on one another.

"If I laid down in a bed, I'd fall asleep."

"Would you? That didn't happen last night when you laid down in a bed."

I feel the heat rise in my cheeks at his words.

I watch his eyes as I lick my lips. "I suppose we should put in a few hours of work, especially since the locals are already talking and all."

"She's not local," he reminds me.

"She's not the only one talking," I say.

"Can I work on your book?"

I search his eyes for something that I suppose is regret that he's not writing his own words, but I don't find anything but want. A want to work on my book. A want for me.

"If that's how you want to spend your time."

"It's not. But you said we have to work," he says as his hand trails from my back and over my ass as he presses a kiss to my lips.

"Yes, you have my permission to work on my book," I say on an airy sigh.

"Dinner tonight?"

"I'll cook."

"Can I stay?"

"I wouldn't want it any other way," I say before I turn from him, move to the door and unlock it, and then exit out into the store.

CHAPTER 29

"Do you have a day you don't work?" Noah asks me as we sit on my couch, my head rested on his lap as he strokes my hair.

"I go in late on Wednesdays."

I feel his body move as he laughs.

"Why is that funny?" I ask looking up at him.

"You go in late one day a week? No days off?"

I shrug. "When it's all you have in your life, there's no need to take a day off."

"Go away with me," he says, but as if it were a thought that didn't even process, but just jumped out of his mouth.

That has me sitting up, studying him, and then I straddle his lap. His hands come to my hips, and admittedly, I might grind myself into position before I work into the conversation at hand.

"We don't have time to go away," I remind him.

"We do. I'm saying a few days. One if it's all we can get. We could go to Denver and stay at the Brown Palace. Or go down to Colorado Springs and stay at the Broadmoor. Or even rent a cabin in Estes Park."

I study his dark eyes as his hand moves from my hip, up and

under my shirt, his thumb lazily tracing the sensitive skin under my breast.

"You've done some homework," I say.

"I only have so much time here, and I want to spend it all with you."

Doesn't that hit hard?

This thing between us is temporary, and I know that. I've already battled with this, but when it comes up, it stings.

"What do you plan on doing on our time away?"

"You," is all he says, and I throw my head back with a laugh.

"You're never going to finish that book."

"I'll finish it. Deadlines are in place for a reason."

I can feel him grow beneath me as his hand moves to my breast and now his thumb brushes my peaked nipple.

"Estes Park," I say again moving myself against him. "If we're in a cabin, no one can hear us."

Those dark eyes of his grow darker, and his hand comes back to my hip again as if to position me into the right place on his lap.

"You do tend to use words some people might find offensive," he says and I grin down at him.

"Do you find them offensive?"

"Fuck, no," he growls. "I love that I can make you say them."

One thing about having some random sexual encounter in my fifties—there's no reason to hold back. Noah makes me feel everything. And though I could easily turn that around and make it all about his experiences with other women that make him so skilled, it doesn't play in my head that way. He likes to pleasure me, and he does an exceptional job.

"One night," I say and he eases his head back against the couch to look up at me.

"One?"

"We can't afford more."

"One night it is." His fingers dig into my flesh. "I think we're going to need to go to your bedroom so you can use those words. It appears that I have a little—something, going on." He moves beneath me.

"There is nothing little about that, and I'm happy to use all the words."

From the moment I walk into my store on Wednesday, I'm putting out fires. Books that were supposed to arrive the day before are stuck in Denver and patrons are none too happy when they can't have their preordered book that released this morning.

Mrs. Packer's store had a water leak and it managed its way under the door between our stores. Luckily Lily caught it as it happened and nothing was damaged. Katie gave Sylvia St. Clare my phone number, and knowing that this woman, who has kept me on the phone for the past forty minutes, has a thing for the man I'm sleeping with, hits me wrong.

She's been nothing but nice, but I already don't like her.

"And I know it sounds strange and all, but the sticky notes we use to write people's names on the books so that I can personalize them while they're there, yeah, don't get the super sticky ones. They leave residue and sometimes just don't come out well. Ya know what I mean?" she says as I'm taking notes at my desk.

"I do understand."

Noah walks into my office with a bag from the deli down the street and sets it on my desk. I look up at him and I must have a look of distress because he mouths the words, *Are you okay?*

I roll my eyes and nod, then turn around my notepad where I've written Sylvia's name at the top.

His eyes go wide and his cheeks turn a color red I've yet to see.

I'm not sure what the true motive is, but he leans in and lingers a kiss on my lips as Sylvia talks about the kind of tea she would like me to serve at our author talk, because she doesn't want people to have to spend money on anything other than her books.

When the call is finally over, I look up at Noah, who has set out our lunch on my desk, and now perches against the desk watching me with great interest.

"You didn't sleep with her, right?" I ask, defeated.

"I told you I didn't," he confirms.

"I'm just a bit disgusted that I'll have to share my space with her. I didn't want to have shared you too."

The corner of his mouth turns up. "Nothing to be jealous over."

"Me? Jealous?" I leave it there, because, yeah, I'm probably jealous of every woman that came before me. Though, funny enough, I have no jealousy over Abby.

"I'm sorry she's causing you some unwanted anxiety," he says as he takes the folding chair from between the two file cabinets and sets it next to me. "Fuel up. We're going to work on your book now."

To that I drop my shoulders. "I don't have time for that. My writing isn't important. This event is top of the list."

Noah turns me in my chair so that our legs fit together, thigh to thigh. "You need something for you."

"I have you, in this moment," I say as if reminding each of us that this is all the time we have.

"Two hours," he negotiates.

"One."

Noah runs his tongue over his teeth. "One hour. Uninterrupted. During business hours."

I snort out a laugh. "Why during business hours?"

"Because after hours, you're all mine," he says, lifting a hand to the back of my neck and pulling me toward him, kissing me so thoroughly that it takes me a moment to remember what we'd agreed to. "One hour. All mine. No interruptions."

I nod. I can't say no to this man, and isn't that a bad thing?

CHAPTER 30

Lily's eyes have narrowed until I'm not sure she can see through them. "Em, this fucking event is next week. Do you know how much we still have to do?"

"I do. I'm asking for this as a friend," I say in a heavy whisper as the store is full of patrons who just happen to be taking in the town on a Wednesday afternoon.

Lily huffs out a breath and leans against the counter, her arms crossed now. "An hour now, two days while you're off having a sex-cation," she says so matter-of-factly it doesn't register with me for a moment. "You know I have a life too, right?"

"I'm more aware of that than anyone. I watched your kids for more than one sex-cation," I remind her.

She puckers her lips as if she hadn't considered that too.

"Don't get hurt, Em."

Now I narrow my gaze on her. "Why would I get hurt?"

"He's leaving."

Wasn't she on the other side of this before? Wasn't she the one telling me to live a little, or am I making that up because normally, that would be exactly what she'd have said.

"I'm fine. I'm not going to let this make or break me. We're having a nice time while he's here. He's going to help me with my book. Who knows; maybe someday I'll have my own signing here," I say and wait for her expression to change, but it doesn't.

"You deserve something like that. You deserve to have anything you touch turn to gold."

"Deserve it or not, I can only have it because you're here with me." I reach for her and she takes my hand.

"Ride or die, bitch. You can't get rid of me."

When I step back into the office, I'm not even sure Noah notices until I shut the door behind me. And then, only briefly, does he look up.

"How fast does a wild fire move?" he asks as he's writing notes in a notebook I've seen him take out of his bag from time to time.

"It depends on a lot of factors. We once had over a thousand houses destroyed in a matter of a few hours when a fire started and we had eighty mile an hour winds."

That has him looking up at me. "In the mountains?"

"Just at the base of the foothills, not far from Boulder. It nearly wiped out an entire city."

"Recently?"

I nod. "Just a few years ago."

He blinks up at me and then looks down at his notes. "So, specifically in your book. I'm just trying to track the timing of the fire."

I sit down in the folding chair he'd put there when we ate lunch. "There is a lightning strike that starts it. I guess the way I see it, it smolders in that area and then with the dry ground cover, it starts to move."

He nods thoughtfully. "All while Autumn and Logan are ..."

He leaves it hanging.

"Yes."

Noah puckers his lips. "So the fire wipes out her wildlife research and his lumber mill?"

"Yes. Then they have a fight on their hands, right? First the fire, then the rebuild. She wants what's best for the wildlife she's studying and he's a business man using the forest for profit. I mean that's the gist of the enemies to lovers anyway. Wildlife supporter versus the lumber mill in this case."

Noah nods thoughtfully. "I think you need some angst while they're in the throes of passion."

To that I raise a brow. "Angst? They've been battling each other for half the book. Now they're in, what I consider, a very detailed moment, and you want me to give it more angst?"

"Hear me out. They're not paying any attention, right? It's storming outside, but there is no rain. Anyone working in a forest all the time would pay attention to that. Wouldn't even the air feel different? It would crackle around them more than just because of the sexual energy." He places his hand on my knee. "Maybe deep inside one of them thinks they should look outside when the room lights with lightning and they should react to the crack of thunder. They're not that far from ignition, so wouldn't there be a tremendous noise?"

I roll my lips between my teeth. He's right. I have them doing it up until they're tired and someone comes to the door to tell them to evacuate.

"Shit," is all I can say.

We lock eyes, but it's as if we're scanning one another for the answer, and it has to come from me.

Simultaneously we both stand and switch places as if this were a rehearsed dance we'd taken part in hundreds of times before.

I sit down behind the desk and look at the screen. The cursor blinks right in the middle of the most heated sex scene I've ever written. I can feel my cheeks warm.

The words on the page were written years before I met Noah

Carter. But as I read them, I can feel them. Perhaps this book was in some way a wish that came true.

I scan my eyes over the words, looking for that moment where I can change the direction.

"Here," I say, pointing to the screen. "This would be the perfect place for one of them to come up for air, consider looking out, but then get taken back down by …" I leave it linger there.

His eyes flash, and I wonder if this is the exact spot he was thinking of too—or is he thinking of the take back down that has my heart flutter as well?

"Write it in," he says.

I lock my glance in his direction. I've never written anything while someone watched and I can feel every hair on the back of my neck stand in protest.

Not only am I going to create something in front of someone who does this for a living, it's the sex scene.

Noah obviously doesn't have the same reaction, because he's watching the screen, waiting for the words to appear.

I move my fingers in and out, as if I have to warm them up before they execute the maneuver, and then I rest them on the keyboard.

Looking at the screen, I move the mouse to the right place and begin to change the feel of the scene. Throes of passion, words of angst and pleasure, lightning. She lifts her head toward the window and he takes her under with another kiss, another pulse, another whisper, another—.

The air in the room is thicker now. My palms are damp and I retract my hands from the keyboard and wipe them on my pants as Noah cranes his neck to read what I've written.

"I can't type and look up at the screen," he says, his eyes still scanning the text.

"Typing 101," I say.

"Yeah, I failed typing 101. Hunt and peck works out perfect

for me," he admits, then touches the screen where I've added the text. "Go deeper on this."

I read the line he's pointing to, and again, my cheeks heat.

"Go deeper? Isn't that what he's doing?"

A small chuckle escapes Noah. "This is a pivotal moment between them and the entire story. Everything comes together and falls apart in these pages."

He's right. When I wrote it I thought it was just that love scene that came at the right time. But when he works through it, it's so much more.

I chew on my bottom lip as I remember the first time with Noah. I channel all of the anxious energy knowing I was going to sleep with a man who I'd only just met, who I hadn't had very many nice things to say about, and who would then leave.

My fingers touch the keys, retract, and then hover.

Noah moves in closer to me, his hand now on my thigh. "It's right there," he whispers, but when I look at him, he's not looking at me, he's looking at the screen. He's in bed with those characters, and I'm not even sure he knows it.

I may be the one writing, but it's showing me the genius that is this man. So why is he so blocked?

I look back at the screen and begin to type. Maybe it's his hand on my knee or his breath in the room, but the words flow through my fingers.

Soon, the love scene that was there to heighten the tension and to bring these two people—opposing forces—together, now has that angst that Noah was talking about. It reads even hotter now that there is some uncertainty and they are each choosing the other in that moment. It becomes life or death and they can't even pay attention to the details because they are so wrapped up in one another.

I turn to look at him now and he's smiling at me as if he's the one that wrote what is on the screen. "That's it. That's what I was looking for."

Everything in me heats now and I move to kiss him.

His hands come to my cheeks and when he eases back that smile is still there.

"Now, in the next chapter," he begins and I realize he's all work now.

I ease back in my chair and listen as he goes over his notes. The affair I'm having with this man is never going to compare to the professional I'm working with now. There is a great chance I might not like him again when this is over.

CHAPTER 31

I don't usually have to admit when I'm wrong. I live alone, no children or a man to answer to. I own my own business, so everyone answers to me. But, when I thought I wouldn't like Noah by the time we were done working on my book, I was wrong. I like him even more. In fact, I respect him in an entirely different way. There is a reason he's as successful as he is.

I gave him the hour he'd asked for.

Hell, I would have given him all night, but Lily came knocking after an hour.

"You get back to work. I'm going to go back to the hotel and pack a bag," he says standing and folding the chair, sliding it back between the filing cabinets.

"You don't want to rush back in the morning?" I tease as I save the version of my book we've worked on for the past hour.

"No. I want to spend every moment with you until you have to walk back into this store. I'm also going to make plans. We're going to Estes Park, staying in a cabin, and using all of those pretty words you have."

My cheeks heat when he says that.

Noah moves to me, kisses me gently, and picks up his bag. "I'll be back before you close."

I try to stay focused for the rest of the day, but I find that hard to do. My mind keeps going back to my manuscript. I find myself grinning, thinking about the scenes we worked through and how they're so much better.

I'm not even paying attention when Katie walks up to the counter and places her hands flat on the top.

"You're going out of town?" she says as if she's trying very hard not to be disappointed in me.

"I'm going to Estes Park, for just one night."

"One night, but two days gone."

I nod slowly. "Yes," I draw out the word. "Lily will be here and so will Julia."

Her lips are pressed in a thin line. "He owes his editor pages by Monday. Monday, Emma. Monday," she repeats for good measure.

"He knows this?"

There's pink rising in her cheeks, but she keeps calm. "Of course he knows that. He's known that since the start."

I keep a cool eye on her, my nerves steady. "Then I'm sure he'll have them to them in time. He's a professional, after all."

Now she moves her hand to place it over mine. "Be careful, Emma," she warns as she turns and heads to the back of the store where she and Julia are rearranging the romance and thriller sections.

I don't want what Katie has said to me to take up space in my head. I have another week and a half with this man, who is seated next to me in my car, and I don't want to have to worry about his perceived work ethic.

His head is craned so he can see out the window at the full moon that lights up the road. "I can't believe you make this drive every single day. It's just so beautiful," he says.

"It never dulls. Because it's nature, it changes daily."

He sits back in his seat and turns his head to look at me. "You do have a way with words, Ms. Reynolds."

I don't know why that has me laughing. Maybe because I wasn't even sure he knew my last name, or remembered it, despite that I'm sleeping with the man.

"I know I said I just wanted to spend time with you tonight, but I was thinking about the scene after the fire when they both realize they have to rebuild and the other isn't good for their cause," he says as I pull into my driveway.

"Why is my book so important to you?"

"It has my mind working like it hasn't worked in a long time. I feel energized by it."

When I look at him, I see him differently. This isn't the moody, arrogant man who walked into my store over a week ago. This isn't the same man I'd caught asleep sitting upright in a chair.

This man has a spark in his eyes now—his clear eyes.

"Do you want to work on it tonight?" I ask.

"Do you have it on a laptop or something? Or maybe we can brainstorm, or—"

"I can pull it up on my laptop," I say carefully. "But what about your book?"

I have to ask. Katie's voice keeps rattling in my head. I honestly don't know if she's more upset about me being involved with Noah because I'm keeping him from working, or if she's worried about my wellbeing.

Noah purses his lips. "I got a few words in today when I went back to the hotel. It's coming along."

I want to pry, but I won't. What will it matter to me if he turns in his pages or not? In another week, he'll just be a memory.

Dinner was hurried and forgotten on plates as we pushed my laptop between us. Noah's comments and suggestions come between praises and accolades for what I have written.

Self doubt and excitement play a game of Ping-Pong in my brain as I erase entire paragraphs and add new ones while Noah watches.

"Do you think I can actually get this published?" I ask, wondering if he does see potential in it, or if he's just avoiding his own work.

"I want to show it to a junior agent that works with my agency next week."

That has me closing my laptop. "It's not ready for that."

"It's not ready for publication. It's ready to have someone objectively look at it," he says as he rests his hand on mine.

"I won't be ready next week. I have too much to think about next week. You can't ask me to—"

"Wait till you meet her. You'll want to show it to her," he says as if he knows this for a fact.

"I don't want to work on this anymore," I say and he nods slowly.

"Can I interest you in a slow dance on the balcony?" he asks, leaning in closer to me.

"You could interest me in almost anything."

I watch as he searches my eyes for something, though I don't know what. Does he still want to work on the book? Are we just taking a moment to take in one another?

"I want to tell you something," he says, his voice serious and low.

"What's that?"

Noah moves his chair closer, his hand still covering mine. "Abby was everything to me," he says and I feel a knot in my throat. I didn't expect him to say that. I don't know what I expected, but that wasn't it.

My jaw tenses. "Of course," I say, but he lifts his finger to my lips to silence me.

"Nothing in my life has been the same since she died. I don't eat. I don't sleep."

The more he talks, the more that knot chokes me until I wonder if I'm even breathing.

"I write out of habit, and luckily it's good enough to make a living from. But I don't enjoy it, not anymore, not as much as I've enjoyed working with you on your book."

Blinking hard, I try to clear my throat and breathe.

His thumb traces over my knuckles and it sends a kind of electricity up my spine that could have me bursting from the chair or dying here.

"Until I met you, I thought that any kind of happiness was over for me. I didn't know I could care about anything again."

I continue to blink, only now my cheeks are wet because my eyes have filled with tears.

"Emma, this week has changed my life. It's given me purpose again. It's brought me joy. It's everything I hadn't realized I was missing. No other woman could have made me whole again, but you have."

I press my lips between my teeth because they've begun to tremble.

"Really?" I eke out the word and it's small in comparison to how I'm feeling.

He smiles sweetly. "Really. I don't know what will happen in another week, but you'll be no less important. I want you in my life, Emma. It might take some work, but ..."

"Yes!" I blurt out the word as if he's proposed marriage to me, but he hasn't. In fact, he's still talking about leaving, isn't he?

But what does it matter? I fucking love this man, though I'm not going to tell him that exactly.

Noah sits up straight and his smile widens.

"We can still see each other when I go back? I mean, we can work this out?"

Basically, I guess, he's asking me to be his girlfriend—long distance? My head is spinning now and the work we've just done is no longer pinging around in my brain. Now the thoughts of long weekends in New York, or carefree ones on my deck fill my head.

"You make me happy," I say to him and it sounds so elementary I nearly tell him to forget it, but he's smiling at me, and I can't think of anything else.

"Thank you," he says as he lifts his hand to my cheek.

"For what?"

"For making me whole again."

CHAPTER 32

There is a ball of guilt that weighs heavy in my stomach as Noah and I drive toward Estes Park.

I should be enjoying the look he has in his eyes as we drive over the tight mountain roads. He looks like a child seeing nature for the first time.

He's mesmerized by the winding road, the mass of trees, the view when we come to a valley. Nature in Colorado is much different than any nature he gets in the city, I'm sure.

Instead, I'm worrying about Lily, Julia, and Katie. They were all willing help take care of the store for the next two days, but they're not happy about it. Happy for me; yes. Happy to have me gone; not at all.

"How often do you make this trip?" Noah asks, his head craned to look out the window, much as it had been the first time I took him home with me.

"I don't," I say.

He sits back in his seat to look at me. "You're kidding? You do realize just where you live, right? I mean, you know all of this is out there and you don't make this drive often?"

The ball of guilt is still heavy, but a smile settles on my lips.

"When was the last time you went to Times Square and just looked around? When did you last take in a Broadway show?"

His smile turns into a cocky grin. "My agent's office is one block from Times Square. I was there two weeks ago. And I saw Wicked a month ago."

"Oh," I say having been put in my place, but all I want to ask is who he went to Wicked with.

He reaches across the car and touches my cheek and I shift him a quick glance before I turn my attention back to the road. "But, in reality, I never go to Times Square and it was a fluke invitation that took me to Broadway."

I raise a brow.

"When you come out, we'll visit those places together," he says, resting his hand on my thigh. "I look forward to sharing them with you. Maybe in the fall you and I can drive and see the colors too. Though I'm sure this is equally amazing in the fall."

I shift a smile toward him and breathe in the moment. We have future plans.

As I descend from the mountains into the town of Estes Park, Noah is again on the edge of his seat taking it all in. And that's when he sees it. The most notorious landmark in the entire town.

"Oh, my god!" he shouts, moving closer to the windshield.

His eyes are wide and he looks like a small child. When his palms come to the dashboard, I actually snort out a laugh.

"Are you serious? Did you forget that was here? I thought that's why you wanted to come here," I say, watching his awe blossom as the glory of the Stanley Hotel comes into view.

"Are you kidding me? I was so focused on the cabin website for a sex-cation, that I forgot to look at the town itself. I didn't even put two and two together."

"Did you just really call this a sex-cation?" I challenge.

His wide eyes shift to me now. "No. Lily did," he says, ratting out my best friend. "But, c'mon."

I can feel my whole body heat. I'm humored, horrified, mad,

and freaking excited by the mention of it, but all the same, I can't believe Lily said that to him. On second thought, yes I can.

Noah turns fully in his seat to look at me now. "Can we go up there?"

The smile that tugs at my face is so natural, I could never tell him no.

"You're fanboying, you know that?" I ask.

"The Shining, Emma. The *fucking* Shining!"

Laughter rolls from me now. "This is the Stanley Hotel, not the Overlook," I try to deadpan, but it's worthless.

"You're not going to deny me this, are you?"

"That will take hours out of your sex-cation," I remind him with a mocking tone.

"Stephen King, Emma," he says with as much emphasis as he had about the hotel. "My idol! My fucking idol!" he shouts and I actually jump.

"And you wonder why I worried you were going to throw me off the deck in the dark. Your horror brain is in full gear."

I can feel the laser focus of his stare on me. "You do realize that this romantic man that I've become is new, right? I'm all horror all the time. I can quote the movie to you. I could watch the movie with my eyes closed and know what's going on."

"I've never even seen the movie," I admit.

"I don't think this relationship is going to work," he says easing back in his seat. "We have nothing in common, but sex."

I laugh again. "We have a private ghost tour at two o'clock," I say softly and manage to catch his priceless expression.

Those wide eyes are on me again. "Are you kidding me?"

"Why would I kid about something like that?"

His hand is back on my thigh and there is a firmness to it. "How did you do that?"

"It just so happens that one of the tour guides is a resident of Pine Haven and a huge fan of yours. They preorder all of your books, and I've been hiding you from them for a week. So expect to sign a few books for payment, take a few photos, and have the best tour possible."

He lets out a long breath. "You are the best fucking girlfriend in the world," he says as he eases in his seat again, a permagrin on his face.

That ball of guilt in my stomach has just hardened again, but in a whole different way. *Girlfriend.* I never thought someone would use that word to describe me again—ever.

CHAPTER 33

There is a part of me that wishes Katie was with us. I'd love her to see this new side to Noah Carter, the broody horror writer.

Walking through the halls of the Stanley Hotel with Norman, our private tour guide and another massive fanboy of the author, has Noah Carter reverted from horror writer to an enamored child. He's in awe of Norman and hanging on his every word.

I, on the other hand, have the hairs on the back of my neck standing up, there is a chill that penetrates through my clothing, and I swear someone keeps whispering something in my ear. How does Noah tolerate this stuff and make up more horror to go with it? Why would anyone want to write murder when you could write happily ever after that makes you believe in humanity?

We're standing outside of room 217, the infamously haunted room at the Stanley Hotel. I've already been told this differs from room 237 which is featured in the movie, as if I care in the least.

Norman made it clear that the room is always booked, but the next guests haven't arrived yet and, "Not everyone can hack it," he says.

We are enthralled with Norman's tale of the room when Noah

reaches for my arm and I actually scream. Both he and Norman throw their hands up in surrender and stare at me in equal horror.

"Are you okay?" Noah quickly asks.

"What did you see?" Norman follows, the key to the room held in his fingers.

"You just scared the shit out of me when you touched me," I say with my hand pressed to my chest.

Two sets of eyes lighten with humor and Norman puckers his lips. Noah, however, actually laughs.

"Are you scared?" Noah asks.

I shift a glance between the two men. "Yes," I admit. "This is freaking me out. Feel my fingers," I say, pressing them to his cheeks.

"You're freezing."

"How do you tolerate this?" I ask Norman.

"You can hear them, can't you?" he asks with a bit too much enthusiasm.

Noah leans in. "Can you?"

I swallow hard. "Can we just wrap this up?" I force a smile to my lips. I want Noah to enjoy this, but I hadn't anticipated hating it so much.

"This is *the* room," Noah says wrapping a protective arm around me looking at Norman move toward the door with the key.

I know it's *the* room. I've been listening to Norman go on about it. Though admittedly, I haven't paid too much attention. There is a low hum in my ears and it distracts me.

"It's supposedly haunted by Elizabeth Wilson who died in here in 1911. She was the head housekeeper that—"

I don't even let Norman continue.

I push away from Noah and hurry down the hall to the staircase that leads to the lobby. With each step my knees grow weaker, but somehow I manage to the lobby, across it, and outside into the brisk March air—and sunlight. I don't even care what anyone thinks about my abrupt retreat from the hotel. Certainly, I'm not the first person to run down those stairs and out of the building afraid that I might die of fright.

Again, I let out a tiny scream when my phone buzzes in my pocket and I pull it out to see Noah's text.

Are you okay? You're freaking me out. Where are you?

I have to warm my hands to make my fingers work to reply. *Outside. Take your time. Enjoy your tour. Don't tell me anything about it.*

He sends me a laughing emoji followed by a ghost. *This is the most fucking awesome thing I've ever done. We're in the room!*

Well, at least I can plan good things. *Don't hurry. I'm okay outside. You and Norman take your time.*

Are you sure?

To that I laugh. *I've never been more sure about anything—ever!*

I'm enjoying myself sitting on the front steps of the hotel, listening to that Jennifer Zeppelin audio book that Noah had me reading from the other night. Luckily, I know he's walking toward me, so I don't scream when he's standing next to me.

I pull my earphones from my ears and tuck them into the case.

"Are you a thoroughly satisfied man?" I ask looking up at him, the sun bright at his back.

"I owe you one," he says, smiling down at me before lowering himself to the step next to me. "This is the best sex-cation ever." He winks and I can't help but chuckle at him.

I love this lightness to him, and those circles that once darkened his eyes are long gone. And maybe, just maybe, that was my true purpose in getting involved with this man—to protect him from himself.

"You mentioned sex-cation, but I'm going to guess your head

is so full of inspiration that you would like a few hours with your laptop or notebook to write down everything that's swimming in your brain."

He wrinkles up his nose. "That would have pissed off Abby," he says.

"At least I know she had a flaw," I say with humor lit in my voice and by his reaction, I know he took it as it was intended.

"Do you mind?"

I reach for his hand and interlace our fingers. "I don't mind, just don't share what you write with me. I don't want to know just how demented you really are."

Noah laughs as he leans in and presses a kiss to my cheek. "You could work on your book," he offers. "We can sit on the porch of the cabin, enjoying the view. We can share a bottle of wine and that bag of M&Ms we picked up at 7-Eleven."

Now that has me laughing. "You think there are M&Ms left?"

"Well, then we'll stop in town and get some cheeses or something."

"Classy."

"I thought so," he says as he lifts my fingers to his lips.

"So this just turned into a work-cation?" I ask watching this man whose mind stirs behind happy eyes.

"There's still plenty of time for sex," he promises.

"We'd better get to it then."

"We'd better."

CHAPTER 34

He's writing.

Noah's fingers fly over the keys of his laptop. He was right, his hunt and peck typing seems to be a good method for him.

Though I'm longing to reach my fingers into his hair where he's tunneled his own, watching him work is intoxicating. He moves his face when he works, no doubt mimicking the characters he's writing. I know Lily has accused me of the same.

I have a notebook in my lap, a pen poised in my fingers. The book I've been working on for years isn't what I'm thinking about now. It's a new story, one where a man happens into a woman's world and turns it upside down. A broody man who really is a cinnamon roll. He's older. He runs his fingers through his hair. He doesn't say much, but when he does, he rocks her world.

Maybe it's my story. Maybe it's the story I want.

I worry my lip and continue watching him. I think he's the story I want.

The pen falls from my fingers and Noah looks up from his computer.

I don't even think to pick up the pen.

This is selfish, but I can't help it. I drop the notebook to the chair as I stand. He watches me as I begin to unbutton the front of my shirt.

He's more aware of our surroundings sitting the on porch of the cabin, as he scans a look around, but there's no one there.

Noah licks his lips as he watches my every move, eventually closing his laptop and standing when I let my shirt fall.

There are no words. There is no need for them. I turn from him and walk toward the cabin.

From the corner of my eye, I see him pick up my shirt, his laptop tucked under his arm as he stands and follows me.

I never see him lock the door to the cabin, or discard his laptop on the table. All I know is that by the time I make it to the bed, stepping out of the rest of my clothes, his hands are on my shoulders and he turns me to face him.

His gaze takes in every inch of me, and there's nothing but appreciation in his eyes. I'm comfortable with him doing this, it's a new feeling for me. I've never been this secure in my nakedness with any man—not even when I was married.

Noah's hands come to my waist and he brushes them up my sides, his fingertips leaving a tingling trail.

"Thank you," he says softly, his breath on my throat before he kisses my skin. "I shouldn't have been working so hard."

"Forgiven," is all I can manage as his hands wander up to cup my breasts.

"I'll make it up to you," he promises, his mouth skimming my jaw.

"Uh-huh," I say almost silently because I can't control my breath as one of his hands moves down the front of me.

"I'm going to love you, Emma, all night long," he says lowering me to the bed.

There are no more words, well, not words meant to hold conversation. As the night progresses there are only those words he promised me he'd make me say over and over again.

~

There is a bliss that hangs in the air between us as I drive back toward Pine Haven, through the awakening forest, with its browns giving way to hues of green.

The sun peeks through the treetop canopy forcing me to put on and take off my sunglasses, yet I'm more aware this morning of the sun's absolute glory than I have been in a long time.

Next to me, in the passenger seat, Noah has his computer on his lap and his fingers again fly over the keys. I know he got up in the middle of the night and worked too. This is what I had assumed he would look like the entire week in my office, but I think only now he's unblocked and is creating.

There is no conversation, and that's okay. I have enough conversation happening in my head.

Though they all agreed to cover for me while I was gone, I know that when I get back to the store, Lily and Julia will side eye me for at least a day. I don't know how Katie will be with Noah. And then there's the fact that by the time we get back, Sylvia St. Clare will be arriving.

He said they had that one kiss, but in my head it was more than that. Yeah, I know that's not true, but it's hard to separate my imagery of it since I the man next to me is really a stranger.

I shift a glance at him, his head down and his eyes laser focused on the screen, and I realize that, no, he's not a stranger. I know this man better than anyone—doesn't that say something?

As we descend out of the forest and into the valley, the car fills with that sunlight that has been playing peek-a-boo with us. It's then that Noah lifts his head.

"God, that's beautiful," he says taking in the town below us.

"I know. This is why I couldn't stay in the city. This beckoned me back."

There is a lightness to him now. That dark cloud that hovered over him since the moment he'd walked into my store is lifted. Will I be the only person that sees that?

He closes his laptop and takes in the surroundings. He's like a child on an adventure, I think, soaking it in.

And, while I drive, I soak him in. We have one week left. Sure, we've agreed to a long distance thing, but in reality, we have one week.

CHAPTER 35

The decision is made to not go home right away, or in Noah's case, back to the hotel. Instead, we decide to go back to the store.

He wants to work.

I want him to work.

I know that it will be appreciated.

When we walk through the front door, I stop and take it in. This is not the store I left on Tuesday night.

The shelves are moved around. There are twinkle lights everywhere. The front window is a mix of books from all the attending authors, though Noah's are the most prominent ones.

Even though the plan is that the Q&A sessions are to now happen at Mrs. Packer's store, there are a few more reading nooks set up, as well as the table where there will be author signings.

"Well, you both look satisfied," Lily says from behind the counter. "Though, I thought you'd still be partaking of your—"

I hold up a finger to cut her off. There is no reason in the world she needs to say the word sex-cation in the store when there are customers.

I think that's when Noah realizes just how many customers

are in the store and he hurries past me, laptop under his arm, and into my office, closing the door behind him.

"Everything okay?" Lily's humorous eyes have now gone wide and worried.

"He's inspired," I say and there's a smile that surfaces on my mouth as I look at the closed door.

"You rocked his world."

That might be the case, but that wasn't it. "Have you ever been to the Stanley Hotel?" I ask.

"Yeah. Who hasn't?" Lily says as she opens a book on the top of the stack next to her to add to the computer.

"Did you feel anything? See anything?"

Her interest is piqued and she lifts her head to look at me.

"Did you?" she asks.

I lean in. "I ran out of the hotel."

The grin on her face says she's amused by my story. "And demented thriller writer?"

"Hasn't stopped writing since we left the hotel."

Now she crinkles up her nose. "So no sex-cation?" she whispers.

"Oh, no, there was plenty of that, but he's been working almost non-stop too. Whatever happened in that hotel lit the fire for him."

Her grin is back. "Everyone will be glad to hear that."

There is calm in the store, even though we're crazy busy. The event starts on Thursday, but there are already people starting to arrive.

After lunch, Katie blows in like a small tornado and beelines straight to me.

"You're back already," it's a statement, not a question.

"We came back this morning. That was the plan."

I can't decide if there is some relief on her face or if it's irritation. But, she drops her shoulders, so I'm going to go with relief.

"You had a nice time?" she asks.

"Wonderful."

"Good. Is he at the hotel?"

I shake my head. "He's in the office, working," I say with confidence.

Now a small smile curls up the corner of her mouth. "Working?"

"Working," I say. "The trip was what he needed. He's been working non-stop."

Now her eyes brighten. "That is really good news." Then, she lays her hand over mine. "You might have been the best thing for him," she says before she turns and heads toward Mrs. Packer's.

Her sentiment, though appreciated, stirs some doubt in me. I can't just be his muse and sleep with him so he'll work.

I shake away the thought. That's not what she said.

I turn and look at the door. Behind it, a genius is creating a masterpiece. There should be some pride in knowing I helped free his mind so he could work. Too many people seem to be depending on him.

Of course, it goes further than being the muse. There is a need to check on him.

Instead of barging through the door, I walk to the back of the store, make him a cup of coffee, and head back to the office. But Katie has beat me to it.

In her hand she has a coffee from Pack-a-Punch, and she's handing it to him. This has me holding back, watching the interaction.

His body takes up the space between the jamb and the door—he's keeping her out, but she doesn't look fazed.

Then there's the moment he sees me. My heart melts when his mouth lifts into a smile, and Katie turns to see me.

"I wanted to give you a new list of questions for the author Q&A," she says, holding out a stack of papers to me.

I move in and take them. "I thought you already emailed me these."

"These are Sylvia's," she says, but I can see her face trying not to contort into displeasure. "She had some specific questions she wanted to be asked."

"Doesn't that take away a bit of the spontaneity?"

Noah shakes his head. "There is no spontaneity with that one. She's a planner. You should see her plot a book," he says, and my insides tighten. How much time have they spent together if he knows her process?

Katie winces at Noah's comment. "She's just a very prepared kind of person. It shouldn't be a problem, right?"

Well, when she words it that way, she's baiting me right into the answer. "No problem."

Katie smiles. "Wonderful." She turns back to Noah. "Dylan is flying in on Sunday," she says and Noah's eyes go wide. "He's bringing Rachel Anderson."

With the woman's name, Noah's face shifts again. There is a lightness in his eyes and a smile toying with his lips.

"I'll be ready," he says.

Katie gives him a curt nod, smiles at me, and heads back into the store. At this point, I realize I don't even have control over my own store now. She does. And my team follows her. But sales are up, so I won't complain.

Only now I have to deal with this tense feeling in my shoulders and the gnawing in my belly. Who in the hell is Rachel Anderson, and why did Noah light up like that?

CHAPTER 36

The store is dark. Everyone has gone home. The twinkle lights in the front window display give a warmth to the quiet space.

It's nearly ten o'clock, and I haven't bothered Noah because I can hear him in there working. There is the methodical noise of his fingers on his keyboard, and they've been going non stop since we came back from Estes Park.

A few times I've taken him something to drink and a snack. He's emerged to go to the bathroom, and we've shared a few stolen kisses in the back room. Otherwise, he's been working.

I don't feel the need to bother him right now, even though I'm exhausted and my bed is calling me. Tomorrow I need to be on my A-game. Especially if his agent is arriving and whoever Rachel Anderson is.

Pettiness did get the best of me. I'd been working on my book at the front counter, and I had to look up Rachel Anderson. There are ten million Rachel Andersons. Narrowed down, I searched New York, then more specifically her relationship to Noah. Nothing came up there. There is some relief, but his smile at her name still has me uneasy. That's on me, I know that, but still…

I finally got a hit when I did a search that associated her with Dylan Collins, Noah's agent.

Rachel Anderson is an associate literary agent under Dylan Collins at the agency that reps Noah.

Her photo on the website is a stellar one. I'd want to work with her if I were an author looking for representation. She has a look of professionalism with her just-the-right-length blonde hair with the perfect curl. She has blue eyes that twinkle right off the screen, but they have knowledge behind them. I'd guess she might be in her thirties, but she doesn't scream book nerd at all.

Unfortunately, she screams that *I'm* insecure and worried that the man *I'm* having this brief, but promising affair with likes this much younger woman.

When I hear the knob on the office door turn, I quickly swipe away Rachel Anderson's face from my screen and go back to my manuscript.

I turn around to see Noah stretching in the doorway. His arms are lifted over his head and his shirt rises, and exposes his stomach, which fuels me with need to touch. The office light illuminates him from behind like the god I really see him as.

"It's ten o'clock," he says, rubbing his eyes.

"It is."

"You should have come to get me when you closed the store. Why are you sitting out here in the dark and I'm in there working when we could be at your house or in my hotel room?"

I chew on my bottom lip, still studying this man that I know my heart aches for already.

"You're writing. I want to give you that time."

He snorts out a laugh as he moves to me, standing so he's pressed between my legs, in my space. "I'm always writing," he says as he lifts his hands up into my hair.

"Always?"

"Usually," he says as he dips his head and brushes his lips

across mine. "Let's stay at the hotel tonight. I'll order us up some room service and we can watch crappy TV."

"I have to be back here at eight. I don't have anything else to wear."

"Bring your suitcase from this weekend and we'll have them do the laundry," he says now trailing kisses down my neck. "I want to be with you, and my place is closer."

My eyes close as his mouth works against my sensitive skin. "You're not good for me, Noah Carter," I say as my breath thickens.

"I'm good to you," he says and I laugh.

"That you are."

Noah is the kind of man you wouldn't notice in a crowd, unless you were a die-hard fan, but he's the kind of man that can get stuff done with a smile and wink.

My clothes from our trip are being cleaned.

Dinner was delivered and set up on a table while we were in the shower. Something like that would have once made me very uncomfortable, but I suppose I was much too comfortable to care that someone was in the room.

Now we're laying on the bed, wrapped in hotel robes, watching late night TV when we should be asleep.

"I never had this," I say, my head rested on Noah's chest, his hand brushing down my hair.

"What? Late night TV?"

I chuckle. "No, comfort like this."

He adjusts to look at me. "You and your husband never did this?"

"No."

"Why?"

I shrug. "I don't know. It truly was a doomed relationship from the start."

He squeezes me to him. "Abby and I did this all the time."

"All the time?"

"All the time," he says again, his hand still holding me in place against him. "The moments where you can just have peace with someone is the best."

"And we have that?" I ask. Noah shifts to look down at me.

"Of course we do. Look at us," he says and I take it in, not having even put it all together until that moment. Noah and I are comfortable just in one another's presence. This isn't just sex. This is a full on, two-week-old relationship, which only has a few more days left.

"Em, can't you see yourself doing this with me for years to come?"

I blink up at him. I don't want to tell him that I can. He'll be gone in one week. One week!

Now the comfort seems strained. I move from him slightly, adjust the robe so that I'm fully covered, and fold my hands on my lap. Noah does the same to mimic me.

"We're going to see each other after, right?" I ask.

"We talked about it, yes."

"I know. I just don't see how it's going to work. I mean I can't leave my store all the time. You have movies being made and books to be published and more to write. And you have your family and Abby's family to spend time with, and—"

"And you're trying to come up with reasons that this isn't going to work before we even give it a go."

I pull in my lips. That's exactly what I'm doing.

"You'll come visit me?" I ask, but it's weak.

"Every chance I get." Noah scoots over the inch to press our bodies together, still sitting up next to one another. "And you will come to New York as a tourist and let me show you around."

"I know all the sights," I remind him.

"Not the way I do."

"You never leave your apartment," I remind him, now looking him in the eye.

"And maybe that's the only sight I want you to see," he says as he leans in and takes me under with a kiss that leads us to unwrapping our robes.

CHAPTER 37

Sundays will forever be my favorite day in the store. Mrs. Packer is closed. The flower shop is closed. The town is sleepy no matter the season.

Shoppers are those who are out walking the town, either checking in, or making one more round before they check out.

The patio at the pub across the street will eventually get busy, and some of those patrons will make the walk to my store.

I don't sell a lot, but I clean. I read. I think.

Today I'm waiting.

Noah didn't come into the store with me yesterday, opting to stay at the hotel and work. Katie was much too enthusiastic with his choice, and I suppose it was for the best. Over dinner, he'd rattled off some enormous number of words that he'd written and then went on about another story he'd started. I guess this is what he'd come to Colorado early for—to work. He still calls me his muse, but the more he says it, the more I don't want the job. What happens when my magical power over him runs out?

When the door to the store opens, and the woman in the long puffer coat drops her hood and stomps the snow off her boots, I find it a bit hard to breathe. I'd recognize that blonde hair and those piercing, all knowing, blue eyes anywhere.

Rachael Anderson has just walked into my store—alone.

She scans a look over the store, her eyes stopping on the poster of Noah. A smile pulls at the corner of her mouth as she pulls off her gloves, shakes her head, runs her hand over the cover of his book on the table by the door.

Everything inside of me tightens as she lifts her eyes and zeros in on me.

The smile on her mouth grows wider as she walks right toward me.

"You're Emma Reynolds, aren't you?" she asks, already holding out her perfectly manicured hand to shake mine.

"Yes," is all I can manage as I hold out my hand and her petite one takes hold.

"I knew it. I'd know you anywhere," she says, much like the few people who have caught Noah and been star struck when they talked to him. "Your store is so cute. I looked it up online, but the pictures don't do it justice. And then you have that old coot's picture at the door," she says as she laughs and it's full of love and humor.

I blink at her, still not sure why she's in my store alone. She was flying in today with Noah's agent Dylan. When did she get into town? Why isn't she with him? Was this why Noah didn't come to the store with me yesterday or today? I mean if he's at the hotel and she and Dylan checked in at the hotel, wouldn't she want to be with them? Him? She's obviously smitten with him. I've seen it with my own eyes now—right? No one looks at his picture like that—well, no one who works with him.

My heart is racing and I know my hands are shaking now. I've talked myself into some stupid scenario.

"God, I'm daft," she says, tucking her gloves into her coat pockets. "I'm Rachel Anderson." She holds that manicured hand to her chest. "You must think I'm some lunatic."

Yes! Yes, I do!

Now a line forms between her brows. "Didn't Noah tell you I'd be coming to see you today?"

"Noah didn't say anything about it," I say, but I think about how he smiled when her name was mentioned.

"Well now you must really think I'm some crazy woman coming in here. He was supposed to tell you I'd be coming to meet you. I can't trust him at all," she says and I wonder if I can trust him.

"Why are you coming to meet me? I mean, I know the event will be here and all, but ..."

Her eyes get that shine back and her smile returns. "I've come to talk to you about your book."

I blink once. Then I blink again. "My what?"

"Your book." Her eyes have gone wide. "You are Emma Reynolds, right?"

"Yes."

"I'm interested in your work. Noah sent me the first few chapters, and it's exactly what I've been looking for. And of course it comes with a hefty recommendation. I'm currently building my client list, and I have some editors looking for just your style of voice."

I'm shaking all over now. My hands and knees are shaking and I'm worried I'm not breathing.

This woman has come to me to talk about my book. A book she wants to rep. A book that Noah sent her pages from. A book that Noah sent to her without my permission. I'm furious. I'm excited. I'm speechless.

Rachel reaches a hand to me and touches my arm. "Are you okay? I'm sorry, I should have let him come with me, but they were in a meeting and I couldn't wait to meet you so I told him I was just going to pop over."

I'm supposed to be grateful. The man I love is helping me with my goal.

Do I love him? I hardly know him.

This isn't the point!

"Noah sent you my book?" I ask, my voice shaking as much as my hands and my knees.

"He sent me the first three chapters. He said you'd been working together on it, and let me tell you, it really has promise."

"You really think so?" I ask, but inside I doubt everything this beautiful woman is saying. Not to mention that I'm battling some very persistent anger in the direction of Noah Carter at this moment as well.

"I do. I was hoping I could get my hands on it and read the rest of it while I'm here. I can't promise it'll sell, but I think it has merit."

My throat is dry.

We're standing in my store just looking at one another. I at her in disbelief, and she at me in the same way, though I'm sure its because I'm not reacting as she thought I might. This is great news. Isn't it every author's dream to have an agent come to them and say, "I want to rep you"? But it's not how it works, is it? Shouldn't I be putting out queries and getting rejected? That's all I've ever heard, authors get rejected some hundred times before someone says, "Sure I'll look at it." The odds are against me, so this can't be happening.

"I understand if you're not interested in me looking at your work," Rachel finally says. "Some authors don't plan to go the traditional route, and independently publishing romance is equally as successful."

Rachel reaches into her purse, pulls out a business card, and hands it to me.

"My cell number is on the back, but I'll be here the rest of the week helping Dylan and Noah." She smiles, but her lips are flat. "Call me if you're interested talking about it."

I look at the card and then back at the woman who is turning to walk out of my store, dejected by me. By me!

"Wait," I say and Rachel turns back around. "Do you really think it might be sellable?"

"I do."

"You really want to read it? I mean, yes, we've been working through it, but it's still a little rough."

Her smile fills out now as she walks back toward the counter. "All drafts are rough. But if you're willing to let me look at it, I could have notes for you this week."

My heart is pounding in my chest. This is it. I could have this dream and it's nearly being handed to me—but is that only because I'm sleeping with Noah?

"How would you like it? Printed? Emailed? Flash drive?"

Rachel laughs. "Do you have time to print it? I work better with paper and pens."

"Old school. I like it," I say. "It'll take a bit to get it all printed."

"I'll go shopping then," she says and turns to go shopping. In my store.

CHAPTER 38

When I'm involved with someone, radio silence isn't my idea of things going well. Admittedly, I woke up with Noah and headed to work. It's now seven o'clock and I've decided to just show up at the hotel.

I've gone through every emotion today, most of which has been elation after I handed Rachel my manuscript, but there still is nervous anger that rolls through me. And now that I haven't spoken to Noah in nearly twelve hours, meaning he hasn't replied to any of my texts, I'm shaking again.

When the elevator opens to the lobby, Katie steps out and my stomach tightens even more.

"Emma," she says with a smile and I watch the elevator close without me. "What are you doing here?"

I know she knows what's going on, so why do I feel the need to blow it off as if I'm just casually here? But I'm not going to.

"I came to see Noah."

Her smile tightens like it does when she's worried.

"He and Dylan have been working all day. Could I buy you a drink?"

I study her. Is she trying to keep me away from him on purpose?

"No thank you. I'm just passing through before I head home for the night," I say, but I hear it in my voice, that rattle of insecurity. She hears it too.

"Let me know if you change your mind," she says, the crease between her brows deepening.

I smile, push the button to call back the elevator, and step inside when it comes. I push the number for Noah's floor and step off when the doors open again.

Noise filters down the hallway, from Noah's room. Voices. Laughter.

Turn around, Emma. Go home, Emma.

Instead, I knock.

"One second," a woman's voice says, and I'm certain I'm going to be sick.

"It's probably the room service I ordered," a man's voice says, but it's not Noah's.

When the door opens, I'm staring up at a man I don't know.

"Oh. Hi," he says. "You're not room service."

I swallow hard. "Did I get off on the wrong floor?" I look at the room number to assure myself that this was the room I woke up in this morning. "I'm looking for Noah."

The woman laughs and the man opens the door wider. She's seated on the bed in a small red dress. But I've seen her face enough times to know exactly who she is. Sylvia St. Clare is sitting on Noah's bed in a seductive red dress.

"He ran out for drinks," she says and I know this is my moment to turn and run. "But damn, that has to have been at least an hour ago," she says, turning her attention to the man holding the door.

"I think he ditched us," the man says. "I'm sorry, Dylan Collins," he holds out a hand for me to shake.

"Emma Reynolds," I say as I take his hand, and that has Sylvia standing from her position on the bed.

"You're the bookstore owner," she gleefully says as if I'm the celebrity in the room—or just outside of it. "Let her in."

"No. I should be going. I just hadn't heard from Noah today. Needed to make sure he was taken care of."

Dylan still has my hand in his. "So you're Emma?"

"I am," I say, looking at our clasped hands.

"Thank you. He needed you."

"I beg your pardon," I say, considering yanking my hand from his and running toward the stairs.

"She's lovely, isn't she?" he asks and Sylvia nods.

"Just like he said she was," she agrees.

"I really should be going," I say.

Finally Dylan lets go of my hand. "Congratulations, too, by the way. Rachel has been singing your praises all day as well."

"Oh, well …"

"A great muse and a great writer," Dylan compliments me. "Why don't you come in and wait with us? He has been gone a long time. No doubt he'll be back soon. I've had him working quite hard today. He deserves a break."

That's when my phone buzzes in my pocket and I hurry to pull it out, Dylan finally releasing my hand.

There is a picture of the keypad to my garage door. *Number please. I thought you'd be here, but I had to get out of town.*

I do everything I can to keep my face neutral.

"Thank you for the invite. Message from home. I need to get back. Just let Noah know I stopped by."

"I'll do that," Dylan says, but there is a sly smile on his mouth now too. He knows what just happened.

I turn and hurry toward the elevator, punching the button numerous times as if it will call it faster.

.   .   .

The drive home has lost its beauty, well, for the evening I guess. Tonight as I hurry toward my house, I only realize just how dark it is, and how far out of town.

When I do come up to the house, I slow. The lights are on and there is smoke from the chimney. I can't help but to come to a stop just feet from the driveway.

Swallowing hard, I look at the house that is never alive when I get home. It's always dark. Always cold. It waits for me to light it up and warm it. Tonight, it did all of that without me—with him, waiting for me.

Again, so many emotions run through me and my head spins with elation, depression, anger, love.

I pull into the driveway and open the garage door. As I settle, turn off the car, and lower the garage door, the door to the house opens. Standing in the doorway is Noah, a glass of wine in each hand.

He looks as wary as I feel, but when he smiles it brightens inside of me.

Oh, I have a lot of words for him tonight. After all, he gave my book to Rachel without my permission. But in this moment, I question that. Did I give him permission? Maybe I did.

I draw in a breath as he shifts in the doorway, no doubt wondering why I'm taking so long to get out of the car.

I want this, I decide. I want it a little too much.

I want Noah Carter waiting for me every night when I get home from work, but I'll never have that.

I want him to write all day, because I'm his muse, and spend all night thanking me in his special way.

But again, his life is in New York, and mine will never be.

He turns and sets the glasses down on the bench in the mud room, then walks toward the car. His expression is lost, and as he pulls open the door to the car, I begin to sob.

"God, Emma. What's wrong?" He kneels down next to the car,

which is wet from the snow on the ground and the puddles I've driven through to race home to him.

I blink to clear my eyes.

"Take me to bed," I say and the expression on his face changes, but only slightly.

"Don't you want to talk? I'm guessing you want to yell at me for a plethora of reasons."

I do—don't I?

I shake my head. "If we talk, I might. Right at the moment I think I'm going to yell at you because there was a sexy woman on your bed in a red dress."

His eyes go wide and a horrified look crosses his face.

"On my bed?" His voice rises and the mood shifts again because I laugh. He's so clear to me, and he never did engage with Sylvia more than a kiss—and I know that in this moment more than when he told me.

"Take me to bed, Noah, before my day of emotions crash around me."

He pushes the button on my seatbelt, stands, and holds out his hand to help me from the car.

Following my direction, he leads me into the house, past the wine glasses that will wait, and straight to my bedroom where he makes quick work to help me forget that I'm mad at him.

CHAPTER 39

The Book Affair Literary Event is only two days away. Noah has chosen to work between my house and his hotel room, since Dylan is in town—and Sylvia.

Sylvia has made herself a fixture at my store, and has chosen Lily to be her minion. Okay, minion is a harsh word, but really it's true. She has opinions on how the display should look and where the banner for her book should be. Of course it's wherever Noah's already is. Lily is smart enough to pull Katie into the conversation whenever she's around.

Mrs. Packer's store has had a near makeover, and I would have thought the woman would be a bent out of shape over the attention and having these *youngsters* touching her stuff. But she's fine with it. I also think she's eaten at least one batch of her own brownies to deal with it.

There has been a steady stream of customers for two days and Rachel has poked her head in to talk to me, but I don't even have a moment. She seems okay with it, as she finds somewhere to be useful and digs right into any job.

I'm not sure I can deal with anything she has to say right now. That book was not in the right state for an agent to look at it and want to represent it. All of the harsh words I had for Noah seemed to have been forgotten the past few days. I realized I could be mad when he was gone, there was no need to sour what we had with anger over something that could have the potential of something great.

"Emma, I saw some chairs at the antique store down the street that are just ah-mazing," Sylvia sings out the word. "I've asked them to bring them up for our Q&A on Friday. We can put those others in the back or something."

I know that I'm staring at the woman with wide eyes and a blank look by the way she begins to inch back. "I think we should call them and nix that. There is no room in the back for my other chairs," I say.

"We could just put them outside for the few hours. No harm," she says with a swish of her hand as if to wish it that way.

Katie must see us having this conversation because I notice her hurry toward us. "What's up, ladies?"

I shift my eyes to Sylvia who purses her lips as if she's intimidated by the always organized and put together Katie from New York.

Katie holds all the cards, and it kills Sylvia. And, as long as I don't say a word, this will be hashed out in no time.

Sylvia composes herself and poses—yes, poses. "I was just telling Emma that the antique store will be bringing chairs over for my Q&A. They're wonderful, and on loan of course. We can move the others out for the time being and arrange the area for my—"

Katie holds up a finger, but the smile negates the curt gesture. "Your Q&A will be in the coffee shop. Only signings will be here, and that's already set up," she says full of that New York confidence she strolled in with three weeks ago.

"You know that coffee shop is too small for that event," Sylvia scoffs. "Noah has multiple sessions and one is at the hotel."

"Yes, his sales numbers are astronomical," Katie says with great enthusiasm. "But even his Q&A here is at the coffee shop."

Sylvia wrings her hands together as the door the store opens and Dylan and Noah walk through. I see the expression on Noah's face, and on any other day, he'd walk back out or take a detour. But because we've been waking up together every morning for nearly the past two weeks, he drops his shoulders and heads to my side.

He's not one for PDA, especially when he's around colleagues, but today, he wraps an arm around my waist and kisses me gently on the cheek.

"This place is busy," he says looking around, and I notice a few people notice him.

Sylvia's shoulders push back. "We were just discussing a change of set up," she says and I feel Noah stiffen next to me.

"Oh, I think Katie and the ladies have it all under control. Pretty amazing isn't it?" he says and there is a pride that swells inside of me. This is my man. And just as quickly, the thought of the dwindling number of days I have left with him hits me as well.

Noah turns me toward him and takes my hands. "Go get your coat. We're having lunch at the hotel."

Before I can say anything, Sylvia steps a little closer. "I'll get my coat too."

Noah shakes his head. "Nah, this is just for me and Emma and Rachel."

That has me giving his hands a squeeze. I haven't been able to give her any of my time, and certainly this isn't a good time either. But, Katie manages to shift Sylvia in another direction, and Dylan heads toward the coffee shop.

"Why are we having lunch with Rachel?" I ask.

"Because she hasn't been able to pin you down for more than two minutes."

"We're too busy for this," I argue.

"Nope, you're due lunch. Lily and Julia are fine. Katie is here too. Dylan is staying if they need him." His smile is wide. "Rachel needs to talk to you."

"We never did fully discuss you giving her my book," I say narrowing my eyes on him, but I'm not sure it's as threatening as I intend.

He grins. "Are you going to be mad at me right now over it? I can stay here and work too if you'd rather."

Hell no. I don't want a moment away from him.

"Just tell me is she happy with it, or is she going to tell me to fix everything?"

He snickers at that, raises my fingers to his lips, and presses a kiss to them.

"Yes."

I groan. "That's not an answer to my question."

"Honey, in this industry, no matter how excited they are about a project, they're going to tell you to fix everything." He pulls me to him, wrapping his arms around me and I loop mine around his neck. "I'll be there with you. And, I promise that you can dig your nails into my thigh under the table if you need to."

How could I pass up that kind of offer?

He presses his forehead to me, and even in the crowded store, I just don't care who sees us. Being in this man's arms fills me like nothing else ever has. This is a moment more intimate than sex or being wrapped up on my couch in the dark watching a movie.

I am still wrapped up in Noah when the door opens again. Out of the corner of my eye I watch as three women walk toward us, standing awkwardly as if waiting for us to break.

"Noah?" the woman, who is obviously the younger woman's mother and probably the older woman's daughter, says softly, causing him to turn his head. "Hi."

Three sets of wide eyes scan over us and Noah all but pushes away from me.

"Hi. Hi," he says again, stumbling over his words and nearly his own feet. Suddenly that stiff and rigid man I met three weeks ago is standing between me and these three ladies. His eyes which were bright as he pulled me to him are dark and sad again. I swear, even the color of his skin has faded and he is paler.

Finally, he moves to hug each of them, but their eyes keep shifting back to me.

"What are you all doing here?" he finally asks.

"We wanted to support you. Another New York Times Best Seller and another movie. That's a big deal," the woman who had first spoken says.

He nods as if he'd again forgotten all of those things.

"This is a big trip for you," he says to the older woman, kissing her on the cheek. Then he shifts his attention to the younger woman. "And you graduate next month?"

That's when it hits me and I know who these people are. I know why he pushed away from me so quickly. I know why their eyes feel hot as if they're judging me—because they are.

This is Abby's mother. Abby's sister. Abby's niece.

CHAPTER 40

Noah did what he could to compose himself, and introduce me to his wife's—late wife's—family. But to say the grace of the moment fell short would be an understatement. He didn't even stand near me as he fought to even remember my name.

Her family, however, was gracious—or came across as being so as he introduced me as the owner of the store.

But now, I'm full of extra nerves sitting with Rachel in the restaurant of the hotel while he's showing his in-laws around *my* town.

"I'm glad Noah couldn't make it," Rachel says as she sets her napkin in her lap when our meals are delivered. "I don't mean that to sound as bad as it does. It's just that I want to get to know you."

I follow her lead and drop my napkin in my lap, and then on the floor, nearly hitting my head on the table when I reach to pick it up.

"I'm sorry," I say on the verge of tears that I somehow manage to swallow down. "I think my mind is in a million different places. I'm not sure I'm good company this week."

Maybe if I make this all about the event and the time constraints, she'll cut me some slack.

Rachel picks up her fork, holds it in her fingers, and watches me. "I know the timing is bad for this. You have so many other things going on right now."

I force a smile to my mouth and pick up my fork. "An hour isn't a big deal."

She knows I'm lying. She knows I'm a mess.

Rachel sets her fork back down. "Let's just cut to the chase, then we can eat and get back to work. This week is going to fly by, isn't it?" Her voice lifts. My mood plummets.

I don't want to be reminded of the timeline. Not only will time fly by, but Noah is now distracted. I've lost any time I'd have had with him. This week will fly by, and he'll be gone.

Swallowing hard, I stab a carrot off my plate and shove it into my mouth just to concentrate on something else.

"Your book," Rachel says, and the emphasis on the word book makes me know that things weren't as ready as she thought. She's about the apologize for wasting my time. She's going to give me a pep talk about how to finish it and make it better for some other opportunity. Somewhere in there she'll tell me that maybe I can cut my teeth by publishing it myself and assure me that others who are doing that are having great success.

I wonder if she notices when I bite the inside of my cheek instead of the carrot. Now is not the time for a fucking hot flash!

Then I realize she's been talking this whole time and I haven't heard a word, only the buzzing in my ears.

"I mean, I know you're busy, but if we could carve out maybe four hours this week, I know it'll be ready for me to show it to her," Rachel says and I blink hard trying to come up with anything she's said.

There is no recovery from this.

I set my fork down, draw in a breath, and focus on her.

"I'm sorry, what did you say?"

Rachel's smile widens. "I want to send your book to an editor that's acquiring and I think your voice is exactly what she's looking for."

I have to blink a few times to put Rachel back into focus.

"You think you can sell my book?" I choke out the question and she smiles as if she understands my reaction.

"I do. Emma, you have a gift. I knew that when Noah sent me the chapters. He knows it too. Writing isn't for everyone, but those of you who are good at it, well, you set the bar."

She likes my book. She likes my voice. Noah believed in me.

Noah stole the chapters and sent them without my permission.

Noah did that out of love—okay, maybe lust?

I reach for my glass of water only to find that my hand is shaking so much I'm lucky I don't spill the entire glass in my lap.

Rachel Anderson likes my book.

"Perhaps this isn't the right time to sign with an agent," she says picking up her fork and stabbing a piece of lettuce. "But I'd like to sign you."

An agent.

I just got an agent!

My glass of water is still sloshing in my hand. "You're sure?"

She takes the bite and chews thoughtfully, then sets her fork down again and wipes her mouth. "I can't promise anything, but as your agent, I would do everything in my power to—"

"Yes," I interrupt her, set down my glass, and clasp my hands in my lap just to give me the strength to get through this lunch. "I would be interested in you representing me."

She smiles wide. "Now, full disclosure. I'm just an associate agent, which I'm sure Noah told you. This could be a big break for both of us."

"Well, you have to start somewhere, right?" I say and my voice is filled with nerves and optimism.

"You're right."

Rachel picks up her water glass and holds it out toward me. I will my hands to stop shaking and lift mine.

"Here's to starting somewhere," she says and I tap my glass to hers.

As I sip my water I wonder where Noah is right at this moment. I want to share this with him, but in a way that we can enjoy it. I'm very afraid I'm not going to get that opportunity with his in-laws around.

I sip my water again, and pray that I don't choke on my own doubt. No matter how it came to be, or what happens between us, Noah believed enough in me to share my work and find me Rachel. I need to find the gift in that and be okay with it being all I might have left of him when this week is over.

CHAPTER 41

I have no idea where Noah ended up the rest of the day. All of my text messages have gone undelivered—unread, which means he turned off his phone.

Lily screamed when I told her the news about Rachel wanting to sign me for representation.

"I told you it was a good book," she'd shouted when she pulled me to her.

A month ago that would have been all I needed. She would have run to Mrs. Packer's store, bought a brownie, and we would have celebrated. Now, it loses its brightness knowing I want this celebration with Noah—but he's not around.

Sitting on my back porch sipping wine, alone, I watch the stars twinkle in the dark sky and I wonder what is really in store for me? Will this be the first of many times I celebrate good news alone? Will it someday be as unimpressive as Noah makes it seem? I can't imagine that, but how do I know? It means nothing to him to be a bestseller on the most prestigious list or to have movie deals. Seriously, is this what's coming, or is this a pipe dream? Will Rachel fail at getting my book in front of anyone who matters?

~

Julia's eyes are wide when I walk into the store through the coffee shop with a Pack-a-Punch cup in my hand. Wednesdays are my late starts, but I'm here at open.

"We're covered. You don't have to be here," she says as I walk toward my office, my sunglasses covering the puffy eyes I'm rocking this morning. Besides not sleeping all night, I drank most of the bottle of wine I'd opened, oh, and I've been crying. You know, your average pity party.

"I'm better off here," I say walking past her and into my office.

The light is off, not that I expected anything different.

Until three weeks ago, the light was always off when I walked into my office. No one else went into the space that I kept for myself.

I close the door, still without noise, and turn on the light.

Since Noah had been working from my house or the hotel for the past few days, the office is empty of him—except a coffee mug that never got walked to the back room.

Turning on my computer, I watch my manuscript come into focus. I've worked so many hours on this story. As my life changed, the story changed. As men came and went in my life—those who were good and those who broke my heart—the story changed. And now, because of a man I've fallen for, this story will get to be seen.

I know for a fact that if I give it too much thought, I'll back out. Imposter syndrome is a real thing, especially in this uncharted territory I'm currently in.

I need to close out of this program and not touch this book again until I work with Rachel, or I'll change it completely, because my story has changed again.

Saving the draft on my screen, I close down the program and open my emails. Rachel has sent me a list of potential times to work together this week, as she coordinated times with Katie.

The thought makes me smile. Sure, I was going to be everywhere and involved with the event, and I was feeling mighty special. But now that they are making time for me, *me!*, I wonder if this is how it feels to be one of the authors there here to celebrate.

I can't imagine that I'll ever be as calm about it as Noah is. I don't ever want to be that calm about it. I also don't want to be as demanding as Sylvia.

Picking up the mug he left on the desk, I stand and walk out of the office and to the back of the store to wash it. It's funny that washing the rim where Noah's lips touched makes me miss him more.

"Hey," his voice comes from behind me and I nearly drop the mug into the sink.

Once I compose myself, I turn to face him.

He's standing in the doorway, leaned in the casual way he does that makes everything in me go hot.

"Hey," I say back, then reach for a towel to dry off the mug.

Noah steps into the room, closes the door behind him, and moves to me. Quickly I set the mug and the towel to the side.

He doesn't kiss me, but he comes right to me and rests his forehead to mine and his hands rest on my hips. For a long moment we're silent just taking in air that stirs around us.

"I'm sorry," he says, his eyes closed and his forehead still pressed to mine.

My hands grip the counter behind me. I'm afraid to touch him. I'm actually afraid I'll push him away.

"Why are you sorry?" I ask, my voice unsteady.

Noah draws in a deep breath, but still doesn't move. "I handled that poorly."

Yes he did.

Now he eases back to look into my eyes, still, I don't touch him.

"I didn't expect them, and it threw me off. Last night my

sister-in-law commented about my reaction and it was then I realized what I'd done."

"You don't owe me anything. I know this is temporary," I say, but my voice cracks and my words have him easing back from me further.

"It's not."

"C'mon, Noah. We're grown adults, we can handle this. We can have sex and go on." I slip from beneath him and move about the small room, stacking books onto piles that are already counted out on the table. "I don't need you. You don't need me."

He runs his hand over his face and I wonder if he's even slept.

"You don't believe that do you?" he asks.

I put the books I've stacked back on their original stacks, realizing that I'm messing up more than just this relationship.

"You're in love with your wife," I blurt out the words and they sting as much on the air as they did in my heart.

Noah blinks hard. "Of course I'm in love with my wife. But I have to remind you, she died. She's not here."

"But you can't let go."

"Am I supposed to?" His voice rises. "It's not the same as if she ran off with some man and got pregnant."

Now his words are sharp and I know they were meant to sting and they do, but I deserve it.

"I'm sorry," he says pressing his fingers to his eyes. "It just threw me off having them here. But they're my family. They still keep me as part of their family. Abby is always going to be part of my story. I can't change that, Emma. And it doesn't stop me from loving you."

My jaw goes slack and I'm having a very hard time breathing.

"Don't say that," I say, but my words are shaky with tears.

"I mean it," he says as he walks toward me. "I'm not going to just suck this up and decide it was a mistake. It wasn't. I haven't felt alive since Abby died, but you've given me back purpose.

You've made me feel again. You've made me work again. You've made me see again."

Noah reaches for my hand and pulls me to him.

"I didn't reach out last night because I didn't know how. I know what I did to you yesterday, and I'm embarrassed. I should have held your hand and told them who you are to me. I just didn't know how. But they know."

"You're not cheating on her," I say on a wet sob.

"I know that. They know that. They want to meet you again."

"Maybe we should—"

"Meet them," he interrupts. "They're very excited to know another author." He smiles and I find it hard not to do the same.

"You talked to Rachel?"

He nods. "She has big plans for your book and I think she can do it. It'll be something new for both of you."

"What if I can't do what she needs me to do? What if I fail?"

"What if you don't?"

Again he presses his forehead to mine. "Next year this event is in New York. You can stay at my place," he offers.

"Who says I'll be there?"

"I do. I know talent when I see it—steal it—show it to an agent," he says and I laugh as he wraps his arms around me.

CHAPTER 42

The fit check photo I sent to Lily was not well received.

You look like an old woman. Wear something casual, like you would any other day of the week. Add some bling and an extra coat of mascara, she texts back.

I look at myself in the mirror, and I think she's right. I do look like an old woman and it has me changing my outfit.

Everything inside of me buzzes. The store is about to be packed for the next four days. My schedule will be busy from sun up to sun down. Rachel worked with me for an hour yesterday, and has an hour carved out today to work with me as well. Noah was right. She loves the story and wants to change everything about it all at the same time, but I'm giddy to do it.

Noah stayed in town last night to spend more time with Abby's family. I've had a long talk with myself about it, and I have to be okay with it. I mean, I'll never have that part of him. And the part I do have will return to New York in four days. It's not a complete loss. I mean I did get an agent out of it.

I also know he loves me.

I'm grinning as I pull off the sweater I had on and stand in front of my closet in only my bra looking for something else to wear as the successful owner of a small town bookstore.

The thought has me laughing and it feels good. I have forgotten how much I stopped laughing since I moved back home so many years ago. I need to laugh more. I need to laugh like the night Noah and I ate the brownie.

Now I snort out a hearty laugh. God, that was a good night.

I search through my closet and finally pull out a white button up shirt. I pair it with a pair of jeans and a nice belt that I think Lily picked out for me when we'd gone thrifting. Adding more bling, as she'd said to do, and then taming my hair again, I head into town to help oversee the madness that will be the Book Affair Literary Event.

There is a line outside the store as I pull around the back. My heart is racing. This is the greatest thing I've ever seen!

I park my car next to Lily's and she jumps from hers and runs to open my door.

"Did you see that line? Oh-my-God!" She's shouting and pulling me from the car.

"I did."

"We're going to be exhausted," she says with a huge smile on her lips.

"We'll never notice."

"Someday this will be for you," she says and the sincerity in her words have me pulling her into me and squeezing my arms around her.

"I doubt it, but your enthusiasm is just what I need."

She kisses me on the cheek, links our arms together, and we walk through the back door of the store ready for the chaos to begin.

. . .

The first event is at the hotel. There is a welcome breakfast for all of the attendees and the celebrated authors.

Noah has texted me photos of the room and it's at maximum capacity. He said that Sylvia tried to convince Katie to sit her next to him, but he got moved to the other side of Sutton Upton, a thriller writer that Noah admires and Olivia Edwards, a romance author he thinks I should meet.

Mrs. Packer, Lily, Julia, and I are still working because not everyone is at that breakfast. The store is plenty busy and books are flying off the shelves—and not just the books of the featured authors. Dr. Peter Wells will be very happy to know that those three consigned books he wrote about Pine Haven have sold. They've only been on the shelf since he published the historical account of the area ten years ago.

How's it going at the store? Noah's text comes in near noon.

Non-stop! Greatest day ever! I respond.

Any chance you could get away and have lunch with me? Room service?

I send him a picture of the store and the crowd.

I guess not, he replies. *I'm missing you.*

"You can't text that man during business hours," Lily says as she nudges me out of the way to get to the register. "Your face becomes nearly obscene."

"It does not," I laugh, tucking my phone into my back pocket, the grin still wide on my mouth.

"It kinda does," the woman buying the books says, and I lift my head to see Abby's sister there smiling at me.

"Oh," I let the word fall from my mouth. "Hi," I manage.

She holds her hand out toward me and Lily stops scanning the stack of books. "I'm Grace Thompson. Abby Carter's sister."

My throat has closed hearing her name ... *Abby Carter.*

The woman Noah loved.

The wife of the man I love.

The woman who died and broke him—who probably broke all of them.

Lily manages to kick me behind the counter making me snap to. I reach out to take Grace's hand. "Emma Reynolds. I own the store," I add as if she doesn't know everything about me by now.

Grace manages a smile, and it's sincere, but equally nervous as mine. "Would you have time for a cup of coffee?"

As I take a breath to protest the invitation, Lily shoves me.

"She sure does," she says. "I'll keep your books up here and they'll be ready to go when you are."

"Thank you," Grace says, then turns her attention back to me. "Is the coffee next door good?"

"It is," I say.

"Just don't order anything special from the back," Lily adds and I squeeze my eyes shut wishing I'd wake up from this very strange dream.

CHAPTER 43

Grace follows me through the door between the stores and to the counter where Mrs. Packer smiles up at me.

"I think this event is the greatest thing to ever happen to this sleepy town," she says reaching for my hand and holding it between hers in a sign of love and compassion.

"I think you're right," I say and then realize that I'm standing there with Grace. Introductions need to be made, but how awkward is this? "Mrs. Packer, this is Grace." I take a beat. "Noah's sister-in-law," I say, deciding that part is true.

"Well, it's nice to meet you," Mrs. Packer shoots her hand out toward Grace. "He's been a delight to have around the past few weeks. And he's been good for this one," she says, nodding in my direction and I'm sure I'm going to burn and turn into a pile of ash right where I stand.

"It's nice to meet you," Grace returns the gesture. "What do you suggest for someone who's feeling the effects of altitude sickness." Grace smiles at Mrs. Packer.

I eye her coolly so that she answers without offering something from the back.

"I'll whip you up something special. On the house." Then she turns her attention to me. "Usual?"

"Please," I say and she gives me a wink.

"Have a seat. Bobby here will bring it out in a moment," she nods toward her grandson who smiles weakly.

Grace and I find a small table in the corner and sit. She begins to pull off her winter layers and I study her. Her hair might have been strawberry blonde in her youth, but is much lighter now as it's speckled with strands of dull gray. But I can't help but wonder if she looks anything like her sister. For someone who is so important in my life, I don't even know what Abby looked like.

"Thanks for having coffee with me," Grace says. "I hope it's not awkward for you."

I puff out my cheeks. "Can I be honest? It is, but it shouldn't be," I admit and she smiles.

"It shouldn't be. Noah's always been an odd bird when it comes to social graces. It took us a bit to warm up to him, but once you get to see what's under that crusty exterior, he's just a marshmallow."

Her depiction of him has me laughing aloud. "I don't think I could have said it better. He seems like a grumpy old man when you meet him."

Now Grace snorts out a laugh. "Yes, and I met him when he was a young man, and he was the same."

I ease back in my chair. I don't feel any reason to fear this woman now.

Bobby delivers our drinks and hurries away. His grandmother makes him work in the store because she's afraid he'd never interact with humans outside of his video games. He tries, but I'll bet he's much more personable behind a computer screen.

"Why did the other woman warn me about ordering from the back?" Grace asks as she lifts her mug, sniffs, and then takes a tiny sip of her coffee.

"Mrs. Packer is an old hippie who incorporates her love of cannabis into some of her baked goods."

Grace's eyes go wide. "She sells that here? I thought you had to have a special store to do that."

"You do. So she only gives them to people she's friends with. She never sells them, though she'll accept donations."

Grace makes an O with her mouth and then sips her coffee again. "This is really good."

"She has her own blend. I don't know what she gave you, but if it's a Ski Bum, you'll be awake for days," I say and Grace snorts out another laugh and sets her cup down, then wipes her mouth with the back of her hand.

"No wonder Noah is taken by this town," she says. "He's miserable in the city. I think he's alive here."

I realize I have nothing to base this on. But in the past three weeks, I've seen him warm into someone I want to spend forever with.

Grace clasps her hands together as if to pull herself back to the conversation she meant to have with me.

"I'm sorry Noah made it so awkward when we arrived the other day. We did surprise him."

"He said he was confused as to how he should have done things," I admit.

Grace nods then wraps her hands around her cup. "Abby's death hit him hard. There were times I didn't think Noah would survive it either. But, he threw himself into his work and that seemed to be his salvation. And now he's met you."

"Well, we've only known each other a few weeks," I say as if I have to verify facts for her.

"When you find someone you love, you know immediately. Time just gets in the way." Grace lifts her mug to her lips and sips. "Our parents knew each other three days before they married. They were together until my father passed a few years after Abby. My mother always said that when you know, you just know."

I don't know what to say to that. In my twenties, I might have argued that. In my fifties, I understand it, but then again, I might just be too afraid that time is fleeting and maybe we don't have it.

Grace reaches across the table and rests her hand over mine. "I guess what I really want you to know is that none of us expect Noah to be alone for the rest of his life, just because he loved my sister and she's gone. He deserves better than what he got."

I pull in my lips and bite down to keep them from trembling.

"So, Emma," she says, smiling as she eases back in her seat and picks her cup back up. "Tell me about yourself, your store, and your new book deal. We might not expect Noah to be lonely, but we have no intentions of not being in his life either. So I'm going to need to know everything about you."

She's still smiling as she sips her coffee, and I have decided that I'm as taken by this woman as I am by her brother-in-law. If she's anything like her sister, I can see why Noah fell in love with Abby.

CHAPTER 44

Hand in hand, Noah and I walk through the front door of the Italian restaurant, this time with a reservation and request for a back table. Grace, her mother, and her daughter are already seated at the table.

Noah's grip on my hand gets tighter as we walk toward them.

Grace stands to greet us. She kisses Noah on the cheek and then pulls me in for a hug, stepping between us and forcing Noah to let go of me. She wraps her arm around my shoulder.

"This is my mother, Dorothy and my daughter, Amy," she says. "This is Emma, Noah's new girlfriend."

My breath sticks in my chest until Dorothy reaches up to me and touches my arm. "It's wonderful to meet you. It's nice to know this curmudgeon still knows how to be social," she teases and it's Noah that laughs first.

He leans in and kisses Dorothy on the cheek. "I've been known to win over a person or two."

"Yeah, you grew on us," she teases, patting his cheek.

He moves to the open seat next to Grace and pulls it out for me. I sit and he takes the seat next to me, nudging Amy as he sits.

They all fall into easy banter, much like Lily and I do whenever we're around one another. They have a past—a relationship. It's enviable.

I didn't have a relationship with my ex's family. Hell, I didn't have a relationship with him either.

We study our menus, order a bottle of wine which Dorothy suggests, and order our food.

Grace rests her hand over mine as the server pours wine into each of our glasses. "I'm so impressed by the event. Did you do all of the planning?"

I know my eyes go wide. "Oh no. I feel as if I've actually done so little."

"She's also modest," Noah says. "She's done more than she thinks."

His hand comes to my knee under the table and I'm calmed by it and equally worried what everyone else thinks about him doing so, but no one notices.

"The publishing house set up all the venues and have been in town for the better part of three weeks working with the businesses to get everything set up and running," I say.

"Well, everything we attended today was delightful. I got to meet Olivia Edwards during a romance panel," she says.

"She's a favorite. Her book signing is on Sunday at my store."

Grace's lips flatten. "I wish we'd be here for it."

"You're leaving?" I ask, and I find that the very thought saddens me. I think if given the opportunity, I'd love to spend more time with Grace. I've enjoyed getting to know her.

"We leave on Sunday morning. Amy still has classes, but she's almost to the finish line." Grace's eyes light with the love and pride she has for her daughter.

Noah nudges Amy again. "She's going to graduate and change the world," he says, and Amy's cheeks pink.

"I'm going to balance a lot of ledgers," Amy says.

"The world needs that," he says, lifting his glass in toast.

"I couldn't have done it without you," Amy says, nudging Noah as he had to her.

"Good investment," he says, and I wonder what all of that means.

When he first mentioned Abby's family, I thought maybe they casually kept in touch, but did he put Abby's niece through college? No big deal is made of what she said, there are just grateful and proud smiles on all of the faces surrounding me. Maybe this is how he kept that loss of not having his own child in check. If he made sure Abby's niece had everything she'd need, like a college education, then he put some good into the world, right? I mean, I celebrate every win and console every loss with Lily's kids. They are my world, just as I assume Amy is Noah's.

There is a sting that zaps my heart. I wonder how close he is to his sister's kids and grandkids.

I understand that in my fifties I'm not going to be someone's first love. I understand the loss Noah has gone through, having loved and lost Abby. But a part of me wishes we could go back twenty or thirty years and meet each other again. Would we have fallen in love? Would we have a family and be celebrating these milestones? Would we have been too stubborn for one another and never even have considered what could be?

I've always been someone who thinks things happen for a reason.

There's no need to wish I could have something with someone that I'm fairly sure the younger me wouldn't have fallen for.

After dinner, we walk Abby's family to their car and watch as they drive toward the hotel. Noah joins our hands and swings them between us.

"I know it's cold, but what do you say to a walk?" he asks.

"You know that my house or your hotel room has heat. Are you sure you want to do that?"

Noah laughs and lifts my cold fingers to his lips. "You forget what it's like in New York, don't you? Besides it's April."

"It's only April first," I laugh. "And nighttime in the mountains," I retort.

"I just want to check out the antique store window up the street."

It's such a simple request, and I can't help but want to take this walk with him.

I'm not one to consider someone's aura, but I swear Noah has one shimmering around him. There's a lightness in his step, and a smile turning up the corner of his mouth.

Tonight seems to have filled a need in him that I hadn't yet. And I wonder what Grace would have to say about it—did he seem different to her too?

When we reach the end of the block, we stand in front of the window Noah had mentioned.

I've been in the store a handful of times with Julia, who has an old soul and adores antiques. I, on the other hand, I don't have that same love for old things.

"I'm offended by this window display," I say as we look inside.

"Why is that?"

"Um, that's a Cabbage Patch Kid, and there is a set of Donny and Marie dolls. Oh, and a Michael Jackson Thriller poster?"

That has Noah laughing a joyful laugh I've never heard. "You don't like it because you had those toys, didn't you?"

When I turn to face him, there is a lightness to him. It's infectious and I feel it in my soul.

"My toys are in an antique store," I reiterate.

"Have you listened to classic rock stations on the radio? It's all eighties."

"You're depressing me," I say heavily.

"No, depressing is knowing that the eighties was almost fifty years ago."

"Are you trying to harm my self-esteem?"

His smile widens as he looks back at the window that has a help wanted sign and a for sale sign. I don't know the owners of the store, but I wonder if it's a need for employees in order to not sell the store, or if there's another story.

"Do you antique?" I ask him as I watch his eyes shift from item to item.

"I appreciate antiques. I don't collect them. But my parents love antiques. My mother's dream was always to own an antique store."

"Why didn't she?"

Noah shrugs. "Rent in New York is ridiculous. Then my dad got sick for a long time and she took care of him. Then he retired." He blows out a long breath. "Then Abby died and she took care of me."

I squeeze his hand so he knows I'm there feeling all his feels.

"How did she take care of you?"

He bats his eyes, and I wonder how we've gone from looking in this window that seemed to give him so much joy to him batting away tears.

"I was broken. Really broken. I couldn't eat. I couldn't get out of bed. My mom cooked for me. Cleaned my house. I think a few times she read what I'd written, edited it, and wrote ideas in the margins just to keep me working. She's a caretaker, my mother," he says and his voice lifts in admiration for her.

"She sounds wonderful."

"She is. I can't wait for her to meet you," he says finally looking me in the eye.

This is where I'd shake off his comments and remember that he's leaving me in a few days, but not now. Not when he's given me such a compliment like wanting me to meet his mother.

I don't know what's to come, no matter what we've agreed to, but this moment will live with me forever. This man, the one who appreciates antiques—including our childhood toys—thinks enough of me to share these moments with. This will carry me along for a very long time.

CHAPTER 45

Noah's schedule is packed with events at the hotel, a small, ticket-only event at the brewery, and a slew of interviews with TV networks and news networks.

I find myself grinning behind the counter just thinking about the care he takes when he gets ready in the morning to carve in the goatee that he's grown, to match the look on the back of his cover.

"You're grinning again," Lily says as she carries a stack of books to the front from the back room.

"The energy in this town is incredible right now," I say.

"Yeah, and you wake up with a man in your bed every morning," she smirks.

"Bonus for sure." My grin widens.

"And how did dinner go?" She sets the stack of books on the counter.

"It was delightful. I'm quite sure that if I'd ever met his wife, I'd have adored her."

Lily touches my arm. "You're two different people to him, you know that, right?"

"I think meeting her family makes me understand that more. I mean, I'm not a replacement."

"I'm glad you understand that. That man is head over heels infatuated with you."

The very thought makes my skin warm.

My phone buzzes in my pocket and I pull it out to see a text from Noah.

I've had so many tiny bottles of water during these interviews that I'm sure I'm going to float away, he texts.

"You're grinning again," Lily says as she heads toward the back of the store for more books, and I laugh to myself.

You always have refuge here or at my house. I'll never tell anyone where you are, I reply.

I'll let you know.

Those dots appear and I wait for the rest of his conversation.

I'm free from one until two. Can I see you?

I lift my head and look around the store. Lily is here. Julia is here. I have seen Katie pop in and out. I'm sure for one hour they could hold down the fort.

I'll meet you at your hotel room, I add.

He sends a thumbs up emoji followed by a smiley face with hearts for eyes.

One hour. I can give him one hour.

I'm standing at Noah's door when he steps off of the elevator.

"God, that is the best sight I've seen all day," he says as he moves toward me, wrapping his arms around me, and burying his face in my neck.

He doesn't move from me to open his door. Instead, he just holds himself against me.

I wrap my arms around him and just let him take his moment.

"I ordered up some food. It should be in there waiting for us," he says, his breath still on my neck.

After another beat, he pulls his key card from his pocket, opens the door, and we step inside.

There is a room service tray on the coffee table filled with small bites, and when Noah looks it over, he smiles.

"I just need to clean up. I'll be right back," he says as he walks to the bathroom and closes the door.

He seems off, and I don't know what that's about. I pick up one of the glasses of ice water, pull the cover off the top, and sip. Walking toward the window, I look out over the town. My eyes wander down the main street, and to my store. I think about Noah telling me he can see my car when I'm there and the thought that he watches for me warms me throughout.

When the door to the bathroom opens, I look up to see him turn off the light. He's obviously splashed his face with water, and he has on a T-shirt, where he'd had on a button-up when we'd walked in the room.

"Sorry to keep you waiting. I just needed to refresh," he says with a weary grin.

"Is everything okay?"

He walks to me, takes my glass from my hand and sips. "There are a thousand people here. Each room I go into is packed with people. The few that make their way to me have a lot to say. I've shaken a lot of hands and hugged housewives that I'm not so sure aren't using my books as guides to offing their husbands."

That comment has me snorting out a laugh, and for the first time since Noah walked off the elevator, he smiles wide.

"I just had to wash them all off before I eat," he says.

"Please tell me you're having fun."

He sets the glass down on the coffee table and pulls me to him. "I'm having a good time. But for someone who doesn't surround themselves with people, a thousand at a time is a bit much."

Wrapping my arms around him, I study his tired eyes. "I still find it funny that you think you thrive in the city."

"Oh, but I do. You don't have a bagel shop here," he deadpans and I pucker my lips to hold in my smile.

"You're right. We just can't keep up with the times here."

"But there is nothing quite like Agnes' brownies in the city."

"I doubt that."

"She adds a pinch of love," he teases and I press my forehead to his trying to hold back the chuckle that wants to escape.

"I bet she'd send you home with the recipe," I say, though I don't want to even think about him going home.

"It would never be the same as having a brownie in the romance section."

My heart aches at the memory, not because it was a bad one, but the first one—the first one for us.

Noah lifts his fingers to my hair and brushes back a strand. "Sylvia's signing is tonight?"

I groan. "Her Q&A starts at four and her signing at five."

His throat works and he gnaws on his bottom lip. "I'll bet you could use some help working the counter, restocking, stuff like that."

My lips curl up into a smile and I tuck my fingers up into his hair. "I have a really good staff," I say. "Don't you dare come to help us."

"I mean it. I'm happy to help."

"And I know you would. But I also know that would throw Sylvia right over the edge."

Noah puckers his lips. "It would, wouldn't it?"

"So maybe not being there will keep things a little more low key?"

"I couldn't have said it better myself."

"And I'm sure you have writing to do."

He growls. "Now you sound like my agent."

"Someone has to keep you under control."

Noah nips my lips with a kiss. "But seriously, if you need help,

I can send help. I know for a fact that Abby's family would be thrilled to help you."

I consider that for a moment. "Do you think so?"

"I know so."

"Will you text Grace and ask?"

He shakes his head. "You can text her. I'll send you her number."

I think that puts a lot of faith in me when he offers that. "We should eat some lunch before you need to be back in the spotlight."

Noah pulls me in closer to him, resting his forehead to mine again. "Sleep here tonight."

How could I possibly refuse?

CHAPTER 46

The bookstore is packed. Mrs. Packer's store is full of people. There is a line down the street.

My heart races as Lily moves through the crowd with a small plate of food and shoves it at me.

"Eat this. You need your energy before you do the Q&A," she says.

"Oh-my-god! This is out of control," I say, taking the small plate of snacks and looking out over the crowd.

"Yeah, and this is only Sylvia. This isn't Noah."

I blink hard and take that in. "You think there'll be more people tomorrow for Noah?"

Her brows draw in and she looks at me as if I've lost my mind. "Um, yeah. Haven't you seen the pictures of the events at the hotel? He draws the crowd. He's the headliner here."

I have to swallow hard because nerves are stuck in my throat. No wonder he was so out of sorts earlier.

Lily takes my arm and escorts me into my office. "Sit down and eat. I have Grace, Amy, and Dorothy working the crowd. Amy has retail skills like mad, so she's selling stuff. Dorothy is boasting that she's Noah's mother-in-law, so it's kind of funny that she's drawing attention away from Sylvia, but not in a harmful way."

She looks at the chair behind the desk and then at the plate. "Eat. I'll be back for you in fifteen minutes and we'll get the Q&A started."

I can only nod at this point. I'm no longer in control of anything that's happening.

When I'd texted Grace about helping, she called me. They hadn't expected to be part of the event but they were excited to be asked. Noah is a very lucky man to have them in his life, and I know I'm lucky to have them in mine as well.

As promised, there is a knock at the office door fifteen minutes after Lily shut me in, but it's Katie that walks through. Again, she's dressed like New York and I'm instantly jealous. This woman's closet is fire.

"Are you ready?" she asks, her bright red painted lips curled up into a smile.

"I am."

"Wonderful. I hope it's okay that Noah isn't here," she says and that smile fades.

"We talked about it. He didn't think it was a good idea for him to be here."

She nods. "I think he was right. It's enough to have his mother-in-law working the crowd."

I can't tell if she's humored by it or annoyed. Either way, I'd never ask Dorothy to leave.

"Sylvia is in your back room warming up as if she's going to sing some opera," Katie says shaking her head. "Dylan was headed to Noah's hotel to work with him on his book. Rachel is here to support you in any way you need. I think we're ready to roll."

I draw in a deep breath and let it out slowly before opening the top drawer of my desk to pull out my lip balm. That's when I see the sticky note laying there.

Good luck tonight! I love you! N~

I can feel the heat rise in my cheeks and spread across my chest as I take out the lip balm, apply it, and close the drawer with the note still inside.

That man ...

Mrs. Packer's store is wall to wall people. Through the doorway, I can see that my store is full as well, and there is a line at the door for people wanting to get in for the signing. Amy is with Julia behind the counter. Dorothy is in the front row of the Q&A—talk about pressure.

I don't know where Grace is, but no doubt she's being helpful.

My heart is so full at the moment, and it isn't until Katie puts a hand on my shoulder that I realize it's time to begin.

I'd been handed a microphone that's connected to a small sound system that was set up in the coffee shop and another speaker is in my store as well. This way no one misses out on the Q&A.

I introduce myself and Sylvia, who looks at me as if we're the dearest of friends, and not like we've kissed the same man. But now isn't the time for me to think about that.

When Katie gave me Sylvia's questions, I had studied them, made notes, and practiced their delivery. But right before we sit down in the chairs that are from my store, and not the ones Sylvia had managed to convince the antique store to lend us, she hands me new questions.

These questions talk more about her new series coming out, which she admits isn't even contracted yet. She goes off script and talks about her huge fan base and how amazing they are and how they gather just for her.

When I shoot Katie a wary glance she's pinching the bridge of her nose.

Did Sylvia just hijack this whole event claiming that no one else was worthy of the draw?

I continue with the questions which include topics like her new dog, favorite teas, and how she's shopping her books for scripts.

I don't know who her agent is or if they're in attendance, but she sounds a bit rogue.

In the last ten minutes, we open it up to questions from the audience.

They ask about her recent releases. They want to know about certain characters. But the last question has me shaking.

"I'd heard a rumor that you're involved with Noah Carter. I want to know all about that," the young woman, who is standing to the side of the room, a Noah Carter book pressed against her chest, asks Sylvia.

My mouth goes dry.

I try not to look directly at Dorothy, but I can see from the corner of my eye that she narrows her eyes at Sylvia.

Sylvia swats her hand in the air and lets out an airy laugh. "Oh, that Noah. What a playboy, huh?"

My insides twist and I realize I'm gripping the notes in my hand so tight I've crinkled them.

"I don't like to *kiss* and *tell*," Sylvia says with emphasis and there are giggles from those who are enamored by Noah. "But come through the signing line and maybe I'll let you in on it."

Katie's hand comes to my shoulder and gives it a squeeze. I don't know if it's a signal to wrap everything up or if it's her way of standing in solidarity with me.

Seriously, when I'd met Sylvia in Noah's room, I thought she understood the dynamics. I thought Noah had told her all about us. Then again, I thought Noah had told me all about Sylvia. What more is there to say? Why is she playing it up like this? This says there was much more than a kiss, but that's not what Noah had said.

Katie reaches for my microphone and lifts it to her lips.

"Let's give Sylvia a big round of applause as well as our host, and up-and-coming author, Emma Reynolds, owner of The Reading Nook." The crowd applauds as they all stand and begin to make their way to the bookstore to line up.

Sylvia is flocked with adoring fans, and Katie doesn't redirect them. Instead, she moves me to the side.

Sure to turn off the microphone, she sets it on the seat I'd occupied.

"Don't let her get into your head," she says touching my arm. "That was uncalled for."

I'm shaking and I can't even catch my breath. "I know they had something."

Katie narrows her eyes on me. "Did he tell you that?"

"Well," I say and think of what he told me and his reaction to Sylvia being there. "He said they kissed once."

"Yeah, and that's all it was," she assures me as if she absolutely knows. "I'm going to work the signing. You have a full staff. You go to him. I think it's better that neither of you are here in this moment."

I nod. I'm grateful for Katie's attention to this, even if it wasn't what she wanted in the first place.

Dorothy makes her way to us. "What is that woman talking about? Her and Noah?"

Katie rests her hand on Dorothy's arm. "It's nothing. She's a bit delusional," she says.

Dorothy nods. "Yeah, because that man isn't in love with her, he's in love with this one right here," she says lifting her head in my direction.

My eyes sting with Dorothy's words. "Oh, I don't know about—"

She holds up a hand to stop me. "I know what he looks like

when he's in love." She winks. "He looked at my Abby the same way he looks at you. After she died, he looked lost. He doesn't look lost anymore."

My heart is thudding in my chest and I can't help but pull Abby's mother into me and hug her.

When I pull back she touches my cheek. "Go to him. I'll go work this woman's signing table. We'll see how much she says when the mother of Noah Carter's late wife is handing her the books to sign."

Katie actually snorts out a laugh and takes Dorothy's arm. "Oh my god, you're hired. This is going to be the best two hours of the entire event," she says, nearly cackling as she leads Dorothy away.

CHAPTER 47

When Noah opens the door to me, his brows draw in as he studies me.

"Why are you here?" he asks and I know my eyes go wide at the question.

Noah must realize the question hits wrong, because he takes my hand and pulls me into the room where Dylan is seated at the small table. There are two laptops open and papers all over the room.

"Is everything okay? You look absolutely petrified and," he looks at his watch, "the signing isn't over."

At that moment, Dylan's phone buzzes in his hand and he looks down at the text. Shaking his head, he looks back up at me.

"Seriously?" Dylan says, and I nod. "Bitch."

Now Noah's grip tightens. "What in the hell is going on?"

I realize that I'm much too serious in this moment and force myself to let my shoulders drop.

"Sylvia answered a question that, well, it just wasn't appropriate," I say, trying to save face for everyone.

Dylan snorts. "Bullshit," he says then looks at Noah. "Some

fangirl of yours asked about you and Sylvia being an item. She hinted at you guys having something going on."

Noah's eyes widen. "Why would she …" Then his nostrils flare. "Is she really this petty?"

"Dude, you knew she was. I'm actually surprised she's been as civil as she has been," Dylan goes back to scrolling through the file on his computer.

Noah takes both of my hands in his. "She didn't say anything nasty to you, did she?"

I shake my head. "I think I was just a little surprised by her answer, that's all."

Without worrying about Dylan sitting only a few feet from us, Noah moves in closer, and lifts his hand to my cheek. "I told you the truth. You know everything that happened between me and Sylvia."

I nod. I knew in my heart he'd been truthful to me.

"Is Katie with her now? She's not spreading more rumors about me, is she?"

This answer has my lips curling up into a wide smile. I press my hand to Noah's chest. "Katie is there, but Dorothy decided after Sylvia said that, that she'd volunteer to work the signing table as my replacement, and Katie sent me here."

Noah now backs up to arm's length and scans a long look over me. "My mother-in-law heard Sylvia say that and then volunteered to man the table?"

I nod and purse my lips. "She did."

"Oh, Sylvia made one hell of a mistake," he says with a laugh as he pulls me into his side. "Damn, now I wish I were a fly on the wall."

I decide that since I wasn't at the store to close it up after the book signing, I'd go in early just to reset everything.

It appears that Katie knew what she was doing when she ordered more books for Sylvia. Luckily they all sold, since Sylvia had presigned them. It doesn't look like I'm going to have to beg to return them or keep a lot of overstock.

As soon as I walk through the door, Mrs. Packer appears from the door between the stores. She has a large cup from Pack-a-Punch in her hand and a raspberry scone. She doesn't bring out the raspberry scones too often. Last night must have been very profitable for her.

She smiles at me, then hands me the coffee and the scone.

"Did you get some sleep? You look well rested," she says.

"I did."

"I imagine cuddling up to him all night would help me sleep too," she winks at me and I can't help but laugh.

"It's a perk."

Then her face grows serious. "You did miss all the fun though," she says, her brows rising.

"Did I?"

"After that girl asked about Sylvia and Noah being an item, Katie put the reins on that. And his mother-in-law sat at the table, handing Sylvia her books to sign and talked to every one of the people who came to see Sylvia speak. She told them about Noah and how her daughter had been married to him. Then she told them about how you're the one who really is involved with him and how you're now publishing a book."

I feel my cheeks fill with heat. "Oh, dear. I hope Sylvia isn't—"

Mrs. Packer flicks the air as if to knock my words down. "No one cares what Sylvia thought. She sold a shit ton of books. She got her ass kissed. But that Dorothy saved face for Noah, and you go look on your counter. There's an email list for people wanting more information on your book."

My eyes go wide. "What?"

"Yep, Julia said that when everyone came through to pay for the book, they asked about your book. They all want to know what the woman who actually is sleeping with Noah Carter has to write about."

My lips twitch and then spread into a smile. I just can't help it. "They want to be on my email list to learn about my book?"

Agnes lifts her shoulders. "I didn't understand all of it. You know Julia and her social media tactics. I don't know what it all means."

But I do. My heart is so full.

I clean the store, though it does look like maybe it was thoroughly cleaned after the signing. I wonder which of those ladies was running the tight ship.

Katie is the first person through the door right as I open. Again, she looks like New York as she walks through in her heels, pencil skirt, and a blouse that flows in all the right places.

"How was your night?" she asks.

"It was very nice," I say, because it was.

"Dylan said you all had dinner together."

"They were knee deep into Noah's next book, going through it, I think. I felt bad, as if I were interrupting, but Dylan said they could lock themselves in a room for weeks without coming up for air. So it was probably a good thing I showed up."

"He's right," she agrees, then she moves to the counter and rests her arms on it. "I wanted to let you know that I asked Sylvia to head home after last night."

I know they banked on Sylvia being there the rest of the weekend. This couldn't have been taken lightly.

"You did?"

Katie nods. "I know that rumors start and fans want to believe things that just don't happen, but I wasn't comfortable with how she handled the question. And before we got her totally shut down with Dorothy at the table—and I love and adore her by the way—she'd led a few fans to believe that maybe she and Noah had something going on."

I press my hand to my chest, and then fidget with my top button. "Oh."

"Listen, I know we're all adults. Affairs happen. Relationships happen. And, that's fine. It's not fine when you trade it for a sale."

There was something about Katie that I just liked the moment she walked through my door. Integrity, she exudes it.

Now I wonder if she was as hard on Noah as I first thought she was, or if she was protective of him. Either way, she's protective of him now.

"Are you ready for the crowd you're going to have today? I mean, everyone has had a lot of fans, but Noah—this is going to be on a different level," she says.

I draw in a breath and I realize that I'm so full of pride for the man, I might burst. "I think we're ready."

Katie smiles wide. "Okay, you're going to man the table with him and hand him the books. But I sure as hell am going to have Dorothy work the line," she laughs. "I met Abby a few times, and she was sweet, oh so sweet. Now that I've met her mother, I realize why Abby could handle the moody mess that is Noah Carter. She was raised by a woman with that same kind of spirit."

And just like that, I learn another reason why Noah loved Abby, and I'm finding I love her too.

CHAPTER 48

Julia and Lily walk through the door at the same time. They are each loaded down with bags of all sorts.

"What is all of this?" I ask.

Lily sets her coffee down on the counter before dropping her bags. "We learned a little something last night. One, we get hungry when we're having to handle so many people. So, snacks. And it gets hot in here when there are two hundred people standing around, so a change of clothes."

I grin at her. "You did learn a lot, huh?"

"Yeah, and since you weren't here, we brought you snacks and clothes too," she says.

This is why she's always been my ride or die. She's just the best.

Julia looks around the currently quiet store. "Where is Noah?"

"Psyching himself up for today," I say. "He'll come with Dylan later."

Lily wraps her hands around her coffee cup and leans in on the counter. "Is he okay? That Sylvia stuff was kind of a shit show."

I know she'll be truthful to me, though between Katie and Mrs. Packer, maybe I don't want to know more.

"He's okay. Was it really that bad?"

Lily shrugs. "When that woman asked the question and Sylvia played it up, it just got tongues wagging. I mean it was like watching a piece of paper on fire lift through the crowd. You want to know how a rumor starts, well that was it."

"So everyone thought they were involved?"

She bats away the comment with her hand. "It got shut down pretty quick, but it was still a buzz. It was just that Sylvia played it up, you know? Why in this day and age, would any woman want to stake her reputation on some guy she may or may not have slept with? Aren't we past that by now?"

I pull my lip through my teeth. "Why does this all make me feel like I'm sixteen again?"

"Because it's just about as petty. But let me tell you, Sylvia shut down once Katie put Dorothy in that chair next to her."

I can't help but smile at that. "Was she mad?"

"More like confused. As if she didn't realize what she'd even said when she answered that woman's question, or the twenty more of them that came at her before she got to the signing table. When Katie sat Dorothy at the table and introduced her to the masses as Noah's mother-in-law, shit changed fast."

I purse my lips. "But if they know she's his mother-in-law, then I seem like the other woman too."

Lily shakes her head. "No. She set all of that straight because she had an intimate conversation with every single person who bought one of Sylvia's books. Once Sylvia is done being mad about being sent home, she'll realize Dorothy might have shut down rumors, but she sold a ton more of Sylvia's books. You don't have any old copies left. You sold out of almost all of her books," she says grinning proudly.

"That's incredible."

Then she reaches for a stapled stack of papers by the register and slides them my way. "And this is the beginning of your new mailing list. Rachel wants us to get it put into a spreadsheet and to send her a copy. People are wanting your book now too."

"No one even knows what it's about."

She shrugs. "It doesn't matter. What they know is they like you. They like your store, and this tiny mountain town. That's all they need to know."

Lily picks up her coffee cup and the bags she'd dropped to the floor when she'd arrived and all but floats to the back of the store.

I'm going to owe her and Julia big time when this is all over. I guess that's all I'll have to focus on after tomorrow—after Noah leaves.

I'm at the back door. Can you let me in? The text comes from Noah around lunchtime and I can't help but smile down at it.

I'm helping Julia with a sale, but she shoos me away when I look up at her and smile.

The shop is full, and I'm ecstatic. I will never have this many people through my store again, and I know it. I'm trying to remember how amazing this feeling is.

When I get to the back room, I open the back door. Noah is standing on the other side, his arms loaded up with trays of food.

I reach for some of the items. "What is this?"

"It's lunch, for everyone. Dylan and Rachel are on their way. Katie is at Agnes' right now getting everything set up for this afternoon and then she'll be over."

"You did this?" I ask, setting trays on the table and watching as Noah does the same.

"I did, but it's no big deal. It's the least I can do for everyone for everything you've all done for us to be here."

Once his arms are empty, I pull him into me. "I signed on for this, you know."

"I know, and still it's a lot of work. Work you didn't know was coming."

I kiss him gently on the lips. "I'd do it all over again," I say.

"Maybe next time you can be on the other side of it all. The spotlight side."

"That's a long ways away."

"You never know," he says, his hands sliding over my ass.

Three weeks, I think. Three weeks ago this man was nothing more than a name on a few snarky emails and now he's changed my entire world.

"Rachel wants an hour of my time before your Q&A," I say.

"Why don't you work on it during my signing?"

I shake my head. "I think Katie would have an aneurysm. She wants me at the table." I lean in closer to whisper in his ear. "She just knows I'm good for you."

"I know you're good for me," he says matter-of-fact.

"Well, I don't know if you're good for me or not. I don't know how I'll go back to normal when you leave."

"Emma," my name is soft on his lips and I press my finger to them.

There is a tapping at the door and Katie pushes it open. "I knew you two were up to no good," she says looking at us enveloped in one another's arms, but she's smiling. "Dylan and Rachel are here. Are we ready?"

Noah takes a step back, but captures my hand. "We're ready."

CHAPTER 49

The man who takes the seat next to me in Mrs. Packer's store, in the chair that we once occupied while eating special brownies, doesn't look like the same man who walked through my door three weeks ago.

Aside from the fact he now looks like the man on the back of his books, the dark circles from under his eyes have diminished, and even his skin glows different.

He makes a scene of walking in holding hands with me. Not just holding hands, but our fingers are intertwined. He moves to the chairs and waits for me to take a seat.

I would have thought I'd walked into the room with a rock star. The noise from adoring fans is deafening.

He turns and gives a little bow. It's quite cute and his cheeks flush from the attention.

In the front row are Dorothy, Grace, and Amy. Before he takes his seat, he moves to each of them and kisses them on the cheek. Dorothy reaches for his face and gives his cheeks a pat.

My heart flutters at a different pace.

This man.

When he finally takes his seat, Katie, grinning widely, hands us each a microphone.

I wasn't as nervous seated in the same space yesterday with Sylvia as I am now. There seems to be a different buzz to the air sitting next to Noah.

Every person in the crowd has one or more of Noah's books on their laps. I've seen some of them come through the store in the past few weeks. There is an entire row of book club members who wear a giddy smile as if they knew the celebrity first.

"Wow," I say at the energy that electrifies the room. "Welcome to our Q&A with thriller author Noah Carter," I say and again the room erupts.

There is little change on the broody author's face, and I find that even more adorable than when he gazes into my eyes and says sweet things.

"I know you're all eager for the signing, so let's get to it."

Suddenly I feel odd talking to him as if he's someone who just came to visit my store. Not as if he's the man who fixed my sticking door, who turned my book club upside down, ate a pot brownie with me in the romance section, watched me run out of the Stanley Hotel, or has rocked my world every night since.

"The most-asked question submitted was; why thriller and how did you get started writing that?"

Noah crosses one leg over the other, balancing his ankle on his knee. I think in this moment this is the broody author whom I exchanged curt emails with so many years ago and not the man who sees past all of my flaws.

"Why not?" He says dryly and the crowd laughs.

He studies everyone for a moment and then the corner of his mouth curls up and he reaches for my hand. This I didn't expect.

"All I can say is Stephen King."

There is a round of applause at the mention of the name of the beloved author that so many adore.

"This fine lady took me on a private tour of the Stanley Hotel last week." Again a round of applause for the landmark. "Norman over there," he points to the man waving at us, "showed me around and let me be star struck."

"I can confirm you were star struck," I say and he looks at me and smiles. "What was it about Mr. King's books that changed your world?"

Noah considers for a moment. "Let's be honest, it wasn't the books. It was the movies that caught me first. My teenage years were filled with Stephen King movies, and The Shining was my first."

"Is that why you fanboyed so hard?" I ask and he actually lifts my fingers to his lips and kisses my knuckles, which causes the masses to aww.

"That's why," he confirms. At this point he lets go of my hand, lowers his foot to the ground, and leans his arms on his knees. "I snuck into the theater to see it. I bought a ticket for something else, and well, you know the rest."

The crowd in Mrs. Packer's shop laughs.

"I was obsessed by the story, so I bought the book. My mother wasn't about to let me read it, so that too was purchased on the down low and kept under my pillow. And then it became an obsession. It wasn't long before I was filling notebooks with stories. All kinds of stories. Some I'd share with my family, some I wouldn't."

"And those that you wouldn't, are those the basis of the hits that we have now?" I ask.

He turns his head and grins up at me. "They most certainly are."

Noah's eyes twinkle when he says it.

He may not like this part of the job, the public persona, but he knocks it out of the park.

Katie curated the list of questions for the Q&A and gave them to me before we went on. She didn't want a repeat of yesterday. She wasn't leaving much room for open questions.

The hour passes quickly and I love watching Noah work the crowd. They adore him. I adore him.

When we finish, he moves again to Dorothy, Grace, and Amy and hugs each of them, then he pulls me in for a hug that includes a gentle, but lingering kiss. The entire room again erupts and I guess any rumors of him and Sylvia are put on hold. What a crazy ride.

The book signing extends past its two hour mark and rolls into a third. Though Katie works the line to make sure it continues to move efficiently, Noah takes time with each reader. He knows how important it is to his career.

They've asked about his next books and the movies that are in production. I've had many questions about my own book, but I try to keep all talk focused on Noah. He, on the other hand, feeds them as much information as he can on my book and tells them all they can sign up for my newsletter at the counter.

I think I blush each time he mentions it. That stupid book that has been on my computer for nearly thirty years sure is getting a lot of attention. And all because Noah Carter stole it and gave it to someone—because he believed in it—because he loves me.

The thought has me snorting out a laugh to myself and Noah and the woman he's talking to turn to look at me.

"What's so funny?" he asks.

I can't even answer. Every part of it is funny, mesmerizing, a miracle in its own right. Without him finding that book on my computer no one would notice me sitting here next to him. Rachel wouldn't be asking for time with me to work on the book. She wouldn't be making calls in the aisles of my store to editors she knows asking if they'd like to look at it.

Before the next person in line moves in front of Noah, I turn my head to look at him and he gazes back at me.

"I love you," I say and his eyes go wide.

I know I'm caught up in the moment and the feels inside of me are swirling around at a dizzying pace, but I guess I needed to say it.

There is no time for him to react more than he has before the next woman in line lays down a stack of books on the table and begins to gush to Noah about how she loves his twisted mind.

I ease back in my chair and watch the interaction.

It's different now.

He's trying to focus on the woman in front of him, but I know the words I just dropped on him are causing his brain to misfire.

CHAPTER 50

I find it endearing that Dorothy, Grace, and Amy are still at the store well past close. They'd made the trek to see Noah, and they supported him until the last book had been signed.

Dorothy has fallen asleep in my office chair, which Lily pushed out for her to sit in. Grace has made a list of books she'd like me to send her. She doesn't want to carry them on the airplane, but she wants to support my store. If that isn't the nicest thing, I don't know what is. Of course, she'll get them at wholesale.

Amy has been reading Noah's newest book, and reading, and reading. I assume it's a pastime for them all. She's already three-quarters of the way through the book.

When the last guest walks out of the store, Julia locks the door, turns the sign, and leans against the door with a loud sigh.

"I have never seen so many people in one place at one time in my entire life," she says.

"You really should travel more," Lily tells her.

"I don't think I could handle it."

The scene made me think about my aunt's store the day that people came for their Noah Carter books and he wasn't there to sign them. Sure, he wasn't who he is now, in regard to the literary world, but still, there were hundreds of mad people.

I wish I knew then what I know now, perhaps it would have been easier on all of us had I known his wife was sick.

Noah leans back in his chair and laces his fingers behind his head. He's exhausted, and no doubt peopled out.

"I just walked through the thriller section," Katie says. "The shelves are bare."

The smile that slides over my face has to be enormous. I am so happy in this moment I could just burst.

"I'm glad I won't have to call in any favors to send back books," I say.

"I knew you wouldn't," Katie says with a wink and then she looks around the store. "What can I do to help get ready for tomorrow?"

Lily holds up a sheet. "These are our tasks before Olivia Edwards' Q&A and signing tomorrow morning."

"Let's get to it," Katie says and then turns to me. "You two get out of here and take his family with you. Take them to dinner at the hotel. I made a reservation for five people. You have twenty minutes to get there."

I stand from my chair, walk to her, and pull her in for a hug. "Thank you."

"It's my pleasure. I think he could use some down time."

I look back at Noah who has closed his eyes. I think Katie is right.

Noah and I drive separately to the hotel so that I can leave earlier in the morning and he can choose whether or not he wants to even trek into the store. He has one more panel in the morning and then his obligations are over.

The thought puts a lump in my throat.

Tomorrow is it.

Tomorrow is my last day with him and I'll be busy making sure the last of the authors have as successful a Q&A and book signing as Noah did.

I purse my lips so I won't cry. I can't cry. This was the only given. Noah would leave the Monday after the event.

I pull into the hotel parking lot behind Grace and her family. Noah has already parked and is headed toward Grace's car to help Dorothy from the front seat.

This is where I take a moment and pull myself together. I have tomorrow with Noah, but this is my last night with Abby's family.

As I gather my things and push open my door, Noah is standing there, his hand out to help me from my car.

I smile up at him.

He's tired, but there is a joy that surrounds him.

I wonder for a moment if that happiness is the people that came to meet him and gush about his books, or that Abby's family made the trip to see him, or if I bring out that happiness in his eyes.

Taking his hand, I let him ease me from the car and as he does, he pulls me into him. Quickly I wrap my arms around him for both stability and need.

"Thank you," he whispers warm in my ear.

"For what?"

"The list is long," he says. "Just, for everything."

I ease back and look into his tired eyes. Yes, he's tired, but the dark circles are gone and light from the streetlamps shimmer against the richness of his pupils.

"Thank you for selling more books at my store than I've ever sold—ever."

His mouth ticks up on the side. "To be a bookseller's dream," he teases.

"In so many ways," I say.

Noah brushes a kiss against my lips, then takes my hand, and as a collective group, we walk into the hotel.

The night is spent eating, drinking, and laughing—oh, so much laughing. They each have a story of Noah, and yes they include Abby, but I almost feel as if Abby is a long lost friend now.

It's Amy that lets out the gem that has everyone but Noah holding our bellies in laughter.

"He's afraid of dolls. You know, like the ones at antique stores," she says on a laugh.

I turn to him, eyes wide. "So you took me to the antique store to look in the window? Did you think that Cabbage Patch Kid was going to come out get you?"

He lifts his brows. "Those things are horrifying."

"They are a classic piece of eighties history."

He nods. "And as horrifying now as they were then."

I place my hand on his thigh. "I have like four of them in a box in my closet."

"All the more reason you're staying with me at the hotel and I'm not sleeping at your house. Had I known that all along, I wouldn't have gone out to the dark woods to stay with someone so obviously demented."

That has us laughing harder. And to think, I was worried that this man might snap and actually throw me over the side of my deck railing into the dark forest. Who knew I was the one who was disturbed?

Noah sobers as he drinks from his water glass. "My mother would have loved that doll in that window though," he says, and again, I see a love and a happiness shimmer in his eyes that I couldn't have imagined a week ago.

. . .

There are more laughs, and maybe a few tears, as we hug Abby's family goodnight, and goodbye, at the elevators.

"We're so proud of you," Dorothy says as she pats his cheek.

"Thank you. And thank you for coming. It meant a lot."

Dorothy smiles, pats his cheek again, and then moves to me and hugs me. "Don't let him go. He needs you," she whispers in my ear and then pulls back and pats my face in the same way she'd patted his.

There is a lump in my throat as I watch the three women climb into the elevator.

Don't let him go, repeats in my head. What choice do I have?

When I turn back to Noah, he's staring at the closed elevator door. Their visit was what his heart needed, I know this. But their departure hurts. I wonder if he's missing Abby in this moment.

When he turns his attention to me, he smiles. "What do you say to a nightcap?"

I lift a brow. "Aren't you dead on your feet?"

"Yes, and my social battery is drained," he admits. "To be honest, I don't even want alcohol. Maybe a dessert nightcap?"

I move into him and wrap myself around his arm. "They have a raspberry brownie cake here that's to die for."

"Let's get that to go and eat it outside."

"It's freezing outside."

"I know. We'll get a coffee too," he adds as if that'll make his request better.

"It has to be decaf. I need to get to sleep."

"Decaf it is," he says before kissing the top of my head. "Anything for you."

CHAPTER 51

Lily pulls me into my office the moment I walk through the door. I don't even have to ask her why. We've been friends long enough that I knew when she saw my face, she knew I'd been crying.

She all but forces me into the desk chair, turns and closes the door, then turns back to me.

"Spill it," she says, her arms folded in front of her.

I can't even talk.

The tears started in the shower and they haven't stopped. I hurried out of the hotel room, leaving Noah in bed sleeping because I didn't want him to see me like this.

Lily leans herself up against my desk. "Em, what happened?"

"I only have a few more hours," I managed between sobs.

She studies me for a moment and then it sinks in. "Before he leaves?"

I nod, wiping at my eyes, not even caring about the small amount of makeup I'd managed.

"Oh, honey," Lily says as she rests a hand on my shoulder. "You knew this was coming."

I nod. Knowing didn't equate to being ready for it.

"So, go with him."

I lift my eyes and study her. "What?"

"Seriously, go home with him."

Now I laugh through sobs. "I can't leave here."

"Why not? We're here."

That has me rising to my feet and wrapping my arms around her. "I love you."

She laughs in my arms. "I love you, too. So you're going?"

I ease back, wipe my tears, and shake my head. "No. But to know you would send me off and take care of everything, that means the world to me."

"I'm not kidding," she confirms. "You love the man. So go home with him."

I cup her face in my hands. "I do love him, but my home is here."

There is no doubt she's ready to argue with me over the fact that she didn't mean leave forever, but her fight is interrupted when the door to my office eases open.

"Am I interrupting?" Noah's voice threatens to throw me back into a sea of sobs.

Lily grips my wrists and looks me sternly in the eyes as she mouths the word *go*.

I drop my hands from her face and she stands from her perch at my desk before walking out of the office and closing the door once Noah is inside.

His eyes are on me as I wipe my eyes with the heels of my hands.

"You left without waking me," he says, and for the first time I realize he's just rolled out of bed and is now standing in front of me.

Noah moves to me, wrapping me up in his arms.

"I take it you've talked to Katie?" he says, his lips pressed against my temple.

That has me easing back. "No. Why would I talk to Katie?"

Noah eases back and drags his hand down his stubbled and weary face, then rakes his fingers through his mussed hair.

"They changed my flight."

I bat my eyes trying to dry them. "You're staying longer?" Optimism fills my voice and for the first time since I laid down next to him last night, I feel some hope.

He shakes his head. "Dylan left last night. The production company that has movie rights to one of my books needs a meeting ASAP. I have to head back to New York."

I purse my lips. "In this day and age you can't just call in? Zoom?"

Noah gathers my hands in his. "I need to be there, Em."

I bite down on my bottom lip to keep it from trembling. "I'm not ready."

"Come with me," he says, just as Lily had.

I snort out a laugh. "Are you kidding me?"

"No."

Turning from him, I wipe my eyes. "I can't just leave. We are right in middle of this."

He nods. He knows. He understands.

"Come next week. Or the week after."

I turn back to him, crossing my arms in front of me.

"Noah," his name comes out as a sign of resignation. Almost as suddenly as the tears had started this morning, my mind is clear. "We live two very different lives. We knew this was temporary."

His eyes widen and I swear the color has drained from his face.

"What does that mean? I thought—"

I move to him and gather his hands in mine. "We both know you'll go home and get busy. You'll get locked into your life, I'll get locked back into mine."

His throat works and his eyes mist.

"I don't know that at all," he says, reversing our hands so that he's holding mine, now pressed between us. "That's not what I want."

"Want or not, we know it's what's going to happen. We're both too old to change our ways—to start something new."

There is a flash in his eyes. I can't decide if it's anger or acceptance, but he doesn't move from me. Instead, he leans in, pressing his forehead to mine.

"We have a few hours," he whispers.

"We have a few hours," I agree.

"Then come back to the hotel with me and let's spend them together."

Again, I want to argue that I'm too busy, instead, we sneak out the back door and to Noah's car.

We both climb in, throw on our seatbelts, and Noah starts the car.

We are only moments from our getaway when the back door swings open and Katie and Rachel are standing in the doorway watching us with wide eyes.

"We've been caught," Noah says.

"Shit."

When Katie puts her fists on her hips, I realize that this moment is over. We can't just run away from it.

Noah turns off the engine. "Go. I'll come back."

"You can't. You'll disrupt everything."

"I'll come back. I have to leave town by noon," he says now looking at me. "I'll be back to say goodbye, but, Em, I won't be gone forever."

The tears are back, and I let them fall in front of him. "What—what does that mean?"

"I love you too much to let this be the end of it all. I'll be back."

Now Katie is knocking on the hood of the car and Rachel's eyes are wide.

I don't know what he's talking about. I don't have the mental capacity to take in the angry woman in front of the car and the broken man next to me. I can't handle all of this and be expected to go back into that store and care about the authors who have their spotlight day today. But I have to.

I unbuckle my seatbelt and turn fully to Noah. "I have to go. You have to go."

"I'll come by to say—"

I shake my head. "No. Don't come back. I can't handle you coming back to say goodbye."

"Then we don't say it. I'll be back, Em."

"Don't promise me that." I wipe at my eyes. "We'll cross paths again, Noah Carter. Just go knowing that I love you, and in these three weeks, you've changed my life."

There is a mask of confusion on his face and it hurts. I move in and press a hard kiss to his lips.

"I love you," I say again before I push open my door and run past the two women staring at us.

A clean break is the best, right?

Fuck that!

CHAPTER 52

I am fully hungover. Not from alcohol or infused brownies, but from the week coming to an end.

It's eleven o'clock and the store is finally dark and empty. New York has left the building.

Somehow I'd pulled myself together enough to manage through the day. The Q&As were awesome. The signings netted me a small fortune, thank goodness. The questions about Noah were plentiful, but I think I handled them with grace, even if I am sitting on the floor in the romance section with one of Mrs. Packer's brownies in my hand, still wrapped.

The shelves are bare, but they won't be for long. The furniture is back in place, but not in its final place. The week coming up will offer me a chance to put things back to where they were and go on as normal—well, the normal before Noah Carter had walked into my life.

I feel the tears burning my throat, but I know I've cried them all out.

Before Katie left, she'd confirmed that Noah had made it back to New York, but there is no peace in that. What I want is for him to be at my house when I get there. I want the lights on. I want a fire started. I want the things he was promising but I know will fade away as soon as he's back in his own routine. I'm only his muse to the next bestseller. He was only my avenue to the dream of having my book published.

I look at my phone. It's one o'clock in the morning in New York. If I were to text him would he be awake?

No, I won't do that. I made it fairly clear he needed to just get back to his life.

Rachel has sent me emails every morning for the past three weeks. Notes on my manuscript. Names of editors she's considering pitching to. Names of editors she's talked to in brief conversation who weren't interested.

But in the weeks that Noah has been gone, I've been working through Rachel's notes. I've started taking off Wednesday fully, not just in the morning, and I've started a new story.

The one thing about a true romance is that it will have a happily ever after—or a happily for now. I guess it's just my way of writing the story Noah and I should have had—could have had if I wasn't so worried that one of us would lose ourselves in it.

Julia caught me checking flights to New York, and she must have said something to Lily, because she's made mention of it many times.

"Go, Em. Just go," she'll say from time to time when I'm just managing through my day.

"My life is here. His is there."

She shakes her head and goes on, but isn't that how it is? Long distance doesn't work, not for the happily ever after I want. My happily ever after is still my store.

I always wondered how those authors that put out six or seven books a year can write so fast. How do they come up with the stories that captivate millions? Now I know. They've been in love. They've touched it. They've tasted it. They've kept it. They've lost it.

It's been two months since the literary event blew into town. Mrs. Packer has her grandson doing more at the coffee shop with hopes that maybe, someday, he'll take over. For the first time in all the years I've known her, I've heard her throw around the word *retirement*.

Julia and Lily have swapped schedules to better accommodate Julia's new lab schedule at school. And I've written a new novel and a short story. I guess Noah Carter was my muse too.

Julia insists that we keep his books on the front table with his author photo, and I try not to look at it. The man in that picture was broken, it shows in the circles under his eyes. But to look at him breaks me. Admittedly, when no one is around and the store is dark, I linger there and gaze into his eyes.

Book sales of his latest book haven't stopped. We get new shipments of it at least once a week, and we ship out as many books as we have in store.

Rachel and I are finishing the work on my manuscript, and she's optimistic. "Emma, this is going to sell. I just know it. Noah is positive of it too," she says when we meet on Zoom to work out the details of the last chapter.

I try not to appear as surprised by his name as I am. "You've talked to Noah?"

Rachel blinks a few times. "Haven't you?"

"No. What we had was temporary. We both knew that."

I'm not sure what happens in that moment. The sheer look of confusion clouds her face as if she didn't know he went home and I went on.

"Oh," she says obviously trying to clear her thoughts. "He was here the other day and I just …" she waves her hands in the air as if she's wiping away anything that might have clouded her mind. "He just has such nice things to say about you, I just figured ..."

Does he miss me? I mean I miss the hell out of him, but neither of us have contacted the other. I won't do it because, well, I sent him away. I guess he isn't going to do it either, probably because he knows I was right. It was temporary and now we need to both go on with our lives.

And again, why would you want to contact someone who basically sent you home and said, let's forget this ever happened.

When Julia comes in for her shift she holds out her phone to me. "Did you see who they've signed to play the lead in *Caught in the Crossfire*?" she mentions the movie of Noah's newest book.

I look at the phone and see that Gregory Bishop has signed to play the lead. Though handsome enough for the leading man of an action film, I don't see it. Gregory Bishop's last few films were sci-fi adaptations of Kent Black's books, and Noah's character is far from that. Then again, what do I know about casting movies? All I know is that when I read that book now, and I've read it three times since Noah left, I only see Noah's face as the main character. It's Noah that hunts down the murderer. It's Noah that defends the woman, whom I see as me, and takes her to bed and keeps her safe. It's Noah that's the hero.

CHAPTER 53

The flower beds on the street are in full bloom and I didn't realize just how much I needed spring to arrive. Lily has confirmed on more than one occasion that I'm a grumpy old lady since Noah left.

I shouldn't be grumpy. Rachel called me just yesterday to say that the editor she recently pitched is interested in my book. They're working out the final details, but she might have sold my debut novel.

And yet. I'm not sure I feel as excited as I should.

Maybe Noah had it right. It's just not that big of a deal.

When the door to the store opens, an older lady shuffles through with a box in her arms. Lily hurries toward the door to help her.

"Oh, thank you. I guess I thought since the box isn't heavy, I wouldn't have a hard time walking in," the woman laughs.

"Can I take it for you?" Lily asks.

"Actually, I'm looking for an Emma Reynolds."

Lily looks up at me and so does the woman. There is something hauntingly familiar about her, but I can't pinpoint what it is.

She starts toward the counter, the large box still in her arms, but then stops and looks at Noah's picture. A smile widens on her face as she looks at him. She lets out a little noise as if she's satisfied with his face or the book. I'm just not sure.

"You're Emma?" she asks as she sets the box on the counter.

"I am."

"I'm Beatrice, but my friends call me Bea," she says, darting her hand out in my direction.

"It's nice to meet you, Beatrice."

"Nope, I said my friends call me Bea. That would include you," she confirms.

I exchange a quick glance with Lily who is grinning from behind the woman.

"Well, Bea, what brings you in?" I ask.

"I just bought the new antique store down the street. I love antiques. Don't you?"

"I suppose they have some appeal."

"Oh, the stories those old things can tell. Do you know I once opened a dresser drawer and found a thousand dollars?" She places her hand on her chest. "A thousand dollars. It was taped to the bottom of the drawer and there was a liner in the drawer. Talk about a find," she laughs.

"I'd say that makes antiquing more fun."

"It sure does." She pushes the box in my direction. "I brought these for you. I was told you liked them."

"You brought something for me?" I ask.

"Take a look."

Again, I exchange a look with Lily and she moves closer to the counter.

Carefully, I open the folds of the box that Bea has set on the counter. My trembling fingers go straight to my lips when I see three Cabbage Patch dolls inside.

Tears instantly fill my eyes when I look up from the box.

"Why would someone want you to have creepy dolls?" Lily asks, looking into the box.

"You think they're creepy?" Bea asks as I pull out the first doll with yellow yarn braids.

"Creepy as hell," Lily replies and Bea chuckles.

As I study the doll the first tear falls. "Bea, how did you know I liked dolls—these dolls?"

"Well my son told me of course," she says.

I drop the doll back into the box and draw in a shaky breath.

"Em, what's going on?" Lily is now moving around the counter to my side.

I shake my head. "You said you just bought the store?" I ask Bea.

"Yes. We've been looking for some purpose in life, and when he said he'd seen the cutest store ever and thought we should move and open it, well, I couldn't help myself. Then, we visited, found a cute house, and when I came in and saw your cute store, I was a goner."

Lily grabs my arm as if she's trying to grasp the conversation.

"When were you in the store?" I ask.

Bea gives it some thought. "I suppose it was a month ago. A cute young lady helped me out. I bought a few Jennifer Zeppelin books. My son said you and he shared a love of her books."

That has me gasping again, but a laugh squeaks out.

Lily reaches her hand out and covers Bea's hand on the counter. "Bea, who is your son?"

Bea doesn't answer. She just looks up at me and smiles. "He wouldn't have let me leave the city without him," she says and now I burst into tears.

"Noah?" Lily asks now taking my shoulders and turning me toward her.

"He says he has a great chili recipe he's going to try out. It'll be ready by the time you get home," Bea says, the smile wide on her face.

"Noah is here?" Lily asks and Bea nods.

"He was miserable. Nearly as miserable as when he lost Abby. He started packing up his apartment the minute he left this place. And now we're all here," Bea explains.

Lily reaches for a tissue on the counter and hands it to me. "Go. Go now. God, don't wait until we close tonight. Go!"

Wiping my eyes I begin to laugh, but the tears don't dry up. Everything inside of me feels as if it's going to burst, but in the very best way.

"You're good if I go?" I ask Lily.

"Don't fucking worry about me. Go," she says nearly pushing me out the door.

I pull her to me and hug her tightly. Then, I hurry around the counter and pull in Bea and do the same.

"Welcome to town. Congratulations on your new business. I love your son," I blurt out the last part. "I love him."

Bea laughs and cups my face in her hands. "Oh, honey, I know. Now go, and take those creepy ass dolls with you."

I'm mindful of the road. It's steep. It's bumpy. It rained two nights ago and there are still small ruts that are filled with water. But, if I can keep my wits about me, at the end of this long and bumpy road is the man that I love. The man I can't stop thinking about. The man I turned away and now he's here. Not only is he here, he moved his family here.

He's here!

The house has that warm glow to it, even with the sun headed toward the backs of the mountains, the house breathes warmth.

I pull into the driveway and put up the garage door, laughing when I realize he had the code to the garage door and not once did I think to change it after he left town.

Hurrying to turn off the car and climb from my seat, I nearly choke myself with the seatbelt when I yank against it.

Finally free, I open the door and pull the box from the passenger seat.

That's when the door opens to the house and Noah stands there like the god I always saw him as. The light behind him illuminating him in all his glory. His hair is longer. His beard is full. He's barefooted in my house and holding two glasses of wine.

"Lily thinks these dolls are creepy," I say and my voice cracks slightly.

"They are creepy," he says.

"You're here," I say slowly walking toward him, perhaps afraid that he will evaporate and I'll realize this is just a dream.

"I'm here."

"Your mother is here," I laugh, but the sound is wet.

"So is my father," he confirms.

I keep moving, but I don't seem to be getting any closer to him.

Noah steps into the garage, still holding a glass in each hand.

I readjust the box in my arms. "You're here to stay?"

"I was wrong. I don't belong in New York. I don't like the noise, the people, or the bustle. Imagine how much less broody I would have been if I'd have figured that out a long time ago."

I laugh again, and this time I drop the box between us at our feet.

"I love you, Emma. I couldn't be away from you," he says handing me one of the glasses of wine.

"I love you. I've been broody since you left."

He chuckles. "Well then, everyone will appreciate it that we're back together."

I have to touch him, so I push the box out of the way with my foot and move to him, wrapping my free arm around his neck and he pulls me to him with his free hand on my waist. Our mouths come together and there is an electricity that buzzes through us that has my heart racing and my blood pumping.

"Can I stay here?" he asks. "As in, stay for good?"

"I'd be so disappointed if you didn't."

"We can make our own happily ever after."

"It starts now," I say and step back from him.

Noah watches me as I hand him the glass of wine in my hand and open the box with the dolls. From inside I pull out the brown Kraft bag that says Pack-a-Punch on it.

"What is that?" he asks.

I move to him again and plant another warm kiss on his mouth. "Mrs. Packer was eavesdropping and she sends her love," I say, opening the bag and showing him the brownie inside, as well as the newest Jennifer Zeppelin book.

EPILOGUE

I don't remember when I've been more nervous. My palms are sweaty and so is my hairline. This isn't a hot flash, it's full out anxiety.

Noah rests his hand on my knee as it bounces under the table.

"You're going to put a hole in the floor," he says, the gold band on his finger catching the light.

"Why don't you get nervous like this?" I ask.

"Who says I don't? I used to physically get sick before I did a book signing. You're in a unique position," he says looking at the line that has formed down the street from my quaint store. "Most authors have book signings that no one shows up to. Your first book signing looks to be an epic event."

"Sure, not because of the book though."

He snorts out a laugh. "USA Today Best-seller on your debut novel, that's nothing to scoff at."

"They're here for my celebrity husband. I'm married to fucking Noah Carter," I remind him.

"You sure fucking are," he says easing in and kissing me softly on the lips.

"I have to open the door now," Lily says. "Can you two stop making out?"

"I'm going to be sick," I blurt out the words and Noah pushes a bottle of water in my direction.

"Sip. Breathe. Be amazing."

He kisses me one more time before he stands and Dorothy slips in and takes his seat.

Noah rests his hands on Dorothy's shoulders and leans in to her ear. "Take care of my best girl. She's a star you know."

Dorothy pats Noah's hand, but her eyes are on me. "You have excellent taste in wives, my son."

Noah kisses Dorothy on the cheek. "I sure do."

He leans in one more time and kisses me. "You're in good hands. I have to go work the front counter now. My business partner has a book signing to get to."

Noah gives Lily a nod and she opens the door to the store and Julia directs them in a single line to pick up their copy of my book and head to the table.

I know my husband, the broody thriller writer, just wants me to have my happily ever after in my happy little store surrounded by the people I love the most. He didn't mention that his newest book, which he wrote in my office, just hit the New York Times Best Seller list this morning, and it hasn't even released yet. He didn't mention it, but I keep up on it. I know he just wants me to have my moment.

When I look toward the counter, as Dorothy hands me my first book to sign, he winks at me. I couldn't imagine he could be any sexier than the picture on the back of his books, but with that full beard, he proved me wrong.

And here I thought my bookish love would only bring me happy endings among the pages of books. I was so wrong. Broody authors can also be part of happily ever afters.

RATE AND REVIEW

We hope you enjoyed *Bookish* by Bernadette Marie. If you did, we would ask that you please rate and review this title. Every review helps our authors.

Rate and Review: Bookish

MEET THE AUTHOR

Known for her #1 bestselling contemporary romances, Bernadette Marie is a fervent advocate of Happily Ever Afters. As a devoted wife and mother of five, she cherishes the notions of love at first sight, whirlwind romances, and the power of second chances. Beyond her literary pursuits, Bernadette is a dedicated martial artist with a 3rd-degree black belt in Tang Soo Do and holds certification as an instructor. Her passions extend to the tranquility of Tai Chi, exploring Disney parks, and indulging in lunch outings with friends. When she's not crafting compelling narratives or overseeing her own publishing house, 5 Prince Publishing, Bernadette can often be found immersed in a beloved rom-com, effortlessly reciting cherished one-liners.

OTHER TITLES FROM 5 PRINCE PUBLISHING